PRAISE FOR VIVIAN AREND

"If you've never read a Vivian Arend book you are missing out on one of the best contemporary authors writing today."
~ *Book Reading Gals*

"The bitter cold of Alberta, Canada, is made toasty warm by the super-sexy Coleman brothers of Six Pack Ranch."
~ *Publishers Weekly*

"Brilliant, raw, imaginative, irresistible!!"
~ *Avon Romance*

"This story will keep you reading from the first page to the last one. There is never a dull moment..."
~ *Landy Jimenez*

"I definitely recommend to fans of contemporaries with hot cowboys and strong family ties.."
~ *SmexyBooks*

"This was my first Vivian Arend story, and I know I want more! "
~ *Red Hot Plus Blue Reads*

"In this steamy new episode in the "Six Pack Ranch" series, Trevor is a true cowboy hero and will make any reader's heart beat a little faster as he and Becky discover what being a couple is all about."
~ *Library Journal Starred Review*

A RANCHER'S SONG

THE STONES OF HEART FALLS: BOOK 2

VIVIAN AREND

ALSO BY VIVIAN AREND

Six Pack Ranch

Rocky Mountain Heat

Rocky Mountain Haven

Rocky Mountain Desire

Rocky Mountain Rebel

Rocky Mountain Freedom

Rocky Mountain Romance

Rocky Mountain Retreat

Rocky Mountain Shelter

Rocky Mountain Devil

Rocky Mountain Home

Thompson & Sons

Ride Baby Ride

Rocky Ride

One Sexy Ride

Let It Ride

A Wild Ride

A full list of Vivian's print titles is available on her website

www.vivianarend.com

A Rancher's Song

ISBN: 9781999495718
Edited by Anne Scott & Angie Ramey
Cover Design © Sofie Hartley of Hart & Bailey Design Co.
Proofed by Lynda Ryba & Linda Levy

PROLOGUE

Walker jammed his glove more firmly under the rope, adjusting position on the back of the bull. Focusing down on what he was doing, letting everything around him fade away. The noise from the crowd in the stands and the bull under him were loud, but louder still were the rough gasps of his own breathing. Blood rushed past his ears like a drumbeat as his heart pounded.

A steady breath. Another one. Feeling the animal beneath him and trying to work with the wild energy of the beast. He needed great numbers, and that wouldn't happen unless both of them were ready to put on a show.

His leg smashed against the metal rails as the bull shifted violently toward the right, all of the cowboys along the chute either backing up rapidly to stay out of striking range, or leaning in to control the animal.

It was time. Walker lifted his free hand and nodded.

The gate jerked open, and the next second he was flying into the arena, body whiplashing as the bull did his damnedest to remove the human annoyance from his back. Every time the animal's hind legs came down, pain slammed up Walker's spine like a sledgehammer. He made sure to keep his teeth tight together on the mouth guard, riding through the motions, as sharp and rapid as they were, as if he were on an ocean wave undulating through what had to be the most violent rollers ever.

But the ride had a rhythm, and a pace, and in spite of the pain, and the fear, and the adrenaline racing through him, Walker found himself falling into the zone. That perfect place where nothing existed except for the strange connection between him and the beast. He didn't care that he was doing something incredibly dangerous, or that he needed it to last for a full eight seconds. The sensation was beautiful and glorious.

Until it wasn't.

Fear should have reared upward like a raging beast, but no, it arrived slowly. Or so it seemed as the zone vanished, and in its place was the sensation he'd felt before.

Death.

Walker was going to die.

It wasn't about the poetry of the motion now; it was about somehow figuring out how to survive. Pain was one thing, but the icy cold fingers of fear that had wrapped around him were invasive and unstoppable. Walker tried his best to ignore the sensation, but like a wagon that had been inched over the top of a steep hill, momentum built and tension increased.

Bony fingers wrapped around the back of his neck and clung tightly. Death was there with an unshakeable grip, and Walker really didn't want to be thinking that way, but once the thought arrived, he couldn't shake it. Like a low buzz that slowly built in speed and volume until he found himself no longer bounced by the violence of the bull but flying with deceptive smoothness through the air, headed for the ground.

Walker had enough presence of mind to roll as the earth came up to meet him, shoulder and forearm slapping down, his head meeting the ground briefly as he rolled and came to his knees, glancing quickly to see where the bull was.

Only in rodeo were you safer on the back of a wild animal than on the ground.

He lifted his eyes to find he was facing the crowd, audience leaning forward with fear and adrenaline on their faces. A woman turned her head, her long hair whirling, the silvery white strands like spun moonshine, and in that moment everything Walker should've been focused on fled.

Ivy?

He stared, waiting for her to turn back so he could see her face. It had been so long since he'd seen her, but he knew what she'd look like. Pale skin, but bright eyes. A grey so light they turned silver at times, flashing at him as he'd tease and steal a kiss...

"Move it." The order came at the same moment a hand hit him on his already bruised arm, pushing him off balance.

Walker's arms shot forward to stop his fall, his hands hitting the hard steel of the arena enclosure. A flash of bright colours rushed past the corner of his eye. A shadow of pitch black.

Oh God, the bull.

A loud shout escaped as the bullfighter waved his arms and got the animal's attention, turning the beast away from where Walker was still trying to figure out what was going on. Another of the three bullfighters stood on the safety rails and grabbed Walker by the back of his vest, hauling him to the top of the fence before shoving them both over. A second later, the two of them were sprawled on the ground on the other side of the railing.

The furious bull was out in the arena tossing a safety barrel, the bullfighter inside safe even while he was being scrambled like an egg.

"You make a good target, Dynamite, but maybe you could get the hell out of the arena a little faster next time." The cowboy grabbed him by the wrist and hauled him to his feet, a mixture of good-natured humour and annoyance as he patted Walker on the shoulder. "I know you're supposed to be fearless and all, but I pretty much recommend being scared sometimes. It'll keep you alive longer."

The rodeo bullfighter picked his hat up off the ground before dipping his chin and climbing over the railing to rejoin the rest of his team.

Walker stared after the man. He wasn't sure what the bullfighter was talking about.

He glanced down at the dust and dirt on his vest and chaps then up at the clock. 6.96. He must have been bucked off, but he couldn't remember anything from after the moment the panic had begun to slide along his spine.

The last minutes of the event were missing from his memory, and if he wanted to stay alive, that wasn't good.

He waited until his score of zero for the ride showed up on the scoreboard next to his time, good-naturedly taking the jeers from his fellow cowboys. Then he packed his bag and headed for his truck.

When things went wrong he had a place to go. It was a bit like admitting defeat. But at that moment, realizing he could've been seriously hurt or killed, or caused another man to be, acknowledging he was beat was the only choice.

1

"Holy cow, when did Bradley Ford lose all his hair?"

Ivy Fields slapped a hand over her sister's mouth, glancing around to see if anyone was within earshot of the rude comment. "You want to borrow the microphone to ask him? Or maybe we should try using inside voices, instead."

Tansy rolled her eyes, but she was smiling as Ivy inched her hand back. "Fine, I'll be quiet as a mouse." Tansy tossed her head, her blonde hair floating around her shoulders. "I swear the man had flowing Jesus-locks last week when he came into the coffee shop. He's bald as a baby's bottom."

They both turned to examine the crowd who'd gathered in the Heart Falls Community Centre for the afternoon Canada Day events. Everywhere she looked, Ivy spotted familiar faces, although most had changed since the last time she'd seen them, a few dramatically like Brad who—

Okay, the shaved head was *not* a bad look on him at all, just shocking. "He wore a ponytail in high school, didn't he?"

"Uh-huh." Tansy tilted her head to one side. "Okay, it's kind of sexy, I guess. Only there's nothing to grab onto."

Her younger sister had lost her. Ivy frowned. "Why would you want to grab his hair?"

Tansy raised a brow then waggled it.

God. How her sister managed to make things about sex ninety-nine percent of the time was incredible.

"Go away," Ivy murmured.

Tansy eyed her with a smirk. "And in other news...you're still an innocent. Anyway, the short style is probably safer. Brad's a firefighter now. He doesn't need flammables next to his face."

"A firefighter. That's good."

"Yeah, new Fire Chief for the county, in fact. He's a catch, according to local gossip. Maybe you should make a move on *him.*" Her sister screwed up her face then shook her head as she pulled out her phone and checked her messages. "Nah. I think the current plan is still the best."

Ivy wasn't so sure anymore, not as the room continued to fill with locals. Noisy, loud—it wasn't too late to call it off.

Only when she opened her mouth to tell Tansy she'd changed her mind, her sister was already a half a dozen paces away. "Rose summoned me," she tossed over her shoulder. "Enjoy the show."

It had been a long time since Ivy had stood in the local community hall, but the calendar didn't lie. It had been eleven years since she'd lived in Heart Falls, and while she was glad she'd had her time away, it was good to be home.

Returning at the start of July meant she had an entire summer to look forward to getting reacquainted and settled before diving into her new position at Heart Falls Elementary School.

A flash of warmth hit somewhere in her chest as her parents danced around each other in the aisle between tables, her mother juggling trays from the kitchen, her father heading toward the stage where he was acting as auctioneer for today's final event.

The two of them exchanged warm smiles. That too was something Ivy was looking forward to—more time with her family.

She'd missed them terribly. They weren't related by blood, but they were family, nonetheless. She and her three sisters had been adopted by Sophie and Malachi Fields years ago.

Tansy had rejoined Rose on the far side of the room, standing behind a long table that an hour ago had held row after row of pie pieces. Ninety percent of them had been baked at Tansy's coffee shop. Probably with Rose's help, when she hadn't been busy with the table centerpieces. She operated the flower and knickknack shop adjoining Tansy's. *Buns and Roses*—Ivy needed to catch up on how things were going there as well.

Another thing to enjoy. Spending time with her younger sisters, including sitting down with the youngest, Fern, and finding out what the eighteen-year-old's future plans were.

But today was about more than family. Ivy let her gaze drift over the room, putting names to faces, and trying to make guesses about the changes in relationships being acted out silently before her.

It was forgivable if the first place her curiosity led her was toward the Stone family. The oldest brother, Caleb, had his arm resting on the shoulders of a dark-haired woman, and two little girls were dancing around them.

And as a bell rang from the stage to get everyone's attention, she spotted Luke Stone pulling out a chair for a blonde woman as they re-settled at spots beside Caleb. Obviously, they were a couple as well.

She'd been gone so long.

Changes were inevitable, not only here, but in her as well. She'd been waiting for a long time to take this next step, but it seemed her nerves were going to give her hell the entire time she waited for Tansy's bright plan to fall into place.

Oh, well. Nerves wouldn't kill her.

"Thank you, everyone, for joining us for this fine Canada Day celebration." Her father smiled over the crowd with that easy way of his. "I'm pretty sure you all had enough to eat earlier, although I imagine a few gentlemen up here on the stage were nervous enough to skip dessert. Don't worry, though. I instructed my daughters to hold back a couple of pies." He turned to the row of a dozen or so plus men standing in an awkward line to his right.

"You should auction off the pies," someone heckled from the floor.

"Charlie Miller, you already ate an entire pie by yourself." It was Tansy, of course, shouting across the room as people turned toward her with grins. "If you want another pie to yourself, you go right ahead and put in your bid. I'll make your favourite."

"Do I get the pie maker as well?" Charlie teased.

Tansy raised a brow then gestured to the stage. "Considering this is a *bachelor* auction, you probably should take that up with my dad."

Heads twirled back to where Malachi Fields no longer looked quite so jovial as he glared at Charlie. "Maybe we should get on with the main event."

Charlie settled in his chair and zipped his mouth damn fast, much to the amusement of the people around him.

"All proceeds from today's auction go toward the Community Health Center. I believe they've got some funds earmarked for a playground update and some for after-school care. Very worthwhile, so I hope you all contribute however you can."

He turned to the row of local young men and called one forward.

While her dad introduced the first victim, whose ears had flushed bright red, Ivy found her attention wandering. She wasn't interested in a kid barely out of his teens.

No, it was the tallest man in the lineup who had everything in her twisting. He stood with his arms crossed over his chest, the firm bulge of his biceps pressing against the crisp white denim of his shirt. He wore black jeans, the thick fabric barely restraining his muscular thighs, and with a black cowboy hat on his head, Walker Stone was every inch the cowboy Ivy remembered.

He needed a haircut. The bottom edge was curling up in an unruly manner that made Ivy's fingers itch. She wasn't quite the innocent her sister thought. She'd take off that hat of his and lay it aside so she could thread her fingers through the thick strands and watch his pupils go dark.

Or at least that's what memory said would happen. She adjusted position uncomfortably and wondered why she was tormenting herself like this. It *had* been eleven years. Showing up at the bachelor auction and throwing herself at him the first time they met again was a terrible idea.

Of course, it had sounded brilliant when Tansy and Rose proposed the plan the night before while the three of them were curled up in Ivy's temporary lodging, back at home in the same room she'd occupied during high school.

The maple tree outside the window was taller than before, but that same branch reached conveniently toward her window—

Memories made heat flush Ivy's face, and she forced her attention back to the stage where, with a round of applause, her father finished reading the envelope that held the details of the offered date, handing it to the winner of the second eligible bachelor.

Malachi wiggled the next envelope in the air. "We are delighted to welcome home a man who was born and bred in Heart Falls. Although he seems determined to bring himself back in more than one piece. Walker *Dynamite* Stone. Come on up here."

Ivy found herself leaning forward as Walker stepped out from the crowd of young men and joined her father.

They shook hands briefly before Walker turned to the room and offered a dazzling smile, no doubt playing it up a little for his adoring women fans, a group of whom were gathered at a long table in the front right corner. They weren't locals Ivy recognized, but it was possible they were from the surrounding counties.

The auction was a chance to find single men, and someone like Walker was worth the drive. One woman looked as if she were trying to convince her friends to spot her a little extra change.

Ivy was suddenly very happy to have her sisters as back up, because the only thing more embarrassing than bidding for a date with Walker would be bidding for a date and not winning.

"You plan on sticking around long enough to take one of these ladies for a night on the town?" her father asked Walker, leaning the microphone toward him.

"A date with one of these fine ladies? Wild horses couldn't drag me away." Walker offered a wink to the woman waving at him from the near side of the room.

Ivy put a hand over her mouth to stop from snickering. That was such a Walker thing to say.

Her father turned to the room and opened the bidding. He didn't babble fast and furious like some true auctioneer. He took the time to name the bidders when he recognized them and add to the excitement of the event with a little teasing. But it was all in fun and for good cause, and it was exactly what Ivy needed to make her summer plans start with a bang.

If things went well.

The first minute passed, and the bids came slowly at first. Ivy watched with interest as two women in the same group bid at the same time then burst out laughing.

Her father got into it. "Now, ladies. You're going to have to do better than that. Two hundred dollars is barely enough to build a new sandbox. This fine bull rider deserves a few higher numbers than that. Do I hear two fifty?"

"Two fifty," came a call from behind the pie table, Tansy waving her hand in the air.

Both of the men on the stage jerked in shock.

Concern crossed Walker's face before he schooled his features into a smile, but Malachi kept frowning even as he acknowledged the bid. "Two fifty from the young lady behind the pies, who might've consumed a little too many of her own wares and be on a sugar high at the moment."

"Two seventy-five," came another shout, this time from the woman at the front table.

"There we go. There's a good solid bid." Malachi twisted his body toward the nearby group, as if cutting Tansy out of all future bidding options.

Her poor father. He was going to kill his daughters before this day was over.

"Three hundred," Tansy returned. "And I'll throw in a cherry pie."

Walker's lips twitched, but he still looked as if he'd swallowed a bug.

"The bid stands at three hundred and one cherry pie." Her father turned back to the table at the front and held his arms open. "Back in your corner, ladies. May I remind you we're talking about Heart Falls' finest. A bona fide rodeo champion."

"That means he's good in the saddle," one of the women teased.

"Let's keep it family friendly," Malachi reminded them over the laughter. "Do I have another bid? I have it on good authority he also has the voice of an angel."

"Sing for us," went up the cry.

Walker held up a hand in protest, shaking his head. "Now's not the time."

"Three fifty for a date, and the table next to me says if you'll sing something this minute, they'll donate one hundred to the fundraiser." The woman at the front gestured over her shoulder where a group of older men grinned at Walker with amusement.

Walker shrugged, glancing over his shoulder at the bachelors still waiting. "Sorry, guys, but you have to suffer a little longer. Easy money is easy money."

He accepted the microphone from Malachi, staring at the old timers for a moment as he patted a hand on his leg, heel tapping to get a rhythm started. Then he opened his mouth and let the words roll, strong and inviting, bringing smiles to the faces around them as he sang about the end of a long day on the ranch, finishing work, and heading out to have a good time.

A verse and the chorus, not much more than a half-dozen lines, rang out a cappella—and it sounded great. Walker's voice was rich and strong, and Ivy found herself moving in time to the simple words.

He held the final note before cutting off with a bow, hat in hand. Walker pointed a finger at the old-timers, motioning them forward. Laughter and applause rose as he hammed it up for their benefit.

One of the men came to the front and handed over a pile of twenties. Walker shook his hand enthusiastically before offering the money to Malachi.

The room was still filled with noise when Tansy's voice cut through the chaos. "One thousand dollars, and you have to promise to sing at the date."

That was the way to get a bunch of wild, enthusiastic people to calm down—*not*.

The volume tripled, and once again Walker looked slightly sick to his stomach, his smile barely clinging in place.

Malachi looked as if he was either going to join Walker or shoot his daughter. Especially when no amount of encouragement could get anyone else to up their bid.

"Going once. Going twice... This is Walker *Stone* we're talking about, ladies."

"Say it, Papa. You can do it. *Going three times,*" Tansy encouraged.

Another ripple of laughter.

"Going three times..." Malachi looked around the room in vain. He brought his hand against his leg a little less enthusiastically than he had with previous auction winners, but still, he carried on determinedly. "*Sold.* To Tansy Fields, for one thousand dollars."

THIS WHOLE THING had been a bad idea from the start. But now, watching as Tansy Fields made her way out from behind the pie table and skipped toward the front of the room, Walker wasn't sure he could keep his smile in place for much longer.

His younger brother Dustin, who was still waiting in line to be bought and paid for, slipped to his side, leaning against him to murmur quietly, "That's awkward."

It was more than awkward; it was wrong on so many levels. Tansy Fields was like a little sister to him, and watching her bounce forward like a female Tigger wasn't doing anything to change his opinion.

It might be for a good cause, the bachelor auction, and he might be home in Heart Falls, which meant he had to take part or come up with a damn good excuse why he couldn't, but no way he was going to do anything with Tansy Fields.

It wasn't going to be a date by any stretch of the imagination. *No way.* Nothing date-like, especially not a good-night kiss. It was bad enough he'd had to sing—though, thank God, he'd gotten through without something terrible happening.

Something terrible had *happened.* He was supposed to go on a date with Tansy.

She stood at the front of the stage, grinning at him briefly before turning her smile on her father. "Boy, do you look grumpy."

Malachi shut off the microphone and folded his arms over his chest. He lowered his voice as he bent to speak to his daughter. "I'm sure you've got a reasonable explanation for your behaviour, yes?"

She handed over a folded piece of paper. "I have a beautiful explanation. It's all in there."

Walker wasn't sure how any explanation was going to make this better. Heck, if came down to it, he'd refund her money, and they could eat a pizza with her whole family or something for their "date."

Only as he read the page she handed him, the tension drained out of Malachi like a plug had been pulled. The man flashed Walker a wide smile then held the paper aloft as if it were a winning lottery ticket.

"I think in the interest of keeping things aboveboard and transparent, I'll read this to you."

Walker tried not to tense, but something strange was afoot.

"*Bidding* done by Tansy Fields with the purpose of winning one date with Walker Dynamite Stone, at a time, etc., of their reckoning, purchased by—wait, there's been a small note added that says payment includes one cherry pie."

Laughter again, but people were leaning in, listening intently.

"Purchased by—" Malachi hesitated, and Walker wondered if anyone had ever wanted to strangle an auctioneer as much as he did at this particular moment.

Malachi lifted his eyes and looked across the room, a great deal of amusement in his voice. "—*Ivy* Fields."

Relief shot through Walker so hard his legs shook, and as applause burst from the crowd, heads pivoted from side to side. Suddenly, hands rose to point as Ivy stepped forward.

It'd been a setup, and for one moment Walker was absolutely overjoyed. But then reality kicked in, and he realized that it wasn't eleven years earlier, and nothing was going to be simple. Still, he couldn't stop himself from drinking her in as she made her way forward through the crowd.

Her cheeks were rosy, probably flushed with embarrassment at the hoots and hollers. Her silver white hair hung in a braid pulled forward over her right shoulder, the delicate skin of her forearms and hands a sharp contrast with the powder blue blouse she wore.

Her eyes sparkled at him, though, and she wore a smile brighter than he remembered seeing for a long time. Confident, and yet not. Bold, and yet with that core of vulnerability she'd had so many years ago.

She'd changed. Hell, so had he, but one thing was the same. That same draw hovered between them even from half a room away.

Walker stepped to the front of the stage and flipped himself off, landing solidly in the empty space at the front of the aisle that would bring them together.

Another round of cheers went up, and then the shouting changed to words.

Kiss her. Kiss her. Kiss her

The locals knew their history—knew they'd been sweethearts back in the day. It made sense they'd be riled up and willing to tease. The crowd was helping to pull Ivy forward, and hands were at Walker's back guiding him as well.

As if he needed any encouragement.

They met in the middle of the room, and the noise level hit a deafening volume as the chant continued.

Kiss her. Kiss her.

Walker held out a hand, and she placed her fingers in his with no hesitation. It wasn't the crowd's encouragement that made him do it. It was the need in his gut telling him to go ahead and take a bite.

He pulled her against him, sliding a hand behind her back as he brought their bodies into contact, twisting and dipping her, bending forward until she had to arch back and rely on him to hold her safely.

She didn't fight him, not one bit. She just moved in unison as if it'd been yesterday and not years ago they'd been in each other's arms. And when he leaned over and pressed his lips to hers, it was like coming home.

Sweet heat. Hovering passion. They'd been children before, playing at love and testing their physical boundaries. He wasn't a child anymore, and neither was she. And it was clear as he took her lips that if he let it, the fire between them would flare a whole hell of a lot hotter and wilder than it ever had before.

The wolf whistles in the room were deafening, but the loudest thing was the hum of approval from Ivy's lips as he brought her to vertical, swirling her in a circle as if they were finishing a turn on the dance floor.

Yeah, kissing Ivy was like coming home—which was a whole hell of a lot of trouble considering his return to Heart Falls was only temporary.

2

Walker stared into her face as they separated enough for polite company. "You're back," he said stupidly.

"I'm back," Ivy agreed, peeking over his shoulder to the stage. "Are you okay with this?"

He wasn't sure what he felt at the moment other than sheer relief he didn't have to deal with Tansy. "Of course."

Ivy nodded firmly then glanced at the people watching them with interest as Malachi opened the bidding on the next man. "I think you're supposed to go back and cheer on your fellow bachelors so they don't feel awkward."

God. Heading back on stage was the last thing Walker wanted, but she was right. "I remember. You got a number for me to call? To set up our date?"

She handed over a business card then backed away, answering her sisters' calls from the side of the room. "I'll talk to you later, then."

"Later."

Ivy sashayed smoothly down the open aisle. Her hips swayed

from side to side, and it was impossible to tear his gaze away or to refrain from imagining her naked, her long limbs...

He shook himself, checking to see if anyone had caught him leering. No one close by—their attention had turned toward the stage. Unfortunately, when he glanced toward the pie table, Tansy and Rose were grinning at him like fools.

He shook a finger at them.

Rose stuck out her tongue. Tansy batted her lashes then turned to face the stage where Dustin was being hauled forward to be auctioned off.

The good-natured teasing continued as Walker rejoined his crew at the front.

Even his brother Caleb wore a satisfied expression when they bumped into each other on the way out of the hall.

"I don't understand why they've got the auction happening in the middle of the damn afternoon," Walker muttered quietly as Caleb smacked a hand on his shoulder, pushing him aside to let his wife and girls walk ahead of them to the truck. "Doesn't seem right, letting kids see guys get sold off like they're breeding stock."

"Oh, worried about your reputation? That's why you and—Ivy is it?—were in a killer lip-lock in the middle of a G-rated gathering?" his sister-in-law Tamara deadpanned.

Walker didn't *think* he blushed, but...

He glanced at Tamara. "It was all in good fun."

"Exactly. *That's* why the auction is part of the family event, so it *doesn't* get dragged off into territory the town council wants to avoid." Tamara opened the crew-cab door then helped her youngest daughter, Emma, climb onto the running board and into the back seat.

Tamara examined Walker with great curiosity while Emma got settled. "Still, I have lots and lots of questions for you."

"Ivy and Walker were sweethearts in high school." This matter-of-fact bit of data came from his second niece who had crawled in from the other side of the truck and was doing up her seatbelt. Sasha leaned forward and smartly informed Tamara, "Kelli says high school sweeties who stick together forever are movie fodder and not real."

"When do you find all this time to talk to Kelli?" Tamara asked, obviously puzzled. "She works in the barns, and you're at school all day."

"Not anymore," Sasha pointed out, ignoring the question. "Summer holidays started. Kelli says—"

"We'll just wait on what Kelli says until we're on the way home, okay, pumpkin?" Caleb offered Tamara a head shake before turning to Walker. "Come for supper."

"Can't. Things to do."

Caleb raised a brow, and Walker gave in. He'd only gotten back to the ranch a day earlier, and he hadn't spent much time with anyone. "Fine. I'll wash up then join you."

"I'll invite Dustin," Tamara offered. "If that's okay with you."

"Who you asking, me or Walker?" Caleb gave Tamara a pointed look. "Because it seems Dustin is at our table more often than not these days."

She raised a brow back. "I'm not about to tell him to go away, Caleb. He's family."

Walker wondered what the hell was up, but before he could ask for details, they were on the road and headed back to Silver Stone.

He followed his brother's truck at a distance, his gaze lingering on the familiar rolling hills that slowly opened up to reveal the long, low ranch house perched between the barns and the shining surface of Big Sky Lake.

Home. He'd been born here and had grown up roaming these hills, working chores after school then full-time once he'd graduated. This was where he'd learned to ride and rope.

Where he'd stolen his first kiss—from Ivy Fields, no less. The

Snow Princess she'd been back then, and memories swirled around him, hard and fast.

He shoved them away and focused on the here and now, turning into the ranch and parking by the bunkhouse.

He changed out of his dress-up stuff into clean work clothes then made his way to the ranch house, letting himself in the back door. Tasty scents filled the air, and as he hung his hat on one of the hooks in the mudroom, it was clear the place was the same, yet subtly changed since he'd left earlier that year.

New curtains hung at the windows, and he noticed new shelves in the mudroom. Tamara's touch, no doubt. Over the shelves were hand-drawn name tags for Emma and Sasha, pink and purple with glitter. Tamara's feminine touch and his nieces' presence were noticeable everywhere around the house, more so than ever before.

Laughter rang from the main room, and Walker stepped toward it eagerly. This was why he'd come back. A touch of home —maybe it would cure what was ailing him.

Sasha spotted him, jumping up and down. "Uncle Walker sits by me," she shouted.

But Emma had snuck up to his side and slid her hand into his, tugging lightly to get his attention. "I saved you a seat," she told him softly.

His throat thickened. His littlest niece had never been a big talker, so it was good to have her sharing so much more smoothly than he remembered. "How about I sit between you two? Or will you steal things from my plate? I hope not, 'cause I'm hungry."

"Mama cooked lots," Emma assured him, tugging him to the table, the words so much more important because they came easily to her lips.

Tamara certainly had cooked enough, and the food went down just fine. Dustin had showed up as well, ruffling Sasha's hair before hurrying to help carry a platter to the table. Then he'd taken his dose of teasing over the woman who'd bought him at the bachelor auction.

"I'm taking her out next Friday," he said, a flush on his cheeks, but he was happy.

"It's not the same one as last year, is it?" Walker asked. "Because didn't she get a little stalkerish on you?"

"Dustin's previous admirer was not around for this year's auction," Tamara informed him as she helped Emma deal with her plate.

Dustin grinned. "I don't know how you managed that, but thank you."

"No problem. I'm sure she's having a good time purchasing stock in Calgary this weekend." Tamara looked thoughtful, glancing up at Walker. "Calgary Stampede starts this weekend. I thought you'd qualified."

He'd qualified, but competing was out of the question. "I'm taking a little time off," he told her. "I need to do some training before I go back in the arena."

Thankfully, no one asked any more questions, so he sat back and enjoyed the family time and the food.

Dinner finished, Dustin and the girls headed to the sink to do clean up. Emma snuck back and turned on the *Wizard of Oz*, music and singing filling the room.

Dustin groaned in mock pain. "Emma, *no*. We've heard this a million times over the past month."

"The girls are in a play at the end of the summer. Get used to it, Uncle Dustin, because if you hang around, you'll hear a lot more of it." Tamara patted him on the shoulder then moved to put away the leftovers.

Caleb tipped his head toward the door, and Walker nodded, stopping to grab his coat.

"We'll be back," Caleb told Tamara.

"*You'll* be back," Walker said. "I'll be turning in after chores. Thanks again for supper," he offered to his sister-in-law.

"Anytime," she returned. "Stop by for coffee some morning if you'd like. You know where to find me. Only, use the porch, *Dynamite*. We need to get the roof re-shingled before anyone goes stomping around up there."

He grinned. "Rooftop approach reserved for Santa. Got it."

Marching across the well-worn path toward the barns, Caleb at his side, was a feeling as familiar as breathing to Walker, yet...*strange*. Something felt different. Caleb seemed more centered. More whole.

And he...

He was different, but damn if Walker could figure out what was bugging him, other than his feet were restless and his roots felt disturbed. He felt like a tumbleweed that was wishing it was time to dig in deep, but the winds weren't finished with it yet.

They worked in silence for a while, Walker because he wasn't quite sure what he wanted to say and Caleb because the man had the patience of a rock. Walker wasn't sure it was possible to outlast his brother.

When it came to waiting it out, Caleb always had been the best of them.

But apparently, Tamara's presence had brought about another change, because before Walker could find a way to introduce the topic, Caleb did.

"Tamara touched on it, but I guess I should straight-up tell you that we didn't expect you to show up. Not until after the Stampede."

Walker stroked a hand over Hannibal's nose. "Needed a break."

"Not a problem on our end." Caleb looked thoughtful before adding, "Problems on your end?"

Caleb had to have seen or heard about Walker's near-disastrous final run. "I didn't get hurt, if that's what you're asking. Shook me up a bit, though. I guess I need some time to figure out if this is really what I want to do for a while longer or if it's time to get out of the chute."

His brother stopped working, turning his full attention on Walker. Yeah, the near admission he was close to quitting rodeo had to be a bit of a shocker.

Yet if he couldn't find a way to deal with his problem that was exactly what was going to have to happen. And if he found a way to deal with *this* problem, there was the whole other possibility he hadn't even yet mentioned to his family.

The secrets were building, fast and thick.

Caleb's gaze grew as solid and firm as his response. "Find your feet. We're here for you. Whatever you need."

Even as relief rushed over him, Walker felt as if he were all of the companions on Emma's Yellow Brick Road. He wasn't smart enough to figure this out. He'd had a heart once, but it had been taken from him. His courage was in the shitter. And coming home was the only thing he had—yet something felt off.

But he'd spend more time pondering it when he wasn't tying up his brother's night. "I know you've got my back, and I'm glad. Thanks." He eyed Caleb with suspicion. "What's up with Dustin?"

A huge sigh escaped Caleb. "Other than he seems obsessed with my wife?"

Walker attempted to hold back a laugh and failed miserably. "Oh my God, are you jealous our kid brother is getting attention from Tamara?"

"Not jealous, not really. It's just...it's not *right.*" Caleb looked as grumpy and gloomy as he had a year ago, before Tamara had come into his life. "She's...I mean, there's nothing wrong. And she would never...and *Dustin* would never. But...she's *mine,* dammit."

Oh brother. In the category of things Walker had never expected to have to deal with...

He schooled his expression to stay as straight and serious as possible. "I didn't see anything wrong with what the kid was doing tonight during dinner, so unless he's been stepping over the line at other times...?"

Caleb looked sheepish. "No. I'm just grumpy, I guess."

"You said it, not me," Walker teased softly. "It looks as if Dustin is admiring your taste in choosing a lifetime partner this go-round. Tamara can handle some hero-worship without it going to her head."

"Of course she can. And the kid isn't doing anything wrong—you're right about that. He's always underfoot, though. I swear Dustin moved back in when I wasn't looking."

"It's not just Tamara, bro. He wants to be around you. That's not a bad thing. You've been a dad to him for longer than our father was in his life."

Caleb stilled. "You're right. God, I hadn't even thought of it that way."

And most of the time Walker wouldn't have either, but the truth was the years since his parents' accident had been weighing heavily on his mind.

Seeing Ivy had brought back more than just the good memories from their high school days.

One snowy February day, the lives of the Stone family had been irrevocably changed. The stabbing pain of guilt crashed against him, and Walker had to turn away in case it showed on his face.

Luckily, Caleb had moved on to problem-solving. "Maybe it's time I do like Dad did to me when I was first starting out. Get Dustin put on a few more long-range cattle drives. Give him some more responsibility."

"Things that send him away from home a little more?"

"Still with Ashton or some of the hands he knows best." Caleb nodded slowly. "That could work."

"It doesn't sound like a bad idea to me." Walker leaned back against the nearest support post. "If there's any new stock that needs to be picked up in Montana or the Dakotas, he's old enough to do the drive."

"We're not doing any buying for a while, Walker. Budget has been tightened down and watched closely." Caleb's body posture stiffened with the admission.

The confession had all the signs of a big problem. "How much trouble is Silver Stone in?"

Caleb's hesitation was too clear. "Not sure yet. The floods a couple years back did more damage than we realized. And I didn't want to bother you when you'd just left, but we ended up having to cull part of the herd in late February. Even though supply demands were down, we had to buy feed—I should let you talk to Tamara because she's been doing the books, but, yeah. It's not good. We've got that oil exploration thing started, but so far there's little progress. We have to buckle down for now."

It wasn't at all what Walker had expected to hear. Silver Stone Ranch had done well. Maybe not outrageously successful over the years, but they'd always earned more than enough to get by. Or at least that's what he'd thought, although it had been Caleb and Luke making the decisions.

"Well, I'm sure you can turn it around," Walker assured his brother.

"We'll do our damnedest."

They worked together until it was time for Caleb to head back to the house where his family was waiting for him—to his little girls and the woman who'd joined them and filled the place with love.

Where their little brother was probably hanging out, being both a pain in Caleb's ass and a reminder of everything he'd accomplished and worked toward after being tossed into a position of responsibility so many years ago.

Walker turned, feeling very alone and useless.

It seemed inevitable he'd end up on the hillside where his parents' graves were, overlooking the two lakes. He slid off Hannibal's back and let the reins fall to the ground as he stepped toward the simple stone markers.

A lingering gust of wind swept in, icy cold from passing over still-snowclad mountains to the west. That's all it was, but what it felt like was death brushing past, carrying a memory of the hurt and the pain of those early days. The sorrow and the guilt.

Walker stared down at the two gravestones, side by side. "I hate that we never had time to change things, Dad," he admitted. "Of all the shitty days for me to pick a fight."

Although, it had been less about Walker being an ass and more about his father pointing the fact out to him…

Walker had known he was going to be late for chores again, but this time it wasn't deliberate. He'd been fooling around at Heart Falls, tossing rocks against the frozen surface and daydreaming about Ivy when his horse had up and taken off on him.

He'd been halfway home on foot when his dad rode up and held out a hand.

Walker took it, swinging up behind his father. They'd rode in silence for the time it took to get back to the barns.

He'd tried to bolt the minute they got within range, but his dad called him back. "Your horse is in his stall. Give him a brush down before you get to your chores."

"Yes, sir."

Walter Stone looked him over. "That's all you got to say?"

"I tethered him, I don't know why he decided to take off on me. It's not my fault."

His dad raised a brow. "Accidents happen, but maybe you shouldn't have gone out for a ride when you knew chores were due to start."

"I would've only been a little bit late, even if I had to walk the whole way," Walker had grumbled. "It's not a big deal."

"Come on. I might've accepted that when you were fourteen, but you've got a month to go before you're considered an adult by most of the world. Eighteen is old enough to be able to tell time and get your ass in here to do your job."

"I'll work late," Walker snapped.

"Some of the time that works, but not when you're supposed to go out with the crew. And I don't know why I'm having to explain this to you, because this isn't the first time. You need to buck up and do your part. You're not a kid. You can't expect your older brothers to pick up the slack for you anymore. They've got enough on their shoulders. They don't need to be responsible for you as well."

Walter Stone had folded his arms over his chest, disappointment written all over his face, and damn if that wasn't the worst possible thing.

Walker had hated that his dad was upset. Worse, he'd known that he was in the wrong, but spitting the words out seemed impossible.

Which had only pushed him to be even more stupid, because that's what seventeen-year-olds did. "If I'm so damn terrible, fire me. I'll find myself another place and get out of your sight and off your land as soon as I can."

"Now you're just being stupid to try and rile me up. You know we don't want you to leave. This is your home—"

"Doesn't have to be," Walker muttered.

His dad had shut up then, the two of them eyeing each other

as a kind of power surged through the air around them. Finally, his dad had straightened, folded his arms and nodded once. "Make up your mind what's important to you. Your mom and I are going with the Hayes family to Calgary this weekend. You want to laze around on your ass, so be it, but remember it's Caleb and Luke you're letting down. It's the rest of the people relying on you, and in the end, it's yourself. We'll talk more when I get back."

HE'D NEVER COME BACK.

Not the caring man who'd tried to teach Walker about responsibility; just his body, cut from the car along with Walker's mom, and their family friends.

Walter and Deb Stone had been laid to rest overlooking the ranch they'd built with their own hands. Built with sweat and hard labour, and now Caleb was saying it was possible the ranch might be lost.

Walker had a lot of experience with the sensation of feeling out of control, but it never got any easier to face.

He lowered himself to the cold bench beside the graves, the wooden slats worn from the harsh winters and rough with age.

It finally struck him—this was why he felt so strange, so rootless and lost. Because up until now he'd been coasting along and not doing anything worthwhile. He had nothing of value to offer anyone.

It was time to change that. While he still wasn't sure he was capable, at least now he knew what he needed to strive for.

"You were right, Dad. Caleb and Luke have more than enough responsibilities, and it's my turn to do my part and step up to the plate. I'm sorry it's taken me eleven years to really learn the lesson, but I think I've got it now."

He'd come home because home was where a person came

when everything else fell apart. What he needed to do was deal with his fears so he could help.

The ranch needed money? Well, he couldn't do much being a ranch hand other than day-to-day tasks. Out there on the rodeo, though, there was real money to be made. And the other possibility, the one he hardly dared think about because it seemed so outrageous—there was money to be made there too. Lots of it.

Talk about singing for your supper.

But he couldn't make money riding bulls, and he couldn't make money from singing if he was going to be shut down and catatonic with fear when he least expected it. He needed to find a way to deal with these damn panic attacks, and maybe that was something he could do here at home.

But as soon as he got a handle on them—as soon as he found some way to cope—he'd have to leave. If it was his turn to make a sacrifice, so be it.

There was the irony. In order to save his home, he had to leave it.

3

Ivy joined her sisters, leaning against the side of her car where she'd parked at the edge of the walkway, eyeing the little bungalow before them.

It was cute.

Okay, it was one of the places that had the dreaded words "cozy fixer-upper" in the sales pitch, but Ivy had already completed the purchase before moving back.

Even though it was the perfect house for her, she had to admit it wasn't very much to look at yet. "I know it needs paint—"

"Oh, honey, it needs so much more than paint." Rose shook her head as she stepped forward, leaning down to poke a finger at the mostly dead grass. Her dark brown hair fell forward against her cheek, and she pushed it behind her ear when she stood, offering Ivy a grimace. "Please tell me they paid you to take this on."

"Actually," Tansy interrupted, "from what I've heard, the place is sound. The repairs are mostly cosmetic, and there's no reason why we can't get all that done over the next couple months."

Thank goodness one of her sisters had vision. "It's small, I know, but the price was right, and like Tansy said, all of the important things are in good shape. Which is good, because there're no expensive repairs needed, just a lot of TLC. But I think I'll spring for new appliances because even if avocado green is coming back in style, it's not my idea of a good time."

"Paint, appliances, new locks?" Tansy listed as she stepped toward the house. She put a foot on the first step but when it creaked ominously, she backtracked rapidly. "New stairs."

"New stairs," Ivy agreed. "We'll go to the back door for now. But the porch is sound, and they put new shingles on less than five years ago. The house came with some furniture, which is good because I don't have much of my own. I can slowly replace things and buy stuff that fits the space properly."

She led them to the side of the building where a second set of stairs led up to an entrance just off the kitchen.

"The view is spectacular," Rose admitted, turning toward the mountains to let the sun hit her full on the face. "Good thing you're not superstitious, though, sitting right next to the graveyard and all."

"That's usually where they put the caretaker's house," Tansy teased.

"Oh, goody. Does this mean you're going to be moonlighting as an undertaker?" Rose asked.

"Only on the second Thursday of every other month," Ivy retorted. "Come on, I can't wait to show you inside. I need ideas for what colours to paint things so the rooms look bigger."

It felt strange, yet right, to guide her sisters through the tiny home. Right now it was dirty and dingy, but it had so much potential. That was part of what Ivy did in her job as a teacher. She looked not only at where her students were at that moment, but where they could be, and figured out what it would take to get them there. She loved that journey of discovery. It wasn't only the students who learned things along the way; she did, too.

Taking this house from its current sad and dilapidated condition to the point it became a real home would be an adventure, and she could hardly wait to get started.

"Okay, this is sweet." Tansy motioned into the living room.

Between the front door and the living space someone had built a barrier wall with a lot of shelves. The shelving created a front entranceway by separating the door from the rest of the room.

"Paint that white, and it would not only brighten up the place, but you can put knickknacks all over it, and pictures. Could be pretty," Rose suggested.

"That's what I thought," Ivy agreed. "Tansy, add to the list. I need to change all the light fixtures. Nothing fancy, but I want to put in LEDs, and some of them need to be directional to get light right into the corners."

Tansy wrote notes obediently on the notepad she carried. "Light fixtures and area carpets." She glanced at the two of them. "The hardwood floor is nice but trust me, you're going to want something soft underfoot in a few places."

"And *that* has to go." Rose pointed toward a loveseat that had definitely seen better days. "Although, the kitchen table and the mismatched chairs around it are cute."

"I like them as well," Ivy admitted, though she refrained from mentioning they reminded her of the times she'd joined the Stone family for dinner. Their table and chairs were just like that —mismatched, near antiques that looked right together. Although, admittedly, their table was five times the diameter of hers.

Everything in this house was teeny.

They peeked into the bathroom, made more suggestions, and then checked out the two tiny bedrooms at the front of the house.

"I'm going to use one for my office, but I suppose I could put a bed in the other one so if you wanted to stay over, you could."

"Planning for houseguests. That's awesome." Rose's grin faded as she walked into the master bedroom. "Really?"

Ivy glanced around, failing to see the problem. "Look, there's a bathroom off here, which is a miracle in a house this size. It's only got a shower, but that works for me."

"Well, that's good. Can an actual bed fit?" Tansy asked, poking the mattress with her knee before attempting to pace across the floor. "There's not a lot of room in here."

"Not a lot of room at all. How big is a queen-size mattress?" Rose asked. "You're going to be banging the walls all the time."

Ivy rolled her eyes. "I'm not sure how active you are in bed, but if I'm wiggling enough to make the mattress move, I'm going to damage the walls anyway."

Rose snickered before covering it up with a cough.

Ivy gave her a dirty look. "What?"

Her sister raised her hands. "You're such an innocent. How on earth did you make it to this age still being able to say things like that without it being innuendo? *How much action do we get in bed*?"

"Be fair, Rose. If she's asking about you, it's not very much," Tansy teased.

Rose whirled on her sister, fists planted on her hips. "*If* you don't mind."

Oh my God, they were talking about sex. Ivy felt her cheeks heat as blood rushed upward. "I'm not into sexual calisthenics, thank you. And the bed is for me, and not me and anyone else."

Although she hoped that was a lie.

She knew exactly who she wanted to be in bed with, and as she eyed the small space where she had intended to put a twin mattress, maybe her sisters had a good point. If she laid Walker out on a bed that size...

"Whatever are you thinking about, because you look as if you're about to fall over." Tansy stuck her face in front of her. "There are some dirty daydreams going on in there."

"You're so annoying," Ivy informed her haughtily.

"Yes. You still need to tell us what you were thinking about."

Walker. On her bed. Stripped naked.

She'd only seen him naked during stolen and rushed moments, and that had been the seventeen-year-old version of Walker, not the incredible, mature man he'd become. The bull rider was mighty fine. All solid muscle and angles, sharp enough and hard enough to feel against her...

Ivy smiled as sweetly as possible. "That's for me to know and you to never find out."

Rose and Tansy exchanged glances before snatching pillows off the mattress and swinging them forward, catching Ivy in the middle. Chaos ensued.

And for a moment, Ivy let go of all of the *what ifs* and *why dids* that had been tormenting her over the years.

It had been right to go away to university. Her dream of being a teacher had been there as long as she could remember. During her early years when she'd been frail and sickly, books had become her friends and her way of seeing the world.

But once the Fields adopted her, she'd begun to see and do more. They'd taught her how to take care of herself and that being inquisitive was a good thing. They'd taught her about love and acceptance—and so much more. That gift was something she wanted to give back to others.

So as much as she'd been drawn to staying in Heart Falls with her high school sweetheart, making one person happy versus having the ability to change many people's lives—it hadn't seemed like that big of a sacrifice at the time. Especially since it was only going to be for a few years.

The differences in the realities of real-life compared to

dreams were huge. Not only dreams, but even well-thought-out and planned agendas had to be adjusted. She hadn't been strong enough to finish four years of teacher training without taking extra time. Adding in the practicum and student teaching hours—double the time there as well as she caught every single cold and germ, fighting to stay healthy—meant her training had taken far longer than she'd expected.

And then there was the hospital stay that went on forever...

It was only in the last couple of years that her body had finally begun to cooperate. Now she was strong enough to face most day-to-day illnesses no worse for wear than one of her sisters.

She was never going to take her new health for granted—the ability to bounce back from a summer cold or a fever quickly had seemed an impossibility when she was young. Needing to take only a few days off work was a huge difference from ending up flat on her back for a month.

"You're really going to stay in Heart Falls permanently?" Rose curled an arm around her shoulders, and Ivy realized she'd been daydreaming, staring over the Rocky Mountains to the west. The porch chairs gathered around a small table had made a perfect place for them to stop as Tansy wrote more notes and Rose ran back in to take measurements.

And Ivy, apparently, got lost in thought and did nothing.

"It's better for me," Ivy said with a nod, "but that's kind of a bonus to the whole situation. The less I travel and the more I'm around the same people, the better it is for my immune system."

"You could teach online. You could live in a big city and get your groceries delivered to your door," Tansy pointed out.

"She could become a hermit and never see another human being again in her life," Rose said with mock enthusiasm. "Oh my God, of *course*. That's the most perfect idea in the world."

"Shut up. That's not what I meant..." Tansy wrinkled her

nose. "Okay, that's kind of how it came out, but what I meant was I know you love teaching, but is being around a room full of grade twos the best thing?"

"In a small town like Heart Falls? Actually, yes. I'm okay getting exposed to some germs, but ones that are familiar are better for me. My immune system can build up all the normal resistance as long as I don't keep introducing lots of variables."

Rose was the one to nod slowly, but a little sadly. "So, you are never going to be a world traveler."

"I'm never going to be a traveler, period. But like I said, I don't feel as if this is a bad thing. Grandma is here in Heart Falls, and Mom and Dad are happy to stay." Ivy eyed her sisters. "You two seem as if you're happy running Buns and Roses."

They glanced at each other and turned back, nodding in unison as if they'd practiced. "We like it here too," Tansy admitted.

"Although I want to see a bit more of the world," Rose added. "Did you know Ginny Stone is in Italy right now?"

"I didn't. She's living there?"

"She's doing something with organic farming. She's been in France, England, and she's got another couple of countries to visit. Tamara Coleman—I mean Tamara *Stone*—said Ginny will be back for a month sometime soon. Their foster sister, Dare, is getting married, and of course Ginny needs to be around for that."

It was good to get caught up on all the gossip. It seemed every day there was something new to learn about her family, about her sisters.

About herself.

Her phone rang, and she excused herself before answering.

"Ivy Fields."

"Hey, Snow."

She tried to keep from reacting, but it was clear she'd done a terrible job because both her sisters' heads pivoted as if they were on magnets, gazes locked on her face. "Hi, Walker."

Rose shoved two thumbs in the air while Tansy tilted her head as if she were listening and expected Ivy to adjust the phone to make it easier to eavesdrop.

Not happening.

"Thought we should set up an official time and place for our date. Are you free tonight?"

Her sisters continued to make annoying gestures, and Ivy closed her eyes so she could ignore them easier. "I could be. I need to tell my mom I won't be around. Are you thinking supper?"

"I'll be done by five. I could pick you up by six."

Pleasurable warmth spread slowly through her system. "Six works for me. I'm staying at my parents."

He chuckled softly, and the sound sent another trickle of goose bumps over her flesh. "Then I know where to find you. See you later."

"See you."

She glanced down at her lap to hang up her phone, taking a deep breath and composing herself before lifting her gaze and attempting to pretend nothing out of the ordinary had happened. "Well, if you've had enough time to—"

"Oh, no way." Tansy folded her fingers together and pleaded. "Please. You gotta give us the goods."

"Sexy bull rider is picking you up at six. Where's he taking you?" Rose asked eagerly.

Ivy opened her mouth and realized she hadn't bothered to ask. "Out."

Tansy and Rose glanced each other and snickered. "You've got it bad for that man," Rose said softly. "And I hope everything works out, but if it doesn't, remember we're here for you."

"You're such a cheery ray of sunshine, Rose Fields. Of course it's going to work. Don't you remember how he used to fawn over her?" Tansy demanded.

"It was a long time ago, and we were both young," Ivy pointed out.

"Not *too* long ago," Tansy teased. "I told you every time I've seen him over the years he always asks, 'how's the family', and it's pretty clear he's not checking into Dad's health."

The warm blanket of pleasure wrapped a little tighter. "That's good to know."

"We just need to push him in the right direction—"

Nope. Not happening. She didn't need her sisters' help. Ivy went for blunt. "I care about Walker a great deal, and I am interested in seeing where this may go. That's why I let you talk me into the bachelor-auction thing, which, I might add, was way out of my comfort zone."

Tansy had the grace to look ashamed. "You did so well I forgot how shy you used to be."

Ivy didn't think being shy was something that ever went away. "I have more coping methods than before, but I'll say this to you now because I love you both—don't meddle. Thank you for helping me with the auction, but I want to do this on my own."

Tansy let out a heavy sigh and leaned back in her chair dramatically. "Fine. We won't follow you on your date."

"We were only going to do that because it's been a long time since we've eaten out," Rose claimed.

Too tempting. Ivy raised a brow. "Perhaps you're the ones who need to work on getting a little action, hmm?"

Rose stuck out her tongue, and Tansy snickered, their attention off Ivy's upcoming date and back on teasing each other lovingly.

Which was fine by Ivy, because her brain was so full at that moment she didn't have the energy to compartmentalize and deal with their endless enthusiasm. She was looking forward to tonight and the possibility that lay before her and Walker.

She glanced to her right and into the window of the master bedroom. The upper pane was covered with dust, and the lower was wide-open on a room that definitely needed changes.

Perhaps even a larger bed—

But first, she needed to take action of a different kind. There was a certain gentleman who she'd thought about an awful lot without setting her hopes too firmly in place.

Next on the agenda: a date with a Walker Stone.

4

Ivy stared out her bedroom window, nervously playing with the buttons on her blouse. She'd entered a time warp, waiting impatiently for Walker to show up to take her on a date.

Back in high school the tension had been sweet and exciting, and a whole lot of nerves had been involved as she wondered if they'd even get out the door. In those years, her health had been so delicate there were times her mom or dad had made an executive decision and called off the outing at the last minute.

Oh, her parents always tried to make staying home somehow special, but watching a movie while her little sisters snuck in to steal popcorn wasn't the same as getting to go to the actual theater alone with Walker.

As a large truck pulled up to the front sidewalk, Ivy couldn't step away. She should've been hurrying to get down the stairs as soon as possible, but at that moment the memories were too overwhelmingly beautiful to rush.

He'd asked her on their first date the day she turned sixteen. She hadn't been allowed to date before then, but they'd known they liked each other. They'd spent time together at school and all, but nothing had officially happened between them. Her parents' strict rule had meant she and Walker were friends first in spite of the bubbling boy-girl attraction between them.

As Walker got out of the truck and paced toward the front of the house, she drank him in as if she'd been thirsting for years. His long limbs moved smoothly as he glanced around and adjusted his cowboy hat, and when he tilted his head and looked instinctively at her window, Ivy didn't bother to hide.

His grin widened. He tipped his hat before disappearing from her line of vision.

The doorbell rang, and Ivy hurried to finish getting ready, suddenly aware that unlike the past years when she'd roomed with friends or lived on her own, her family was going to answer the summons.

She dragged a brush through her hair, grabbed her purse and headed for the door as, sure enough, her father's voice rang out in a greeting.

"So. We meet again," Malachi teased Walker. "Good to see you."

"Thank you, sir. You're looking in fine shape." Walker's voice rumbled up the stairs as she left her bedroom then had to whirl on her heel to go back and grab her inhaler.

"Plenty to keep me busy. And I've been right here in Heart Falls all the time. You don't stop by nearly as often as you used to, especially the last few years."

Good grief. Ivy didn't attempt to take the stairs with ladylike grace, instead stomping her way down in hopes it would get her father's attention before he made some too-blunt comment. "Thank you, Daddy. You can stop grilling Walker. It's not high school graduation night, you know."

Her father raised a brow. "I certainly hope not. I seem to remember he didn't get you home until nearly three a.m."

She couldn't do anything about the heat in her cheeks, but she refused to look away. "You know we had car problems."

Walker caught her eye and grinned, which made them look even guiltier. The sad part of it was they *had* broken down at the side of the road. And not even on a back road where they could've gotten into some mischief. No, they'd been right on the 22X, out in the middle of everything, but with no phone reception. Walker had walked to get a signal to call for help. And with her delicate shoes, he had insisted she stay in the truck, so their evening had devolved into time apart then enjoying a few stolen kisses while waiting for the tow truck.

Her father raised one brow as she reminisced. "Three a.m., that's all I'm saying."

Walker found his voice, a soft chuckle escaping him. "I can't believe you're still holding that over us."

Malachi relented, patting Walker on the shoulder. "Well, we've obviously forgiven you since here you are, back in town and taking Ivy out. We've been keeping track of your exploits. You've racked up some good results on the circuit this year. Looks as if you're already ranked high enough to head to the PBR in the fall."

Malachi failed to mention the disastrous final event Walker had taken part in, mostly because Ivy was staring daggers at him by this point, warning him to behave.

Of course, warning her father to behave was like trying to rein in a two-tonne elephant.

"Who are you talking to, sweetheart?" her mother asked from the next room.

Ivy had just lifted her gaze to Walker's face, and his lips twitched with amusement, which made her want to break out into giggles as well.

"It's Walker Stone, Mrs. Fields." he called. "I've come to pick up Ivy for our date."

Her mom rounded the corner, a bottle of wine in one hand, an iPad in the other. "Walker. How good to see you. Ivy, do I need to open some wine for this recipe, or can I use the grape juice we have in the fridge?"

She stepped between them, nearly braining Walker with the wine bottle as she passed while intently reading the recipe.

Walker dodged back smoothly before brushing a hand over his lips to hide his smile.

Ivy reached for the iPad to see what recipe her mother was talking about. "What are you making?"

"Something to use up the buffalo steaks the Simpsons gave us. I appreciate their generosity, but I think the poor animal had been around since the last turn-of-the-century. The first roast I cooked was tough as shoe leather."

"Buffalo from the Simpsons?" Walker made a face. "When did they start running buffalo?"

"Back in the early nineteen hundreds, according to Sophie, but I think they got them in last fall," Malachi informed him. "It's not a bad idea, and they've got the room."

Walker nodded slowly, and Ivy realized she was watching him again instead of checking out the recipe so she could answer her mom.

"Now that you're back, you'll be able to get caught up on all of the comings and goings in Heart Falls," Sophie assured him. "How's your oldest brother doing? Him and his new wife, of course—I was so excited when Malachi told me about their secret, surprise wedding with just them and their two little girls. And have Luke and his fiancée set a date yet?"

Ivy scanned the recipe quickly, as she listened to Walker's response.

"Nothing from Luke yet. Our sister Dare is getting married next month in Rocky Mountain House, so that's enough excitement for the family right now."

"And will—?"

Ivy stepped in before the grilling could continue. "We need to go to make our reservation on time. Mom, use the juice. You don't need to open the wine unless you want to drink it. But you'd be better off starting the recipe now for tomorrow—marinating for only an hour isn't going to make the meat less tough."

Sophie banged her free hand on her forehead as if Ivy had made the most brilliant announcement ever. "Of course. You're completely right. Walker, would you like to join us tomorrow night to try some buffalo?"

Ivy was tempted to reach up and pinch the bridge of her nose in frustration, but luckily Walker was holding out her coat to help her put it on.

"Thank you for the invite, but I've got a commitment with the family tomorrow night." Walker took Ivy by the arm and pulled her against him, edging toward the door. They backed away like they used to years ago, making a slow, steady escape before they got trapped by her parents for another half hour.

"Of course you do. But if there's another time that will work, we'd love to have you."

Malachi nodded eagerly as well. "Hey, I have some articles around you'd be interested in. Sophie, where did I put that box of articles on the history of rodeo?"

"Behind my chair?"

"On that new shelf I made you?"

"Might be there. Or on the table. Of course, I might have—"

Walker closed the door firmly behind them, and her parents' words cut off in mid-flow.

They stood on the front porch for a second before his polite smile gave way to a low, rumbling chuckle. "It seems some things never change."

Ivy nodded in agreement. "Can you imagine if they were *trying* to be annoying?"

"Are you sure they're not?" He adjusted the angle of his hat then tilted his head toward his truck. "Hungry?"

She should be, but there seemed to be a whole lot of butterflies dancing in her stomach where her dinner was supposed to go. "I could eat. I bet you're starving."

He pulled open the door and offered her a hand as she stepped on the running board to get in. "No one goes hungry around Silver Stone. JP's got food in the cookhouse for the hands all day long. He never knows when people get off shift. I grabbed a bite before I got ready."

He closed the door on her side then made his way around to the driver side. She was still laughing at his comment. "Is this something all guys do or just ranchers? Have a meal before they go out to eat?"

"Yes." He flashed a grin before pulling away from the curb and heading toward Main Street. The short journey of only a few blocks passed quickly as Ivy stared out the window as they passed familiar buildings. The mercantile. A photography studio. Her parents' book store. Walker nodded at the shop. "It was good to see your parents, as annoying as they are."

"I'm sorry Dad teased about not stopping in more," Ivy said. "I don't know what was going on in his head."

Walker hesitated for a moment, maybe because he was trying to find a parking space outside of Longhorn's Steakhouse, but it seemed there was something else involved as well. "No, he's right. I used to stop by more often."

Ivy hesitated. "You mean, after I left for university?"

"Yeah."

He was out the door before she could ask any more questions, and Ivy pushed it aside as a "thing to think about more and grill my sisters for answers" topic, but for now she had enough to focus on.

"You didn't have to bring me to the most expensive place in town because of the auction." Ivy slipped her hand into the crook of the elbow he offered before guiding her up the front steps of the low-lying building.

An old-time Western theme ran through this part of Heart Falls, with a wooden boardwalk and fake shutters outside the windows of most of the shops. Twinkling lights were draped over miniature spruce trees that stood in pots outside the door.

He hesitated before opening the door for her. "You haven't gone and become a vegetarian or something since you left, have you?"

"God, no. I'm still a carnivore at heart, although I eat a few more green things these days."

He gestured her in, laughing at the memory she must've triggered. The days her mother had pleaded with her to eat something from the fruit and vegetable family. Walker's mother had been alive back then, and Deb and Sophie used to plot together to find ways to get their families to eat healthier.

They settled at the table, Walker shaking his head. "I still remember the time you suggested we hold a sit-in to protest your mom putting shredded carrots in the meatloaf."

"Who does that? What sane person puts anything in meatloaf except their teeth?"

Walker laughed, the long, low sound rumbling through her like a caress, and she let it soak in, let it tangle around her with a sensation like slipping into well-worn jeans. It was comfortable, and soothing, and something that made her feel as if she were completely herself for the first time in a long time.

The hostess handed them menus, but Ivy barely noticed as her attention was drawn across the table. She admired his dark hair and the way his eyes danced over the page as he examined the menu. He'd grown into a fine-looking man. A sense of strength hung about him that was far more than just the muscles draping his tall frame.

She'd always trusted him completely, and while she didn't understand everything she'd heard about him over the past years —his reckless behaviour seemed out of character in her mind—he was still *her* Walker.

Her first love.

Now to convince him that she wanted him to be her last as well.

IF HIS HAND hadn't been forced by the bachelor auction, Walker wondered if they still wouldn't have ended up in this very situation sooner or later. He'd been in Heart Falls off and on for the past eleven years, but this was the first time Ivy had been back for more than a short holiday.

And she was *back*. He'd found that out after the bachelor auction when he did a little digging and discovered Ivy was now the grade two teacher and the assistant principal at Heart Falls Elementary School.

Ha. A little digging—her business card had said as much. But he knew it meant she was going to be around, which meant considering everything between them all those years ago, of course he would've gotten in touch with her.

He wanted to stare. In fact, he was staring. It was a good thing he had the menu memorized, because even though he held the pages in the air in front of him, he was looking past it to steal glimpses of his date.

Ivy wasn't as frail as she had been back in high school. Her frame was still delicate, and her colouring pale-moonlight, but she had more muscle and definitely more curves.

He'd enjoyed what she'd had before, thank you very much. Although at sixteen, the fact he'd got to even touch a female body had definitely put him in the awed-beyond-reason category.

The waitress took their order and left, and a moment of awkward silence arrived, at least until Ivy looked around the room before turning her gaze on him and offering a less than innocent smile.

"You look as if you're plotting mischief," he said, leaning forward with interest.

"I'm enjoying the fact that I already accomplished mischief." Ivy taunted. "Turns out bachelor auctions are fun—I'd never been to one before."

"You didn't need to buy me," Walker told her. "But, yes, I admire your evil tactics. I had no idea what was going on."

Her face lit up. "You should've seen how horrified you looked when you thought Tansy was bidding on you."

"Your sisters are awesome, but no way in hell—"

She snickered, almost a snort, covering her face with both hands as she flushed again. "It was for a good cause."

"Freaking me the hell out. Sounds like a great cause."

Ivy laughed harder. "Stop that. If you get me going there's no way I'll be able to stop, and this is not the place for me to be giggling like I'm twelve."

He couldn't stop himself. He let his gaze drift over her in admiration. "Trust me. No one in their right mind thinks you're twelve."

Her head dipped slightly, and she glanced up at him from under her lashes. "Sweet talker."

"For a thousand dollars I need to recite poetry."

She grew busy straightening her utensils, no longer meeting his eyes. "Please. Don't worry about the money part. Tansy and Rose had been saving tips from Buns and Roses with the intention of giving it to charity. Fern put in a quarter of the money as well."

He wasn't sure if that made him feel better or worse. "You mean your whole family bought me?"

A sharp laugh burst from her. "Definitely not, and if Tansy tries to tell you they did, feel free to correct her."

Their dinner arrived, and for the next hour they filled their bellies and reminisced. Walker told her a bit about adventures at various rodeos, and she told him a few stories from university and her early teaching positions.

By the time two pieces of pie sat in front of them for dessert, they'd barely touched the surface.

"It's been good to catch up a little," he said honestly.

Ivy nodded and took a deep breath. "I've missed you."

Something rolled in his belly. Something alive and wild. "I missed you too."

It was the only thing he could say, because it was the truth.

She picked up her fork and fidgeted, playing with the crust of her apple pie. "It was hard to leave Heart Falls. It was so hard being away at school at the start, but it was exciting enough that time passed pretty quickly at first."

Walker stared at the cherry pie in front of him—his favourite—and refused to look at her. Time had passed, yes, but he remembered that every day had seemed like an eternity to him.

But he was a damn grownup, and it'd been a long time ago, and he didn't need to tell her how much it had hurt that she hadn't been there. Besides, he'd been one hundred percent in favour of her going because it had been the right thing.

Sometimes doing the right thing sucked.

"But as good as it was I wanted to come home." Ivy waited until he lifted his gaze to meet hers. "I've got enough experience to avoid being bounced around, and with the assistant principal position, I can finally settle down."

"In Heart Falls?" He should be feeling something wonderful at her news, but instead a thin line of numbness was traveling along his spine.

She nodded. "I love it here. My family is all here, and my grandma. I've had a taste of living elsewhere, and I can honestly say this is where I want to put down roots."

There was no hesitation as she spoke. Everything about her said she was completely sure. She sounded so confident and excited to be moving toward a new future.

"Good for you," Walker said simply. He wanted nothing but the best for her.

Ivy lay down her fork and took a deep breath. "What about you? Are *you* back in town for good?" Her fingers shook the slightest bit, as if her question was more than a casual request for information.

God. He knew what she was asking. He knew exactly where she was going, because he knew *her*.

Or at least he'd known who she was before she'd left, and that woman, while shy to the point of not being able to speak at times, had still been able to get her point across.

Ivy was back in Heart Falls for good. Was he?

He would have given anything for the answer to be yes; for him to have reached the point he had anything to offer her.

Why did he seem to have nothing but wasted years stretching out behind him? Years he hadn't accomplished anything to help his family or to prepare for this moment?

The knot of discomfort that sat at the base of his neck like some kind of alien infestation had taken control of him, tightened its fingers, and forced him to answer the only way he could. He'd made his choice there on the hillside overlooking his parents' graves. He had to make a difference. He wasn't going to stay.

"I'm only around for a short while. Maybe the summer."

The light of hope in her eyes faded slightly. "Oh. They don't need you at Silver Stone?"

"There's always work for me there. Caleb and Luke are wonderful brothers, but..." He didn't want to do this here. He didn't want to be discussing how they couldn't have a future in such a cold and sterile way, not that moving to a more personal setting would make it any simpler.

He didn't meet her eyes. "Things are tough right now on the ranch. I've got a couple of opportunities waiting that could make some good money. It would give me a way to contribute and pay back the family for everything they've given me over the years."

Ivy reached across the table and laid her fingers on top of his, her touch cool and soft. "I'm sure your family feels you've done a lot to contribute."

"I don't do anything special around the place. Any man can muck out a stall. Out on the rodeo when I'm hot, I can bring home some big purses." He didn't mention the other opportunity that was a million times more crazy, and could be a million times more lucrative—if it worked.

She squeezed his fingers. "Well, I would enjoy your company if you are going to be around..."

"Ivy, honey, don't do this." He spoke softly, but it still felt as if he were poking her with knives.

"I'm not doing anything, Walker. Just saying I like your company. But I heard you. You're not going to be around. That's fine."

It wasn't fine, not on any level. "If I was staying, I would be knocking on your door every single day." His gut ached, and his heart hurt. Finally doing the right thing was brutal—it was like cutting off a limb to hurt them both like this. "I hope you know that, but I can't stay."

An enormous sigh escaped her. She glanced away and

pretended not to dab at her eyes. "Okay. I'm disappointed because I was kind of hoping that we'd be able to..."

She shook her head and held back the words, and Walker felt like one hell of a bastard for dashing her hopes.

He felt sick to his stomach because what he wanted more than anything was to read between the lines and accept what he was damn sure was an offer for them to be together.

Suddenly she smiled at him, pulling herself together with strength that said a lot about the woman she'd become. "I'm proud of you."

Walker wanted to take himself out behind the woodshed and beat some sense into his stupid brain. "What for?"

"For figuring out what's important to you and sticking to your guns. That's what I'm trying to do, and trust me, I know exactly how hard it is to do what you feel is right when the world is tugging you in a different direction. I don't want to tug you from your goals. That's why I'm proud."

Ivy picked up her fork and dug into the last few bites of her pie, focusing on her food, which was great because it gave him a chance to think instead of react.

She was right. As horrible as it made him feel to not get involved with her, he had good reasons. Things to accomplish. Changing his mind on the spur of the moment wasn't going to help his family, and it wouldn't help him deal with the trouble haunting him like a banshee.

Walker took a deep breath then consumed his pie as well, the sweetness settling on top of that small bitter rock that remained in his belly.

He wanted it all. For everything to be right, *and* to have Ivy, and those two things couldn't both happen.

He took her home at the end of the night, and as they stood on the porch outside her parents' house the awkwardness returned, even though Ivy was trying everything possible to make it normal.

She twisted toward him, eyes shining like quicksilver in the pale glow from the porch light. "It was good to get back in touch. And you know you're always welcome."

"I'm pretty sure you'll get an invite to the ranch soon. You need to meet Caleb's Tamara and his girls."

She nodded. "I'm looking forward to seeing Luke and Dusty as well. He looked so grown up on stage the day of the auction, I barely recognized him."

"God, he's nineteen and thinks he's hot stuff."

Ivy snickered gently. "How dare he. I thought that was supposed to be your job description, Mr. Dynamite."

Stupid nickname. But he grinned because it was better to have his reputation be what she was thinking about as they finished the evening. "It's better than Danger-Man, which is what one announcer tried to label me with a few years back."

"I remember that." She offered him a sweet smile. "Well, thank you again for dinner, and I'm sure I'll see you around town."

She lifted up on her toes and pressed her lips to his cheek, chaste and friendly, before squeezing his arm and making her way inside without a backward glance.

In fact, she was gone so quickly he felt as if the porch was whirling. He stood there, motionless, uncertain what he was supposed to do with this lost and lonely sensation.

Finally, he turned and hopped in his truck, aiming it toward Silver Stone ranch in the hopes he could find someone to distract him.

Broken hopes sucked. Broken hearts—

Walker put his foot down on the gas and shoved the thought away with all his might.

5

Walker parked outside the bunkhouse, his usual living quarters while at Silver Stone. He and Luke had moved out of the ranch house years ago when Caleb had gotten married the first time.

He didn't need much, and the bunkhouse had been set up to be comfortable for the hands. Each man had a private room with their own separate entrance, but a shared bathhouse and kitchen area.

He'd never needed much before, but as he looked around the spartan room, it was another dig at how little he'd accomplished over his nearly thirty years.

The small wardrobe had just enough room for his clothes and boots. Hooks on the wall held his hats. The bookcase that doubled as a side table was the only sign he lived here and not someone else. His favourite novels were stacked neatly so he could grab them whenever he wanted.

Hell, he had more property when it came to tack and equipment for his truck then personal items.

His conversation with Ivy earlier had triggered all kinds of emotions. She was settling in, and the kicker of it was he could picture the place she'd turn into a home. It would probably have the white picket fence, and room for two point five or whatever number of kids were average in this day and age.

And that was somewhere he really didn't want his mind to go, so he twirled on his heel and out the door, striding up to the ranch house.

Distraction needed, now.

He'd only been home for a few days, which hadn't been nearly long enough to catch up with his family. And truth be told, as gruff and as silent as his older brother could sometimes be, Caleb had a good head on his shoulders. He'd taken on the raising of their family after their parents' sudden death and had lived up to the challenge, he and Luke, both.

That nauseating sense of uselessness struck again. Walker had been devastated when they'd lost their parents, and at times it still felt as if he were in shock. Stuck in a place of being absolutely useless to everyone and everything, nothing but a burden to be taken care of.

He stomped his way onto the deck, still mentally chastising himself. With his current trouble, he was not only being a burden to his family but to the rest of humanity as well. For someone who needed to change his situation, the sense of helplessness rushing him felt like a heavy anchor dragging him down.

He glanced through the glass window in the door a second before he jerked it open. And thank God he did, because Caleb was most definitely busy. He had Tamara in his lap, hands settled on her hips as she stroked her fingers through his hair. The two of them were staring into each other's eyes as they spoke softly, anticipation and connection clear in their body language.

Walker pivoted, stepping softer with his retreat.

He didn't begrudge Caleb his happiness one bit. His brother had been through hell and back with his first wife, and having found a woman who not only loved him but loved his little girls had put something right at the heart of Silver Stone.

It didn't help Walker get his troubles off his chest, though.

He took a turn through the barns, examining the beautiful horses that were the second half of the ranch income. Again, not something Walker had been a big contributor to. This was far more Luke's work. As Walker ran a hand down the flank of a mare and she eased under his touch, he appreciated his brother's skill even as he worried about how the change in finances would affect Luke's plans going forward.

Walker stepped around the corner and jerked to a stop, backing up rapidly to avoid letting his second brother see him. Damn, he'd been looking for Luke, but this wasn't how he wanted to find him—pressing his fiancée Penny up against the wall.

"Oh God. Yes." Her head fell back, blonde hair falling in waves as her fingers clutched Luke's shoulders, digging in.

"Dammit, Penny. You're driving me crazy," Luke muttered before sweeping her up in his arms and crashing a shoulder against the nearest door. The heavy wooden barrier slammed shut a second later, trapping the two of them in one of the tack rooms.

Walker took off as quickly as he could, but he still heard bodies banging into a wall before he was out of earshot.

Okay, that answered one question. Luke and Penny were still an item. They'd been engaged for a couple years now, but never seemed to be moving any further forward. Not that Walker was about to tell his brother how to handle his relationships considering the only woman *he'd* ever cared about had all but offered herself up on a silver platter tonight, and he'd been a fool and turned her down.

What do you have to offer her? his conscience demanded.

Nothing. Less than nothing, which was precisely the reason

why they were going to stay "just friends" even though the thought was killing him.

Thank God his next destination turned out to be not only safe but twice as successful as he'd hoped. Ashton Stewart had been the Silver Stone foreman long before Walker had been born. As Walker glanced in the window of the man's private quarters on the far edge of the bunkhouse, he saw Kelli James was there as well, the two of them sitting together at a table with a deck of cards.

Ashton's front door held a huge wreath hung in the middle with Canada Day flags festooning the wild spruce branches. It didn't strike him as Ashton's style.

Walker found a free spot on the surface to knock, swinging the door open to Ashton's instant "Come in."

"You got room at the table for a third?"

"Fourth," Kelli corrected. "Dusty is in the bathroom."

"*Dustin*," his youngest brother snapped as he stepped back into the room. "God, Kelli, you look like you're about twelve years old, so it's not your failing memory making you forget my damn name."

"Dustin," Ashton rebuked him sharply before gesturing that Walker should take the empty chair at the table. "You're welcome to stop in."

While his brother sat and reset the crib board, Kelli, who'd been working Silver Stone as a ranch hand for years, eyed Walker with curiosity.

"What? Do I have mud on my face?"

She dragged her fingers over his cheek, pulling back to show a trace of pink on her fingertips. She didn't bother to hide her smirk. "I was going to be nice and not tease, but considering it's barely eight o'clock, and you're already done with your bachelor date, there's just so much to tease about I don't think I can resist."

"You were out with Ivy Fields?" Ashton asked. "How's she doing?"

"Fine. Happy to be back and planning on staying. She's got herself a great job." Walker kept his expression as blank as possible as he grabbed the cards from Dustin's hand and shuffled. "She worked hard while she was gone, and now she's getting rewarded for it. I always like it when people I know come out on top."

Kelli and Dustin exchanged glances that said they weren't buying his bullshit.

Ashton kept staring at Walker, his poker face remaining unreadable. "Good for her," was all he said.

Walker dealt, ignoring the unspoken questions.

He assumed they wouldn't be stupid or rude enough to actually dig in, but he hadn't counted on Kelli and her amazing ability to ignore all the signs that were right there saying *do not cross this line*.

"So. She kissed you on the cheek."

"Yup."

"After what was basically a reunion date, considering you two used to be super-sweethearts."

"Yup." He sorted his cards. Again.

"So, after that steamy kiss you two exchanged during the auction, which I did not see but did hear *all* about, you're saying Ivy kissed your *cheek* at the end of the date?"

"You got a point?" Walker folded his arms over his chest and glared at her.

She grinned back. "Nope. Just making a few comments."

"I'd say something, but I kind of like my head attached to my shoulders, so I'll resist," Dustin muttered before playing the first card.

They played for a while, and all conversation centered on the game, but the questions were still hovering.

Didn't mean Walker had to answer them.

So it surprised him when Kelli finally did say something not remotely in the direction he thought she would go. Up until then, he'd assumed everyone would encourage him to rekindle his romance with his high school sweetheart.

Instead, her words made a whole lot of sense. "You did a good thing by taking part in the bachelor auction, but just because you knew her back when doesn't mean you guys need to be an item now."

"True." Ashton nodded slowly. "Being in a relationship isn't the be-all and end-all some people make it out to be. It's not something to jump into."

"Exactly. There are a hell of a lot of things I want to do before I settle down," Dustin offered.

Kelli snickered. "You're just a baby. Of course you don't want to settle down yet."

"Kelli, behave," Ashton warned. "The boy's got a valid point. You don't have to come back and prod him about his age. Time passes quickly enough, but not if you're with the wrong person. There's nothing wrong with waiting until you find the right one."

"Nothing wrong with being on your own," Kelli offered back.

Ashton lifted a finger and pointed it at her, nodding his head firmly. "Don't want to be tied down, never wanted it. Too much else for me to do. I've already got my family right here at Silver Stone. Don't need to be dealing with some woman fussing about with fancy doodads and whatnot."

Walker didn't stop his snort in time.

The foreman frowned at him. "What're you snickering about?"

"I just couldn't help but notice the decoration on your front door seemed a whole lot frillier than what I'd expect."

Kelli kicked him under the table, but she was fighting to keep a straight face. "Oh, you know when Ms. Sonora gets her mind set on something, there's no telling her to go away."

Ashton sat there as if he were facing the torments of hell. "Tamara told her she was allowed to give everyone a thank-you gift for helping take care of her animals when she was sick this past winter. I didn't know that meant the woman was going to slap fancy plants on my door."

"Ms. Sonora? Are you talking about Ivy's grandma?" Walker asked.

Three heads nodded in unison. "She still lives on that ranch of hers a couple of range roads down. Refuses to move into town like a sensible woman would." Ashton shook his head. "It's not as if we could leave her animals to suffer when she was feeling poorly."

"Of course not," Kelli said instantly, but she turned to face Walker and winked on the sly.

Ashton finished his proclamation. "I like my life. It's simple, it's clean, and my time is my own."

"Amen." Kelli raised her glass in the air. "Well, except for the part about my time being my own, because I'm pretty sure you're in charge of ninety-five percent of my time."

The old man grinned. "That's your fault. If you'd stop hanging around the ranch when you've got time off, you wouldn't have to look at my ugly mug so often."

Dustin held up the deck of cards. "Want to go again?"

Walker nodded his agreement along with the others. They were good company for a man who felt rootless and reckless.

And all of them, maybe with the exception of Dustin, were lying through their teeth. They all wanted more, but for now this was what they'd got.

It had to be enough because there was no other option.

~

Ivy got up on time, prepped for the day, and firmly fixed a smile on her face before she went to knock on her baby sister Fern's bedroom door. Just because she was all kinds of sad inside didn't mean she was going to allow herself to wallow in self-pity.

Besides, diving into Ben and Jerry's for breakfast was not something she wanted to make a habit.

She knocked a little harder. "Fern? You still in bed?"

The door swung open in front of her, but Fern wasn't in her pyjamas. She was wrapped in a white smock, a paintbrush held in her teeth, probably put there so she could use her hand on the doorknob.

Fern grabbed the paintbrush as she twirled away. "Close the door. I've got the window open to air out the fumes, but I don't want the wind moving my papers."

Ivy hurried to follow her instructions, stepping inside and closing the door behind her as Fern hurried back to an oversized easel positioned near the large window. She had the surface tilted to a slight angle with dozens of pieces of paper pinned over it. She picked up more paint on her brush and ignored Ivy completely, rapidly adding colour to each of the dozen pages in turn.

"I'm not trying to be rude, but I can't stop at this point," Fern explained. "It's watercolour, and I'm blending."

"No problem." Ivy made her way to a tall stool she could rest on, watching with great interest as her little sister added touches of brilliant blue and shocking red, and on each page the lines of connection blurred differently to create splashes of purple in a multitude of tones.

Ivy let her gaze drift from the artwork and roam over her sister. Fern gripped the paintbrush with confidence. Her deeply tanned skin looked darker against the white smock, and her riot of tight black curls had been pulled into a knot at the base of her skull. Her dark eyes moved rapidly, boldness in her moves as she added splashes of colour to the final pages.

"Will it disturb you if I talk?" Ivy asked.

"Not at this point. When I'm getting things set up I need to focus, but this is a bit like following a rhythm." Fern grabbed a jar off the side table and held it against her body with her left forearm, wrestling off the top with her right hand before placing it carefully next to the rest of her paints. "There are times I really wish I had three hands and not one," she joked.

"You do pretty well with the one you've got," Ivy pointed out.

"True." Fern was back to work in the next breath.

Ivy glanced at the bedside table where Fern had left her prosthetic. As usual, her sister seemed just as happy without putting on her bionic parts, as she called her device, although, she did love getting new variations. Emails over the years from Fern had always included an update on whatever technology was the next greatest thing.

Ivy turned her attention to the coloured pages. "These are neat—the pictures. What's the plan?"

Because Fern always had a plan. Even back when Ivy had been in her final year of school and Fern in elementary school, it was the eight-year-old who made lists and agendas, broken down into subsections and time frames, no less. Nothing was left to chance when it came to her little sister.

"I'm working on graphics for a game, and I'm trying to figure out what background colouring I want to program into the digital core matrix."

Ivy blinked. "Okay."

Fern laughed. "You're so funny. That's exactly what Mom said."

"As long as you're having fun, I'm glad. I don't understand what you said, though."

Her sister snorted louder. "And...that's what Dad said."

Ivy stepped forward as Fern put her paintbrush into a jug of water, turning to hold out her arms and offer a hug. Fern jerked to a stop and held up a finger for a moment. "Let me get out of this. You don't need to get covered in paint splotches."

She tossed the white coat over the back of a chair then wrapped Ivy in a tight hug. "It's good to have you home," Fern murmured against her shoulder.

"It's good to be home, although I won't be living here for much longer. You'll be able to go back to sleeping in my room if you want."

"I don't mind sleeping in here. I know it's a little crowded with all of my art stuff, but it's got the best light in the whole house so it's worthwhile." Fern ran her hand over her head and tucked away a coil of hair that had come loose. "What are you up to today?"

"I thought I'd go over to Buns and Roses. Want to join me for breakfast?"

Her little sister grinned. "What? We get to go torment Tansy and Rose? Of course, I'm in."

"You're terrible. Want to drive?"

Fern nodded. "I'll meet you downstairs in five minutes."

It was more like fifteen before they snuck away, having finally convinced their mom they were happy to get their own breakfast.

For a small town, there was an awful lot of traffic going in and out the front door of the coffee shop, which was probably a great thing considering the more people, the better the shop was doing.

Behind the counter, Tansy was chatting up a couple of young men with cowboy hats on. Rose spotted her sisters first as she came out on the floor carrying a tray covered with baked goods. "Look what the cat dragged in."

Ivy glanced at Fern. "Which one of us is supposed to be the cat?"

"*Meow.*"

Rose laughed. "Talk in a minute, I'm kind of busy." She walked past them to a corner table, where she unloaded food in front of expectant customers.

"Know what you want?" Ivy asked Fern.

"Hot chocolate, the muffin of the day, and whatever Tansy wants to give me. She's always got something special up her sleeve." Fern waved at someone before gesturing to the side. "You want to put in the order, and I'll grab a table?"

"Sure."

Tansy looked surprisingly happy to see her. "Ms. Fields. Are you still drinking two-shot lattes?"

"Yes, and Fern wants hot chocolate, and we'll both have muffins and whatever else you want to give us for breakfast. I hear that's the way it's supposed to work."

Her sister's face lit up. "No problem. But you have to promise to come around this evening when the shop is closed. I don't mind cooking for you, but I'd like to be able to sit and chat as well."

"We're going to have lots of time," Ivy assured her.

She made her way across the room with the two hot drinks, placing one in front of Fern then settling in the chair beside her.

Once again familiar faces filled the room, along with some new ones. "There are a lot fewer old-timers in here than I would've expected for a coffee shop," Ivy said softly to Fern.

"Buns and Roses is too newfangled. Or that's what the complaints in the newspaper said," Fern told her with a laugh. "Tansy doesn't offer too wide of a menu, and what she does bake is all slightly unusual, so the local farmers still go to Connie's Cafe."

Ivy examined the full room. "It doesn't seem to have affected business."

"Nope. Tansy said the old guys were the ones who never tipped anyway, and all they wanted was cups of black coffee with endless free refills. She can do without their company, but all their sons are showing up here." Fern took a sip of her hot chocolate, her dark eyes dancing with mischief. "Only partly because of how well Tansy can cook."

Ivy stared for a minute at her little sister. "What?"

Fern grinned harder as she tilted her head toward the counter where another set of young men were ordering more food, vying to impress Tansy and Rose. "Face it. They're good businesswomen, and they're easy on the eyes. Add in the fact Tansy *likes* to cook?" Fern shrugged as if it were crystal clear.

Ivy considered rubbing her temples. "And are Tansy or Rose in the market to accept any of this interest in their fantastic qualities?"

"Tansy dates a lot, but she goes for the flavor of the day. Rose tends to go out with the same guy a few times in a row, but never gets serious either."

This was fascinating. Ivy was so glad she had decided to pump her little sister for information, but she'd never imagined the conversation was going to go this direction. "And you? Did you have anybody special this last year of high school?"

Fern shrugged. "Nope. You were the only one of the Fields girls who had a high school sweetie. I went with Ryan McGregor to grad, but we're just friends. I'm not interested in anything but spending time with my friends, guys and girls together."

"And there's nothing wrong with that. Have you figured out what you want to do this year for school?" Fern's interest in art was all over the place.

"I'm not ready to take any formal training, and I'm still trying to figure out what I like best, so I'll keep playing with the odd jobs I find online." She made a face. "Only that means I need to find a summer job here in Heart Falls, and the only thing remotely artistic is getting a job with a painting company."

"I'll ask around if there's anything else you could help with, but yes, you might be stuck doing something menial this year."

Rose showed up at the table, placing two plates with what looked to be an oversized ham and cheese croissant in front of them. "If you want a job here, you've got it. We could use help over the summer, so it's not a charity offer either."

"I know, and I promise I'll give you an answer by the end of the week."

Rose was gone before Fern could say anything else.

They ate their breakfast, the food going down easily between the stories that Fern shared about recent adventures within the Fields family.

It was neat to get the perspective from another one of the kids, and it was good to know that what was visible on the surface was true deep down. Sophie and Malachi were doing well, and they were still solidly in love.

It was one of those bittersweet realizations. That was exactly what Ivy wanted for her parents. She didn't know of two people who were more deserving of their happiness together. But it also threw into sharp relief what was missing in Ivy's own life. All her hopes of being able to rekindle the sweet, intense feelings she used to share with Walker needed to be put aside.

It was heartbreaking, but she knew she needed to continue to live her life. And that meant if Walker wasn't going to be the one standing beside her thirty years from now, she had to get serious about finding someone who would be.

As disappointing and hard as the truth was, she needed to widen her net and consider some of the other fish in the ocean.

"Ivy Fields?"

Speaking of fish. Large fish. Large, muscled, and *grinning at her* fish. Brad Ford towered over her.

It had to be said—he looked good with no hair.

"Brad. I saw you on Friday and wondered if I would run into you sometime."

He placed a hand on the back of the empty chair at their table. "You guys mind? I'm waiting for Tansy to finish putting together the order for the boys at the fire hall."

"Go ahead," Fern answered before Ivy could. Then her little sister laid her hand on Ivy's shoulder briefly. "I gotta go to the washroom. Be right back."

She took off and left Ivy sitting alone with Brad. That's when Ivy wondered if, out of all the Fields family, Fern was the most devious of the lot.

Ivy offered Brad a smile. "I hear you're our new Fire Chief. Congrats on your position, and on becoming a firefighter."

"Thanks. Finished my training a couple of years ago, along with EMT. I worked as a smoke jumper before coming home. My dad needs a bit of help these days, and I'd always planned to return." He flashed a grin. "Congratulations to you, Assistant Principal. This means you'll be the one the kids are hauled in front of when they're bad, right?"

Ivy smiled. "Sometimes. Hopefully not too often."

"And only for the best reasons, right?" Brad leaned back in his chair, and it creaked under his weight. "You have to admit you were the one who got us in trouble that day."

Another rush of memories struck. "I had no idea Bugles were *that* combustible, or I never would've suggested lighting the entire box on fire."

"Yeah, I still blame the science teacher for not giving us better parameters for the project. I mean it's a bit of a setup to ask kids to find common, everyday objects that are dangerous."

Ivy felt her lips twitch. "And now it seems you're in charge of putting out fires. Strange, the symmetry in that."

He laughed; a big, hearty, happy sound that rolled up all the way from his toes. "You're right. I hadn't thought of it that way.

And I guess you're also following the prophecy of that moment, because you're the one who taught me the best way to use the lighter."

Laughter burst free and it felt good.

Ivy was still smiling as he leaned toward her, a question in his eyes. "I saw you at the auction. You and Walker getting back together?"

It should have felt awkward, and maybe if he'd had a different intent it would have, but the interest in Brad's eyes was nothing but friendly.

And that was too bad, because even though it felt far too soon to be thinking about dating other people, in a way it was the right thing to do. If she sat around mourning for the next couple of months, it would prove to Walker that she hadn't accepted his decision.

But she couldn't date *Brad*.

Her voice sounded a little sad, even to her own ears, as she confessed, "My sisters and I set up the auction for a bit of fun and to help the fundraiser. That's why we did the whole Tansy-bidding thing. But no, Walker and I are only friends."

He frowned. "Seriously? You guys were good together."

She raised a brow. "Still matchmaking, I see. Who are you going to fall for? Someone who can keep you out of mischief, I hope."

A soft light came into his eyes. "Oh, there's someone, but she's being stubborn. I'm going carefully with her."

Intrigued, Ivy teased. "Tell me. Do I know her?"

"Probably not. She's not that new to town, but after being gone for a while myself everyone seems new. It's a strange sensation. Meeting people is an unholy mix of being a stranger to town *and* one of the old-timers." His dark eyes flashed with humour. "Nice change of topic, Fields, but I'm not done, yet. I don't believe it. About you and Walker being just friends."

"You'll have to. We had our bachelor date, and that's it." She folded her hands and tried for her best *do not push this subject* expression. The one she'd perfected as an assistant principal.

It worked great on people under the age of twelve, but not on a six-foot-five colossus. Brad leaned in farther and lowered his voice. "Do you need me to beat him up for you? For old time's sake?"

Ivy paused. "You never beat him up for me before."

"I offered to," he reminded her. "When Chantelle lied and told you that Walker told *her* that he was breaking up with you so they could go out, and I found you crying in the gym."

Oh God. "I'd totally forgotten that."

He flexed his arms. "It's pounding time."

Ivy's cheeks hurt from smiling. "Stop. No, you can't beat him up for me, but thanks for the offer."

"You want me to talk to him?"

"Brad." Ivy folded her arms over her chest.

He nodded firmly. "Awesome. So, you're going to talk sense into him yourself. Glad to hear it."

Ivy gave him a dirty look.

"No guts, no glory, Fields. You've gone after everything else you wanted in life, right? Why should this be any different?"

She opened her mouth to protest.

Then she closed it firmly and tried not to look as discombobulated as she felt. He was right. She'd simply given up. Oh, she wanted to respect Walker's wishes, but they hadn't even talked about what he was trying to accomplish. She'd just accepted his *no*, and his confusing excuse about needing to leave town, and she'd moved on.

Stupid woman.

Brad leaned back with a chuckle. "That's what I thought. Hey, we should get together sometime to reminisce some more. We could double date."

"I'd like that." Brad was solid as they came and obviously smart. Ivy eyed him, wondering if he was making a roundabout play for one of her sisters. "I noticed you still didn't tell me your mystery woman's name."

"Order is up, Brad," Tansy shouted from behind the counter.

Brad rose to his feet, grinning. "Her name is Hanna. I'll let you poke your sisters for the rest of the gossip. When you meet her, put in a good word for me."

He turned and left. A moment later Fern was back at the table, glancing at Brad as he dealt with a tray full of drinks and a hefty-size bag of food. "He really should ask you out, but he's been making goo-goo eyes at Hanna Lane ever since he got back to town."

"Don't you go matchmaking," Ivy warned. And of course, Fern knew about Hanna. "Him or me. I don't need help with my love life." Although it seemed Brad had already offered her some fabulous advice.

But she wasn't taking any from her little sisters.

Fern made a face. "I wouldn't dream of it. Although you might want to warn off Tansy and Rose, because they've already got everything plotted out for you for the next couple of months."

Good grief. Just what she didn't need; her sisters organizing her life.

She and Fern sat back and relaxed for a while, Fern's interests in a million different topics making the conversation easy and interesting enough to stop Ivy from going back over Brad's comments.

It was later when she was alone that Ivy pulled them out to examine in detail. Was she going to give up without pushing Walker harder? It made no sense to simply lay down all her dreams like that.

Then again, she refused to make it awkward for him. If he truly knew what he wanted, she had to respect his wishes. The line between giving up too soon and pushing too far was a tightrope to walk. Somewhere between her hopes and wanting the best for Walker, even if it meant not having him, was the right answer. But how would she get there?

Her dreams were restless that night. She still didn't have a solution.

6

Ivy checked her email for the details before punching in the phone number for the Silver Stone ranch.

An unfamiliar female voice answered the call. "Tamara Stone. How can I help you?"

Ivy's gaze dropped to the bottom of the email, and quickly matched the name to the one on her notepad. "I'm Ivy Fields. You were inquiring about private tutoring for one of your daughters."

A curious noise slipped over the line almost like a satisfied hum. "Excuse me. I still get a huge thrill every time someone says that. Yes, I understand you're going to be her teacher this coming year, and after talking to Caleb, we thought it would be a good idea if Emma had some extra one-on-one time with you before the school year started."

Ivy considered. Assistant principal or not, teachers didn't rake in the big bucks. An opportunity to make extra cash would make the expense of the new house go smoother. "We should be able to work something out. Would you like me to drop by the ranch to meet with you and Emma?"

"Please. But if you could come talk to me privately first, I can make sure she's busy."

"I'm free anytime this week," Ivy offered.

"This afternoon? Caleb was thinking of taking the girls riding, if we could say around two o'clock."

Ivy wrote down the time and signed off, working through a few other tasks before making her way up to the ranch.

She was not hoping to see Walker. Not at all.

She was also lying to herself with everything in her. Brad might have poked some sense into her, but plotting how she was going to have a come-to-your-senses discussion with Walker was proving difficult. She wasn't any further along on it today than she had been last night.

Seemed there were some things that were still tough to do for a shy person—and phoning the man up to demand they talk in more detail was one of them.

So when she drove into the yard and saw Walker sitting on his horse, his Stetson pushed back to reveal the strong features of his face, a tingle shot through her. He was such a fine-looking man. Somehow she had to convince him to be *her* man.

The group on horses ambled slowly from the arena into the far field as she got out of her car.

A jean-clad woman came toward her with a happy smile and an outreached hand. Eyes flashing brightly behind bright yellow glasses. "Hi. You must be Ivy. I'm Tamara Stone, the girls' mom."

Oh, yes. "Congratulations on your marriage."

Tamara grinned, her face lighting up with happiness "Thanks. It's been official for a short time, so I'm still giddy." She gestured at the house. "Come in. We can have a drink and talk about what will work best for all of us."

They were steps from the porch when the kitchen door swung open and a familiar face appeared. It was Caleb, a little more worn by the years, but looking fighting trim and very content as he paused to slip an arm around Tamara and hug her tight to his body. "Never thought I'd be the one running late." He turned his gaze to the side and his eyes widened. "Ivy Fields. Welcome back."

"Thanks. I told Tamara congratulations, but I should offer them to you as well. And I'm looking forward to meeting your girls."

He nodded slowly, a wide grin on his face. "It's been a few years. They must've been babies last time you saw them."

"Things change. The world keeps turning," Ivy offered.

Caleb glanced between them, his feet shifting as if he were impatient to keep moving. "I'd love to get caught up, but I promised some little cowpokes an adventure."

"It's okay. We'll have plenty of chances to get together now that I've moved back."

"Go," Tamara encouraged him, attempting to push Caleb to where his horse stood waiting at a nearby rail. "I'll invite her to come for dinner sometime."

Caleb examined her with amusement in his dark eyes. "You're not making mischief, are you?"

"I have no idea what you're talking about," Tamara protested. But she smirked as he leaned in and kissed her thoroughly.

Ivy wasn't sure if she should look away and give them privacy, or if it was kosher to keep enjoying the sight of two people who were most definitely in love.

It was an easy answer. She watched.

Tamara's cheeks were flushed when Caleb stepped back, tipping his hat to both of them in farewell then whistling cheekily as he made his way to the rail. He pulled the reins free and mounted up, moving smoothly as he guided the animal to rejoin the rest of the group.

Ivy's gaze drifted past him to where the others were waiting.

Two young girls sat on small sturdy mounts, Walker and Dusty Stone flanking them.

Walker either hadn't spotted her, or he was deliberately not looking in her direction, which was fine by Ivy because she didn't need to make this moment more awkward than it was already was. He moved lazily in the saddle, circling his horse around the small gathering, using his body to guide the animal, hands relaxed. Moving as one with the big horse.

Something inside her tightened with longing.

A soft cough interrupted her rapt staring, and Ivy straightened with a flush.

Tamara gestured toward the house. "Sorry for getting distracted there, but that man of mine wipes out brain cells far too easily."

Ivy chose not to answer. She wasn't sure if the other woman was offering her an out after catching her staring at Walker, or if Tamara really hadn't noticed Ivy was all but drooling.

It was easier to simply follow up the stairs and into the kitchen.

Tamara indicated the living room. "Have a seat."

Bowls full of peapods rested on the island. Ivy tilted her head toward them. "Or I can help while we talk."

The suggestion pulled a smile and a nod from Tamara. "I'd never turn down the offer of help with my chores. Be my guest. It feels as if we've got a million early peas to shell."

Ivy tugged one of the empty bowls closer and settled in, grabbing a big handful of the green peapods to begin work. "I used to do this with my family as far back as I can remember. The four of us girls would sit at the kitchen table, and Mom would grab a book. She'd read out loud while we did all sorts of chores."

Tamara nodded in approval. "I like that idea. Bet that made the time pass a lot faster."

"It did, except when my dad would join in and things would

get out of control." She let her amusement show as she lifted her gaze to meet Tamara's. "Dad tried to be around as much as possible, only he had a bad tendency to interrupt with what he thought were scintillating bits of information to make the story better."

"I take it that didn't go over well?"

Ivy shook her head. "I think it was a defense mechanism to being the only male in a group of five females. I have to admit his sense of humour rubbed off on all of us. Especially Tansy."

"I've enjoyed getting to know your sisters over the past while," Tamara confessed. "Tansy and Rose in particular. I've only met Fern a few times, but she's got some amazing talents."

"Fern will do fine. She needs to sow a few wild oats before she settles into one main focus."

"Wild oats—in a field full of ferns, roses, tansy and ivy?"

Ivy smiled. "You caught that, did you? I've always considered it a funny phrase considering our last name, but the idea still fits."

Tamara laughed with her before growing serious. "I don't know what you've heard from your sisters, but what we're looking for is help for Emma. She's been a reluctant speaker, and she had her reasons, but we're working through them. She's still hesitant with people she doesn't know, and in tense situations. And because she hasn't spoken a lot over the past few years, she has a few verbal issues. I think she'd do better if she got to know you before the school year began."

"So she's confident I'm on her team?"

Tamara nodded.

"It's a great idea," Ivy said with soft approval. "Might I ask what her reasons were? I don't want to accidentally set off any triggers."

"Emotional abuse and abandonment issues," Tamara said tightly. "A gift from her birth mother, who is out of the picture. Shouting might be considered a trigger, but Emma does okay with her sister going off at her too loudly. And occasionally her Uncle Dustin forgets and he can boom, but she's okay with that."

Ivy's heart went heavy at the thought of any child having been abused. "Someone who loves you unconditionally getting loud is not the same thing as mean or cruel shouting." She nodded. "Thank you for letting me know. I'm glad she's got all of you in her life, and that she's out of a bad situation."

She was glad Caleb was out of what had to have been a heartbreaking position as well.

"Emma knows very thoroughly that she's loved." Tamara took a deep breath. "*Very* thoroughly."

Ivy tried to lighten the conversation, working for as positive as possible. "If she's got some specific school subjects she needs improvement with that will give us a place to start. Then I can adjust our tasks based on what she needs."

"Sounds like exactly what we were hoping for."

"And just to reassure you, speech delays like you're talking about can be gotten over pretty thoroughly. I bet Emma is a smart little thing."

Tamara's hands stilled for a moment. "She is, but you can tell that from...?"

A flush struck at having made an assumption and being called on it. "Okay, I'm guilty of jumping to conclusions, but I grew up with the Stone family. The three older boys, at least, and I spent a lot of time here. Walter Stone might've been a rancher, but both he and his wife were well educated, and they made sure the boys were too."

The other woman nodded slowly. "I forgot you would've known Caleb's parents."

"They were amazing people. It was a shock to all of us when they were gone so suddenly." It had been a long time, but Ivy still remembered how unreal it was. How much they all expected Walter and Deb to simply walk back through the door at any moment because there'd been no warning. "One minute they were there, and the next they weren't. I don't know if it's easier when someone is ill for a long time—having them suffer while you get to say goodbye—but sudden loss is horrible."

Tamara was quiet before answering "There's no good way to lose the people you love, but I think you're right. Getting to say goodbye is better."

She looked thoughtful for a bit, so Ivy stayed quiet, the two of them working in silence on the peas. Their hands moved in an easy rhythm while something bubbling on the stove behind Tamara perfumed the air with the scent of rosemary and salt.

Tamara broke the silence. "You know the family well, then."

Ivy shook her head. "I did, but I've been gone for years. I've visited Heart Falls when I could, but it usually ended up being around the holidays when everyone is busy with their own families."

"I'd love to hear more when you have the time. I admire what the Stones built into their sons. It would be good to know a bit more about them to share with the girls as they get older."

"I'm sure as I spend time with Emma, some of the stories will come out." Ivy glanced around the kitchen, shaking her head. "This place is stuffed to the brim with memories."

"I bet. There aren't a lot of traces of the senior Stones around the house anymore. I think Caleb's ex-wife got rid of a lot of things."

Ivy pushed down a rush of annoyance at what felt like an invasion of privacy, but really wasn't. She *had* been gone for an awfully long time. She couldn't expect things to stay the way they were while she moved forward.

"If there are any books around, you can probably find their names written in the front. The Stones loved to work with their hands, and they knew how to deal with the school of hard knocks, but they also read just about everything. I think that's why my parents approved of me dating Walker back in high school." Ivy smiled. "It wasn't an easy task to impress my parents." She made a face. "Come to think of it, it still isn't."

Tamara laughed. "You're right. That is one thing there are still plenty of. There's a whole wall in Caleb's office covered with books. I never really thought about who put them there."

"Charm'd magic casements, opening on the foam. Of perilous seas, in faery lands forlorn."

The other woman tilted her head, the sun glinting off the edge of her glasses. "Very poetic."

"Keats." Ivy looked Tamara over with interest. Brad's comment about coming back to a familiar place but not familiar people prodded her into moving forward. "I'm thinking I'll start a book club. Would you be interested?"

"Depends what we're reading," Tamara responded instantly.

"Book list will be set up by the participants, so if you want to get in on the ground floor, let me know."

"Sounds like fun."

It was going to be, although she still wasn't sure if she should willingly let her sisters join in. "If I let Tansy and Rose pick books, you'd better be ready for an eclectic mix."

"I don't mind a challenge," Tamara returned.

They did a little planning then, going through some of the notes from Emma's teacher the previous year. Ivy made some suggestions, and Tamara countered them, and in the end they had agreed Ivy would come out three times a week at least for the start of the summer.

"Emma's in the play the Boys and Girls Club is sponsoring. All of her lines are part of the chorus, so if she decides not to speak, it won't be terrible," Tamara told her. "But she was so keen on participating with Sasha, I thought it was worth the risk."

"We'll hold our own rehearsals," Ivy said.

Tamara laughed. "Caleb can fill in some of the parts."

Ivy glanced at her watch. "I should head out. I don't want to be here when they get back and have that as our first meeting. It would be better if Emma knew I was coming and wasn't surprised with it."

Tamara shook Ivy's hand firmly. "Thanks. And I'll let you know about the book club. We also need to set up a time you can come over for supper to catch up with Caleb and the girls. And any of the boys we can wrangle."

Which would include Walker. Ivy schooled her features to stay polite. "Talk to you soon."

She swung out of the yard at Silver Stone, but when the time came to head right on the road into Heart Falls, her wheels seem to turn automatically in the opposite direction. She made her way up the long road that rose toward the mountain pass before exiting onto a single lane that wasn't labelled, but was well known to all the locals.

Ivy pulled to a stop in the parking lot and stepped out of the car, meandering along the path leading to the back of the Silver Stone property.

Heart Falls itself belonged to the municipality, but it was attached to the ranch, and here again Ivy fell into another walk down memory lane. She took her time, sauntering along the narrow trail that led all the way to the bottom of the hill and the pool formed by the waterfall.

Three quarters of the way down there was a bench built into the hillside. A log had been notched out and stacked on rocks to form a solid platform. The sun shone down perfectly, and after sitting for a few minutes, Ivy gave up all attempts at being an adult and stretched out as if she were cat in a beam of sunshine. Warm and relaxed.

So. Her return to Heart Falls wasn't going exactly like she'd planned, but she could roll with the punches. Even today's visit helped her move another step along the way.

She *had* to move forward—there was no changing that fact. She felt a little like her sister Fern as she mentally made a list.

One—she was back in Heart Falls for good. This was going to be her home.

Two—she wanted a home, with everything that meant: husband, a family, and her extended family around her, which was why she was picking this spot to stay.

Three—the man she hoped to build a family with was being stubborn.

What on earth was he talking about, needing to contribute?

She was going to have to move slowly. If he really didn't want to stay in Heart Falls she wasn't going to force him, but it seemed silly not to talk about this more. It would be wrong to not figure out what was going on in his head before she gave up completely.

But if he was sure he didn't want her? She'd find a way to accept that and move on without him. They were adults—she could do it if she had to.

The sun warmed her from top to bottom. She worked on breathing evenly and allowing the truth to soak into her. She *could* move forward, with or without Walker, and yet—

And yet— as she tried to build up enthusiasm for her new to-do list, sadness hovered.

She *wanted* Walker to be a part of her life. It was the thought that had sustained her for so many years, and turning her back on the idea seemed like treason.

Seemed very, very wrong.

7

Walker spent the afternoon laughing with his nieces and enjoying time with his oldest and youngest brothers. It was never a bad thing to head out riding over Silver Stone. But if he was truthful, he'd been a whole hell of a lot distracted the entire time.

He wondered who'd been pulling into the Silver Stone parking area. The instant he spotted Ivy's white-blonde hair, it was as if he'd been plugged into a full wattage amp. Energy pulsed through his very bones.

Daydreaming about Ivy was a really shitty way to spend what should have been a pleasurable couple of hours, and he found himself antsy as they headed back toward the barns.

He slipped up beside his oldest brother and spoke quietly, not wanting to make a big deal over leaving the group, but suddenly too antsy to stay. "If you don't mind, I'm going to ride to the falls. Need a moment to revisit the place."

"Dreamer. Go ahead." Caleb moved in to distract the girls. Sasha fell for it, watching her Uncle Dustin as Caleb teased. Little Emma was the one who examined Walker as he turned his horse away, her big blue eyes staring after him as if she understood something of what he felt. That feeling of being lost.

He blew her a kiss and her lips curled softly.

Thank God she had Tamara now along with Caleb because that sad expression didn't belong in any little girl's eyes.

Although the sensation that had been wreaking havoc with *his* gut wasn't one that any man, woman, or child should have to face, either. The one he felt when the panic rolled in.

His path was clear—whether he wanted to or not, he needed to face that demon and find a way through. Because damn if he would let his family down again. The ranch needed money.

His body wasn't broken. If he dealt with whatever was up with his brain, he could earn enough money riding to throw at the problem. At least temporarily.

His cell phone went off as he reached a clearing in the trees, and he cursed before modulating his voice to be as polite as possible. "Maxwell. Didn't expect to hear from you."

"I don't see why not. Dammit, man. I sort of understand you taking a little time off from the rodeo—that's dangerous shit—but why are you ignoring my calls? I've got people looking for an answer, and they're not going to let you put them off forever."

A few days ago his answer would've been to let them rot, but now he didn't have that option. "Run it by me again."

Maxwell broke out his "everything will be okay if I can explain the basics to this stupid cowboy" tone of voice. "The team I gave your demo to want you to come out and perform with one of their talent. It's backup right now, which isn't a bad thing. With the skills you've got, it's possible you start there then break out on your own."

Singing hadn't been on Walker's agenda. Not ever. "They're jumping the gun a little, don't you think? I mean they only heard me that one time."

Maxwell sighed. "Seriously? Walker. That's what you're

worried about? I'd swear you don't want to be discovered. That's all it takes—*one time*—if you play your cards right. And you had no problem sitting in the studio and making those demos."

"Because the demos and the emergency backup recording were to help Jordan out. It wasn't supposed to be about me." And it'd been easy to sing in a two-by-four sound studio booth, with no one but a technician on the other side of the glass listening to him. There hadn't been any other eyes watching or whatever the hell it was that had caused him to freak out the next time he'd ended up in front of a crowd. "When do you need an answer?"

Maxwell was doing something on the other side of the line that involved paperwork, rustling noises filling the air as Walker brought Hannibal to a stop by the Heart Falls pool and dismounted.

"The sooner the better, but if you're busy training for the fall, I can tell them that. They understand the need to work with the family and prepare for the PBR. They're setting up their schedule now, so I have to have an answer by the end of summer."

Two months' reprieve. Two months for Walker to figure out what was wrong and find a solution to make it right. When he put it that way, it sounded possible. "Okay, Maxwell. I'll have an answer for you by the end of the summer."

"Don't you go forgetting, or get so busy you blow me off again. I want you to give it some serious thought."

"I will."

"Talk to your family. I know you're big on family. I'm sure they'll be able to help you decide. What did they think when you told them about the offer?"

Walker should've kept his mouth shut, but it wasn't in him to lie. "I haven't mentioned it."

Maxwell cursed at the other end of the line. "Dammit,

Walker. What the hell is *wrong* with you? It's like you're willing to piss this away. I should just tell them to forget it."

"No—" Walker snapped, because he couldn't throw away the chance at the money. Even though his skin crawled at the thought of what the deal Maxwell was offering would require. "I swear I'm thinking hard about it, but I need a break. I can't afford to get distracted when I'm riding..."

Truth, but a total lie, since he had no intention of going anywhere near a competition for a while.

Maxwell bought it, though. "Okay. Okay, settle down. I'll talk to Jordan's team, and make nice. They'll wait until the end of summer, but I want you to keep in touch. Figure this out, or someone else will snag the chance of a lifetime."

"Thanks," Walker forced out the words, then hung up more frustrated than he thought possible considering it was an incredible break he was being offered.

Maxwell was right. Anyone else would be jumping up and down to have an opportunity like this fall into their laps.

Walker stepped forward, pacing the trail that meandered around the pool at the base of Heart Falls as the cascade created a musical sound that was a tease and taunt all at the same time.

His memories of his dad telling him he wasn't living up to his potential were wrapped up in this place, and they echoed louder than the water crashing into the pool at the base of the rocks.

He found himself kicking stones aside as he marched to the rocky face of the hillside. High above, the water flew off in an arc, mist covering everything with fine water droplets, soaking his shirt and his hair, gathering into a trickle of water that ran down his face as he stared up at the wall.

So. He had to find out if he could still ride bulls, and he had to discover if he could actually get up in front of an audience and sing without having a panic attack.

He eyed the water. He eyed the wall. Maybe it was stupid, but the idea that struck *seemed* to make sense.

If he knew what caused his panic attacks he could stop them, or barring that, he could learn ways to deal with one when it happened. And since he wasn't about to tell any of his family what was going on and become even more of a burden to them, he was going to have to deal with them on his own.

He slid off his boots, stuffed his socks inside them, and then eased along the narrow path under the falls to just past the falls themselves. To his right was a route up the mountainside that he and his brothers had tried when they were young. They'd climb the rocks, higher and higher, until their fingers would slip and they'd inevitably fall off.

With the pool directly below, he'd fall straight into the water. Unless he was really unlucky, he wasn't going to get hurt.

But as Walker stared up the sheer face, adrenaline rushed his system. If he *was* going to have a panic attack, climbing this monstrosity should be enough to cause one. If he fell, hitting the water would bring him to his senses.

Frustration and confusion and anger mixed inside him. He didn't want to have to deal with the bullshit of panic attacks. He wanted to be with Ivy, and he wanted to stay in Heart Falls, but he wanted to support his family and—

So many thoughts rattled in his brain, whirling over and over until his heart pounded and his brain ached. Screw this. He needed to *do* something.

Walker put his hands on the rock wall and climbed.

A CLOUD SLIPPED in front of the sun, and the temperature dropped just enough to pull Ivy from her blissful sunning. She glanced at her watch and figured she'd actually fallen asleep for at least half an hour.

She stretched as she placed her feet to the ground, taking one final look over the water before—

"Oh my God." Someone was climbing the cliff.

They couldn't be comfortable, not with the way the water was spraying everywhere. And it definitely wasn't safe, because there wasn't a thing around them that wasn't drenched with mist.

Ivy hurried forward, patting her pocket for her phone in case it was necessary to call for help.

She was about halfway down the path when she recognized *who* the idiot was. She wanted to shout at Walker and tell him to get the hell down, but that probably wasn't a good idea.

Instead, she was torn between watching him steadily move upward or racing back to the ranch to find someone who could pound some sense into him.

Walker stopped moving.

She waited impatiently. He must be looking for a new handhold. Or maybe he planned to start descending, although she couldn't imagine why *anyone* would want to climb up or down the rock face.

Only he didn't move. Not his arms, not his feet, not his head.

She waited as long as possible until she couldn't stifle it anymore. "Walker?"

Her voice echoed off the wall back to her.

He didn't move.

"Walker," she tried again, louder this time. But other than the sound of her own voice and the booming of the falls, there was no response.

She was reaching for her phone when his hands shot out sideways, and he jerked as if waking from a sudden sleep. With both hands off the wall, his body fell back, crashing to the surface only a few feet from where the falls slammed against the water.

Ivy raced down the path toward the pool, shouting his name.

Walker bobbed to the surface. She expected him to lift his head and give it a shake, water spraying from him like when they were young, but her hopes were in vain. His back was visible, but his head remained lowered, face down.

Ivy didn't stop to kick off her shoes. She raced into the shallow water, spray flying everywhere as she made her way to the colder depths, shouting his name the entire time.

Her voice was swallowed by the sound of the waterfall's roar.

Less than a minute had passed between him hitting the surface and her reaching his side. Ivy ignored the icy temperatures and hooked her fingers into the material of his shirt, jerking him toward her. The heavy weight of his body dragged her forward until she was up to her neck beside him.

"Walker. Wake *up*."

She hauled him toward the shore because there was no way she could lift him with nothing under her feet to support herself.

The instant she could plant both feet firmly on the bottom, she wrapped an arm around his torso and rolled. His arms twitched again, one of them flailing out and striking her across the shoulders.

She tumbled into the water, loosening her grip on his shirt so she could find her feet.

When she finally caught her balance and scrambled upright, Walker was pulling himself to vertical, blinking hard.

"Walker. Are you okay?"

He finally seemed to see her, his eyes focusing slowly as confusion drifted across his face. "Ivy?"

"What is *wrong* with you? Do you have some kind of death wish?" An enormous shudder shook her from top to bottom as she turned her back on him and stumbled her way onto the shore. The cool wind that had been so refreshing while sitting in the sun made her feel as if she were inside a refrigerator.

"Why are you wet?" Walker asked.

What? In spite of being freezing cold, Ivy paused to examine him. "You fell. You were climbing the waterfall, you idiot, and you *fell*. You weren't moving, so I came in to get you. Don't you remember?"

He shook his head before pausing. "Right. I was climbing."

He was pissing her off, *that* was what he was doing. "Look. I'm cold, and I'm wet, so if you're okay—"

Ivy's dramatic heel-turn-and-stomp-away departure lost its effect when she sneezed. And then sneezed again.

Oh God, she was in trouble. She and sneezes had a history. They *never* came by ones or twos.

She was on her fourth out of control explosion when Walker's arm wound around her. They were both wet, but his big body was like a heat generator, and she cuddled in against him ignoring all logical reasons why she shouldn't.

"Your car's at the parking space at the top of the trail?" Walker asked.

She nodded, but the motion got lost as she sneezed another three times.

"Yes," she finally forced out between explosions.

"I'll take you home."

She wanted to tell him it wasn't necessary, but he had taken off at high speed, returning to jerk on his socks and boots before catching hold of her again and guiding her up the trail. She wasn't going to protest when at this point she really needed his arm around her to keep vertical.

Ivy closed her eyes and let him guide her, burrowing in as close as possible in the hopes the heat coming off him would stop her from ending up in real trouble.

Sneezes, even in batches of a hundred, were not the worst thing that could happen to her after an unexpected dip in a still-frigid pool.

Halfway up the hill, Walker gave up on trusting her stumbling feet, swinging her into his arms. By now the sneezes were not funny; they hurt. Anyone who'd never experienced it probably thought it was amusing, but by the time her body had forced out more than forty sneezes in a row, her bones felt as if they were ready to come apart. Her head ached from snapping forward, and her eyes and sinuses were filling up.

Traitorous body.

He pulled to a stop. "Your keys?"

"Not locked." Forced out between explosions.

"*Keys?*"

Stubborn man. "Pocket."

"Get them."

She held onto his shoulders as he put her feet to the ground, digging her hand into her jeans and pulling them out.

A moment later he had the door open and she was settled on the passenger seat. He tilted all of the air vents toward the ceiling before racing to the driver's side and squishing himself into the tiny space.

A moment later the car was running with the heat cranked on high.

"Stay here. I'll be back," Walker commanded.

Ivy wanted to protest, but she knew better. She was still sneezing, and that wasn't going to stop anytime soon. Her getting behind the wheel and driving safely was impossible until the attack decided to stop.

Walker took off down the trail, vanishing quickly as he sprinted away. She tugged her coat tighter around her shoulders, twisting the air vents toward her as soon as the air grew hot.

Under her the heated seat began to make itself known, but she was shaking too hard to really appreciate it.

Five minutes later the door beside her jerked open. Walker was back.

He took off, heading toward town, and she realized the only place he could take her was...problematic. "My parents," she got out.

"I figured." He sat quietly for a second before adding, "I sent my horse back to the stables alone. I'll have to borrow your car to get home."

She didn't try to answer because everything hurt now, and the sneezes still weren't finished.

By the time they pulled up in front of her parents' house, though, her body was tired enough to have slowed down. Utter exhaustion was rolling through her, and she leaned heavily on Walker as he guided her up steps to the front door.

"Mrs. Fields," Walker called as he brought them in the front entrance, but no one answered. "Malachi?"

Silence.

Walker picked her up again, and she laid her aching head against his chest, no longer trying to pretend she was in control.

He marched up the stairs, carrying her as if she were a feather. "Dammit. They must both be at the bookstore."

"Phone Mom," Ivy suggested, teeth rattling.

"I will, but first, we'll get you warmed up." A shudder shook her from top to bottom, and his arms tightened. "Ivy, honey. You want to hop in the tub?"

Shaking her head was no help. He wouldn't be able to distinguish it from the rest of her involuntary quivering. Getting words out past her shaking lips was difficult. "Want to be dry."

She might've imagined his curse, but she didn't care. She didn't care about anything anymore because it was nearly impossible to keep her eyelids open.

It was infuriating to have her body betray her like this. No grown adult should be sent into shock just from a dip in cold water, but after enough years of fighting her reality, this was the hand she'd been dealt.

All she could do was use her coping strategies to try and not slip further down the path into sickness. Getting out of her wet clothes was of vital importance.

She reached for her buttons, her fingers shaking so hard she couldn't catch hold of anything.

"I'll take care of you." Walker's voice, soft and gentle now, and she let her eyes stay closed because it would be easier to not see him.

So much easier not to watch as he, gently as possible, stripped away her soggy wet blouse and pants Because if she was watching his face and saw even a hint of desire, she was going to do something regrettable.

She also wanted to find a large object and smack him over the head with it. "What were you doing on the rocks?"

He made a soothing noise as he took the blanket off of her bed and wrapped it around her shoulders. "Something foolish. I'm sorry you got caught up in it."

"Troublemaker."

He reached around her, undoing her bra and slipping it off her body under the cover of her blanket. "Yep. You and me, Snow. A ball full of trouble."

Fire and ice. That's what she was thinking because he was peeling her wet panties down her legs, and her eyes popped open just to torment her. His face was set like the stone of his name, as if he were trying desperately to get through this.

Because it was difficult to touch her? Or difficult not to touch?

Her head ached too much to give the dilemma anymore thought. When he picked her up and laid her in the middle of her bed, pulling the blankets over her, she decided she'd have to think about it sometime when her teeth weren't rattling like castanets.

She lay there and shivered, breathing shakily and trying desperately to find a way to suck heat out of the air.

The mattress dipped. A heavy male body joined her, skin connecting with hers as Walker folded himself around her.

"Oh my God."

Somehow those words came out crystal clear. Walker was in bed with her, both of them naked, in her parents' house.

Maybe she was further gone than she thought, and now she was hallucinating.

"I need to warm you up. Relax, honey. You're going to be okay."

A thick band of muscle curled around her as he pulled her in tighter, that furnace inside him operating at full volume. He put out more heat than standing in front of a wood-burning stove.

It was really too bad she was beyond exhausted and couldn't enjoy this as much as she should. Muscles pressed against her, his warm breath sliding over her shoulder as he nestled his face in the curve of her neck. Their legs tangled together, the hair on his limbs scratching like erotic sandpaper.

It took a while before the knot inside began to melt and her body relaxed enough so that blood could flow again. Her head ached, and her muscles were tired as if she'd run a marathon. But she was warm, and she felt safe.

Of course I feel safe—I'm in Walker's arms.

As she drifted off the last thing on her mind was still confusion.

What had Walker been doing in the first place?

8

Walker held himself with an iron-clad control until Ivy's breathing slowed and her body relaxed against him in the most torturous of ways.

It was surreal to sneak out of Ivy's room after pulling on his wet clothes, considering all the times and days when they'd been in their teens and he would've liked nothing better than to be in bed with her.

But most definitely *not* in her parents' house.

He used the phone in the kitchen to make the call, his cell useless after its dip in the pool.

Mrs. Fields answered the call at *Fallen Books*. She took the news that her daughter was tucked into bed and sleeping with amazing fortitude. "I'm heading home right now. Stay with her."

No way was Walker going to ignore the order.

So he turned around and went back up to Ivy's room, pulling the chair from her desk and sitting close beside the bed. A wisp of hair had fallen across her face, but he didn't dare move it because she'd finally settled into a heavy sleep.

Staring at her made something inside him ache.

The door to the room opened. Sophie Fields came in quietly and Walker left, totally ignored as Ivy's mom moved quickly to the bed to check on her.

For a moment he thought he'd gotten away without having to explain everything. Nope—

Malachi Fields was waiting for him at the bottom of the stairs.

"I took a tumble into the pool at Heart Falls, and Ivy got it into her head to come rescue me," Walker explained quickly. Even as the words escaped, they sounded stupid.

Malachi raised a brow. "Why would she think you needed rescuing? Last I heard you could swim."

And here came the troublesome part. Walker assumed another panic attack was involved, but his brilliant idea of the water making him come to must've been wishful thinking. "We'll have to ask her. I got her home and warmed up as quickly as I could. Hopefully she's okay."

Ivy's father was looking at him with more than disapproval. There was fear in his eyes—fear for his daughter, which was turning rapidly into anger against Walker. And Walker was pretty fine with that when it came right down to it.

Malachi straightened, his eyes flashing a warning. "I hope she is as well. But you might want to rethink your relationship with my daughter. I understood you weren't planning on seeing each other anymore."

Of course Ivy would've talked to her parents after their date. Walker wondered what she'd told them. "No, sir."

The older man stared daggers. "That might be best. If it's what you want, don't keep dragging this out. It's not fair to either of you."

He wasn't saying things like "maybe you're too dangerous to have around my girl," but the gist was there. Malachi was a protective father ready to step in the same way he had over ten years ago.

Walker wanted to protest that he hadn't *asked* Ivy to jump in to save him, but the reality was— God, he didn't want to think about what could've happened if she hadn't been there. "Yes, sir."

Mr. Fields shook his head then gestured toward the door. "Come on. I'll drive you home. I was going to stop in at my mother-in-law's, and Silver Stone is on the way."

It was too far to walk, and without a phone he couldn't call one of his brothers to come pick him up. "Thanks."

Thank God the awkward, silent ride was over quickly.

Walker waited until later that night to call and see how Ivy was doing. He got Sophie on the line who was reassuring, but she determinedly put off letting him talk to Ivy.

It wasn't until the next day he got his phone to work and found he had a text from her.

Ivy: *I'm okay after my dip. You?*

He thought for a bit before responding: *Worried about you.*

Ivy: *I'm stronger now than I was. I can deal with disasters easier.*

He was pretty sure there was a smart comment in there regarding *him*, but he chose to ignore it because he had no other option. Not unless he wanted to up and tell her the entire story about his panic attacks.

Walker: *good. Thanks for giving me a hand.*

Ivy: *don't make a habit of it.*

And that was it. She didn't ask for any further explanations, and that in itself had him more confused than expected.

The Ivy he'd known at school would have dug in her heels, figuratively, and not given up without getting to the bottom of it. She'd been physically frail, but she'd had a will made out of the strongest iron.

It seemed she was taking him at his word and moving on.

So Walker tried to do the same. He fell into chores with a vengeance, as well as working out and running to stay fit. Countless sit-ups, hanging crunches, and balance exercises until his abs throbbed and his torso quivered. Being tossed about on the back of a bull was a dangerous pastime made moderately safer by being in rock-solid shape.

Besides, pounding out miles and pushing iron was a good way to work off frustration.

It was good to labour with his family and to push his body hard, but every time he caught himself thinking back to the panic attacks, that strange sensation of hopelessness returned.

Why did they take control sometimes and not others?

He drove a couple hours south to a rodeo training center and helped some younger riders with their practice rides. Watching and waiting for a clue to jump up and smack him in the face.

A day later he got pulled into branding, working in the fields, and roping with his brothers.

Luke and Dusty were there. Caleb had convinced his friend Josiah Ryder to come out. The five of them spent an entire afternoon with Ashton and a bunch of the other hands all crowding in and helping where they could, the animals milling around in organized chaos.

At one point there were more cowboys than animals in the area. Walker turned and stared over the land, admiring the view that was a part of his soul.

"Hey, stop daydreaming and get to work."

Walker jerked back to attention, tipping his hat at Ashton. "Just waiting for everyone to catch up."

The older man raised a brow. "Nice try, but it didn't work when you were eighteen and I caught you staring off into space, and it's not going to work now. Get up," he warned with a laugh.

Walker took the scolding even though he *had* been waiting his turn. It was too good to be with his family and friends, labouring in the heat and sun.

When he did get distracted a few minutes later and ended up on his backside in the dirt, laughter rang loud and clear while he took the teasing with a smile. This much at least was right. Family, hard work. If it weren't for the financial worries hanging over them, Walker realized he could be happy spending his days like this forever.

They were all covered with dust and slick with sweat by the time they were done for the day.

Back at the barn, Dustin hurried through cleanup before racing away at a high speed.

Caleb rolled his eyes.

Walker didn't bother to hide his amusement. "Dustin got a hot date?"

Caleb sighed but offered a faint grin. "He's heading out with Ashton to Uncle Frank's. They'll take the calves we don't need."

"Seems pleased." It looked as if Caleb's idea was going to work.

"He's out of his mind with excitement. He's off to tell Tamara and the girls."

Oh man. "Hang in there." Walker offered.

Caleb nodded. "Tamara's aware of his...*infatuation.* She thinks it's cute, but it'll be good to not have him underfoot for a week."

"Are you and Tamara coming out tomorrow night?" Josiah

called from across the barn. "Kelli mentioned this morning that the girls are having a sleepover with her."

Caleb raised a brow as he looked at his friend. "Think that one through a little harder. I'm going to have an empty house with my wife, and you want to know if we're going to leave it?"

Josiah snickered. "Sorry. Don't know where my brain was."

Caleb took off. Luke, Walker, and Josiah continued to work with the horses. Luke guided the veterinarian through the animals that needed to be checked, and Walker joined in, trying to help where he could.

"What're you doing tomorrow?" Walker asked. "Sounded as if there's something special going on."

"A new owner took over Rough Cut. Ryan set up a line dance night."

Walker laughed. "That's a selling feature?"

Josiah looked at him as if he were an idiot. "Seriously? I suppose, you being a rodeo star and all, you don't have to know this, but women love line dancing. It's like smorgasbord night."

Amusement danced in Luke's eyes. "It's not as if you have any trouble finding women either. When are you going to stop eating from the buffet table and make a selection?"

"Who says I haven't already?"

"Bullshit," Luke snapped. "You just told us you're happy there's a new hunting ground in town. You wouldn't be saying that if you'd already picked a woman."

"If I haven't claimed them, I'm still on the market."

"I take it you don't like your balls too much, saying that when you've got your eye on a woman. Or you're not too worried about it getting back to them."

Josiah shrugged. "I didn't say I was through with the all-you-can-eat buffet, *yet*. And I don't go *through* the entire buffet, I choose the best. I like to take one thing at a time and really enjoy it..."

"...before moving on to the next?" Luke eyed him. "You're lucky my sister isn't around so I know you're not talking about her, or I'd feel obligated to beat the crap out of you for making that kind of comment."

"You're the one who talked about moving on to the next one. I didn't say anything of the sort," Josiah pointed out.

"Oops," Luke muttered.

"Catch me up," Walker said, trying to change the topic before Josiah dug himself into a grave. "I've been gone for long enough I don't know who's taken and who's still single among the girls we went to school with."

"Why are you interested? I mean, you already laid claim to Ivy, considering that kiss the other day. Or was that all some kind of a show for the auction?" Josiah looked as if he really wanted to know the answer, but it was hard to tell with him because the man had the best poker face of anyone around.

Walker forced himself to make it sound real. "Ivy and I were together in high school, but we're not interested in each other like that now."

Liar.

Luke was staring at him as if he were shocked by the admission. Then he went on to answer the question, although his answer was no better than another taunt, thankfully aimed at Josiah. "None of the Fields girls are married or dating, although Rose seems interested in Josiah," Luke said.

"Oh, bullshit." Josiah didn't even glance up from where he was working on a hoof. "She's never looked at me twice, and I've certainly never given her any sign I wanted to get together with her."

"You're the local vet, bro. You're like all the shiny doctor stuff with ranch knowledge thrown in. I think Fern has a crush on you too."

"They're way too young for me," Josiah said. "Luke, your

friend Glenn is closer to them in age. You should toss him their direction. Since you're already taken, I can't suggest you try."

Walker considered. "Where *is* Penny these days?" He hadn't seen her since the day he'd nearly interrupted them in the tack room.

"On a trip to Europe with her dad." Luke looked distracted. "She's not back until late August."

"Bummer."

Luke made a face. "They offered for me to come along, but I figured I should stick around."

Josiah's jaw dropped. "Seriously? You turned them down?"

"I don't have the money to pay my way, and I'm not going to bum a ride and expect Mr. Talisman to pay for everything. But I didn't want Penny to miss out on the trip, so yeah, it sucks, but we're keeping in touch." He turned to Walker. "Speaking of which, Glenn is coming with us to bring horses to Red Deer, since you said you didn't want to go."

It was one way to evade seeing anyone he knew at the rodeo that would be happening. "Glenn still lives in town?"

"Three range roads to the east, yeah."

Glenn had never been one of Walker's favourite people. He wasn't sure why the thought struck, but it did with annoying intensity. Glenn was staying around the community—able and probably willing to get involved with Ivy.

Frustration ran up one side of Walker and down the other, and he found himself saying a curt goodbye. He stomped his way to the bunkhouse and scrubbed up, the hot water pounding against him. Dirt and sweat swirled down the drain, but his black mood refused to wash away.

And when he slipped back to his bunk and lay on the bed, the four walls closed in around him, thoughts of Ivy taunted him. Her asking if he was sticking around, her coming to save him...

Her looking at him as if she wanted nothing more than to be

swept into his arms and...

Walker jerked upright and threw his pillow across the room in frustration. He had nothing to offer her; nothing to offer his family. Only a gut full of anger and frustration, and far too many unanswered questions.

The world had carried on while he'd been farting away his time. Even their small town was changing and turning with the tide, yet here he was, frozen into immobility. No decisions made and no future until he did.

He pulled out his phone and stared at the messages from Ivy. *Don't make a habit of it.* Make a habit of what? Getting into disasters and hauling her after him? Thinking about her?

Wanting her?

This was bullshit on so many levels, and he'd fucking had enough. Screw this.

Walker jerked on his clothes. Maybe it was wrong, but it was the *right* kind of wrong. He wanted to see her, and he wasn't going to sit here doing nothing when that was the one thing that he *knew* for certain he did want.

He jammed his feet back in his boots, slammed on his hat, and headed for his truck.

Ivy had turned her waking hours into a blur of work and family. She'd avoided any terrible repercussions from her dip into the Heart Falls pool. She'd been a bit shaky, but whether or not it was the miracle cure of Walker's naked body pressed against hers —and she totally wasn't ignoring the potential good in knowing *that* information—other than sleeping for nearly twelve hours then having to put up with her parents' concerned questions the following day, she'd felt fine.

But the momentary setback made her determined to get into

her new home as quickly as possible.

For the past week, everyone in the Fields family had been over at the tiny bungalow, scraping off old wallpaper, painting, and generally fixing things up.

Rose stepped back with a happy hum as she glanced around what Ivy had to admit was a tiny, but perfect, master bedroom. "I love it. There's still not enough room to swing a cat, but it's peaceful, and it's pretty, and I'm totally jealous."

The walls were a faint dusty rose, the window trim white, and the overhead light had been covered with a soft, creamy light shade that bathed the entire room with a candlelight glow.

"It's the only room done in the entire house, but I think Tansy was right. The place has good bones."

Rose stepped around the edge of the bed, running a hand over the quilt that Grandma Sonora had given Ivy as a homecoming present. Pale squares in pastel colours matched perfectly with the old-fashioned feel of the room.

"I think you were smart to start with this room." Rose lifted her eyes to smile at Ivy. "It means you can move out, right? You don't have to stay with Mom and Dad anymore?"

Ivy didn't need to feel guilty for wanting to be out from under their roof. She was a grown woman, but it was good to know someone else understood her urgency. "I love them, and they're wonderful, but it's time be on my own."

Rose nodded. "Why do you think Tansy and I live over the shop? It's a five-minute walk from Mom and Dad's, and we could live there rent-free, but when it's time to move on...we move on."

Still, it was good that her sisters had each other. Ivy looked at Rose and wondered if she knew how precious the relationship she had with Tansy was.

Heck, the relationship they had between the four girls was something beautiful considering they'd all come from such different backgrounds. *Choice* had made them a family.

"Definitely time to move on," Ivy agreed. "Help bring in my things from the car? I didn't let Mom see me pack them. I thought it would be easier if I got some of it out of the way without her knowing."

Because after her incident with Walker, it was even more important for Ivy to prove to her parents she could stand on her own two feet. She knew they understood she would always come to them for help, but it was her decision about how her life went.

They'd moved in half of the boxes when, to her surprise, a far too familiar truck approached.

Rose paused with her arms wrapped around a box of books, staring with disapproval at Walker's truck. "What's he doing?"

"Driving past, I hope." Ivy turned away as if that was the end of the conversation. She grabbed two suitcases from the trunk and marched toward the house. Working hard to act lighthearted and not at all curious.

"Liar." A soft snicker escaped her sister.

"Shut up," Ivy muttered.

Along with everything else—frustrated at his first refusal, confused by his stupidity at the falls—Ivy was pissed off at Walker Stone. Not because of anything specific he'd done, but because trying to figure out how to approach him was tormenting her.

Just the thought of him sent her system into hot flashes. She'd been dreaming about him. Sweet dreams where they'd be walking side by side in the park after school, their hands linked and shoulders bumping innocently. And then the dream would turn, and he'd be stripping her bare and covering her with his body and...

In all the years she'd been gone, she'd never had a quarter this kind of reaction to any other man. She'd begun to think her entire libido was broken, but obviously not. She remembered distinctly that, even while shivering madly in her bed, some of the heat between them had not been generated because of the furnace beneath Walker's skin.

Nope. It seemed she was hotwired to the *Stone* frequency.

And now, after a week of stewing herself into a tizzy, he was driving up like he didn't have a care in the world? She didn't know if she should jump up and down with excitement or scream in frustration.

A hand landed softly on her shoulder, dragging her attention to her sister's face. Rose's dark-brown eyes had gone soft. "Sometimes people don't know what they want. And sometimes people know what they want, but they're not quite sure how to get it."

"Which camp am I in?"

Her sister shrugged, dark hair falling around her shoulders as she moved. "I think you know what you want, but you're not sure if it's okay to take it."

"I don't think Walker would like to be spoken about as an *it*."

"He's not an it," Rose said dryly. "But there's something up with him and has been for a long time. We know he likes you. Honestly, the man has been panting after you for years."

"Oh, please."

Rose continued as if she hadn't been interrupted. "We *know* this from how often he asked about you while pretending he wasn't hanging on our every word. You said he didn't want to get involved, but it doesn't make sense."

Which was exactly the part that was bugging her. Ivy nodded as his truck slowly turned up her driveway, no longer uncertain of his destination.

As confused and mixed-up as she was, Ivy knew her sister was right. Walker was confused and mixed-up about a lot of things as well.

They had enough history, they had enough of *them*, there was no reason why she shouldn't dig a little deeper and see if she could convince him to change his mind.

Between the conversation with Rose, the one with Brad days ago, and the fact Walker was offering himself up to her doorstep like a special delivery package, it seemed fairly serendipitous. This was the opportunity she'd been looking for.

She screwed up her courage and turned to Rose as Walker's boots hit the ground. "You should head out."

Rose's lips curled into a smile as she raised a brow, the delicate arch oh-so-meaningful. "Call me later."

She pulled on her jacket and headed down the porch steps, passing Walker with no more than a quick wave as if she had urgent business elsewhere.

Walker seemed to have an urgent target as well, at least until his boots landed on her stairs.

The first step creaked ominously under him, and he glanced down, his face transforming with a frown. "Need a hand fixing that?"

"Maybe." Only this wasn't the time to discuss home repair. Not when she had more important plans.

She gave herself a firm pep talk. Just because she was shy didn't mean she was a pushover. It also didn't mean she had to let all of her goals go by the wayside. If Walker didn't know exactly what he wanted, maybe she could help him figure it out. He'd said he had nothing to offer her, but he was wrong. He had exactly what she needed, but for some reason he wasn't able to see it.

So she'd get around his reluctance by wording it in a way he *couldn't* resist.

Walker pulled to a stop in front of her, all long limbs and delicious cowboy, denim and plaid, sturdy stance and intense eyes. "We need to talk."

Oh boy, did they ever. "Come in."

9

Walker was going with his gut, because the only thing that had gotten him to Ivy's place was the sense that not being there was wrong.

"Leave your boots on," Ivy ordered as she pushed the door open. "Everything needs to be redone, so unless you've been mucking out stalls..."

A soft chuckle escaped him, surprising him with how easy it felt. "I know better than to show up with shit on my boots."

She glanced at him, amusement on her face. "I can't help that I have a strong sense of smell."

The words came out softer than he'd heard recently. Not that he blamed her, considering he'd been a bastard and then a fool the last two times they connected.

She led him into the kitchen area, which was a bit of a shambles but at least had a sturdy table with a couple of chairs that were clearly to sit on.

Ivy gestured him at one before turning to the counter and moving boxes out of the way so she could plug in a kettle. The fronts were off all of the cabinets, the empty shells a bright purple colour which contrasted hideously with the orange countertops and oven and the brown backsplash tile.

"Interesting colour choices," he drawled.

The only normal things in the room were the white fridge and the stainless-steel sink, although that looked as if it had seen better days.

"I don't know for sure, but I have a feeling the previous owners were either a little bohemian or colour-blind." Ivy turned to face him, leaning back on the orange countertop and folding her arms over her chest.

He let his gaze drift. She'd pulled her hair back into a ponytail, a few fine wisps falling around her face, the strands shimmering in the sunlight coming in the window. A hint of red on her lips with a bit of shine, and as he took a deep breath, the scent of cherries lingered on the air.

Now that was just cruel. Cherry lip gloss he wasn't allowed to nibble off?

Just as tempting were the curves behind her sturdy cotton shirt, her waist dipping in before flaring out to hips that were oh so touchable. He knew, from far-too-intimate recent history, every inch of Ivy was covered with soft skin he wanted to stroke.

He pulled his gaze upward, sure he would find either an amused look or a censorious one for being caught leering. But instead, to his delight, Ivy was checking *him* over.

She took a deep breath and let it out slowly, a smile slowly rising as her gaze settled on his forearms and hands. Walker glanced down to make sure he didn't have anything unusual stuck to him, but they seemed like a normal set of hands to him. He'd rolled up his sleeves, and while he had a few scars on his knuckles, his short-clipped nails were clean.

They were just hands, but from the way she was looking at them, Ivy thought they were a bowl full of candy.

Her lashes fluttered upward, and she lifted her gaze, a flush of red flashing across her cheeks and making her look like summertime.

He picked a safe topic. "You've got your hands full, renovating this place."

"I'm looking forward to it," she said. "It's been a long time coming."

She wanted to say something else but caught herself. Walker found himself itching to know the next thing, wanting to hear deeper thoughts than the surface Ivy, and to wipe away this polite façade between them.

She moved forward and pulled out the chair beside him. "How are you feeling after your climbing adventure the other day?"

Confused. Worried. "Embarrassed as hell you had to rescue me. I didn't mean to put you in danger."

Heat flared in her eyes for a moment, silver flashing sharp as a dagger. "I'm glad I was there. You could've been seriously hurt."

There wasn't an answer to that. She was right, although he hoped he would've snapped out of it eventually. "I expect I was winded from hitting the water. Just a foolish lark, but I shouldn't have gotten you messed up in it. I'm glad you recovered okay."

Ivy's lips tightened as if she wasn't about to let the topic go before she sighed heavily. "Stubborn rock."

A snort escaped before he could hold it back.

Amusement twinkled in her eyes again, thank God, because that's what he needed. He needed to see *his* Ivy, all tender and sweet, restoring something that had been missing in his soul for so long.

Pathetic. Sitting in her ramshackle kitchen was enough to make him happy.

She went to the counter and poured them cups of tea, placing one in front of him along with a box of cookies before settling in her chair and deciding it was time to mess with his mind.

"Getting back into the dating scene is making me uncomfortable. More uncomfortable than I expected."

Good.

It shouldn't have been his first thought, but it was the only thing that rushed through Walker's brain. "Abrupt change of topic."

"Well, it seems as if you don't want to tell me why you were playing Spiderman, so I figured I should go ahead and talk about something that's on my mind."

She was thinking about dating, and it was uncomfortable, and since he wasn't the one she would be dating, now he was uncomfortable. "Sorry it's awkward."

"I need your help."

They were venturing into dangerous territory. "What can I do?" He regretted the words as soon as they were out of his mouth.

Because *they* weren't dating. Even though he'd come over to her place for some ungodly reason...

She played with her cup, staring into its depths. "I'm a little uncertain on the whole contact part."

Walker hesitated. "Contact. As in getting in touch with them via cell phone, text or whatever?"

She lifted her gaze to his, quicksilver eyes so cold they were burning hot. "Contact as in *physical* contact. It's been a long time for me, and while I know it's not a case of getting rusty or anything, you know I'm really shy."

"You seem to have improved in that area," he offered deadpan. "You talking about sex, Snow? Because I'm pretty sure I didn't ever get you to actually say the word back when we were in high school."

And this was one impossible conversation. Not at all what he'd expected, although truth be told, he'd kind of just rushed out with no real agenda other than he needed to be with her.

Her cheeks turned red at his words, but her gaze was rocksteady. "It's still hard to say, and a lot harder to do. I mean the thought of doing. So I was wondering if maybe...if you'd consider...*it*. Help me warm up a little."

There was a special place in hell reserved for men like him. Men whose first thought after being offered sex by a timid young woman was to throw her over their shoulder and haul said woman to the nearest flat surface.

Walker closed his eyes, pretending he hadn't just been propositioned by the woman he wanted more than his next breath. "I don't know if that would be a good idea."

"Oh, I understand how bad of an idea it is, but at the same time I think it's exactly what we both need. I suppose we don't have to do *it*," Ivy offered. "Just fooling around might help."

Goddamnfuckinghell. "Ivy."

Her gaze remained pinned to his. "*Walker*. I know you said you can't offer me anything, but you honestly can. I haven't been with anyone since you, and I trust you. Getting to figure this part out slowly over the summer could be a good thing, and I want you to seriously think about it—"

He hadn't heard the last dozen words she'd said. Everything after 'I haven't been with anyone since you' was a bit of a blur. "Wait. What? You haven't been with anyone?"

Ivy shook her head, her eyes lowering for a moment before she dragged them back up into position. The steel rolled back into her spine as she waited for him to respond.

Which he couldn't do yet because he was a dumbass cowboy and needed more information. "You haven't been on a date since you left Heart Falls?"

"I've been on dates. And I've had a few kisses but nothing else. Not really." The faint colour in her cheeks flushed up to volcanic levels. "I do have some toys I use on a regular basis, so it's not as if I have no sex life at all."

Walker was about to fall over, killed by her casual reference to masturbation. "I—"

Nope, he couldn't do it. His vocal cords had frozen because his brain was far too busy sending him images of Ivy lying naked on her bed, hands caressing herself, reaching between her legs.

He felt lightheaded enough he had to lean forward and support his head in his hands and take a couple of calming breaths.

A soft hand landed on his shoulder, patting him reassuringly. "Walker?"

He looked into her face and saw no sign she was teasing or leading him on. Nothing but earnest Ivy, sweet and desirable, and every bit of his past and all sorts of things that he longed for in the future that he couldn't have.

Except he could. Because she was offering herself to him, once again, and this time he was too much of a bastard to turn her down. "I can't promise you anything, Ivy. I still don't know what lies ahead."

She nodded. "I understand, but this is something I want, and I think you want it too. I'm not asking for promises. I just want now. I've had too many days when I didn't know I was going to have a tomorrow. And maybe this is a stupid idea, but if it's going to make us both happy, why not?"

"So even though we might not end up together, you want us to be together now?"

"If by 'be together' you mean having sex and being in each other's beds, yes."

He might be a fool, and his entire life might be steamrolling past without him at the wheel, but damn if he wasn't going to grab on to this one with both hands. "Hell, yes."

~

For one terrible horrible moment she'd thought he was going to once again be all considerate and gentlemanly and turn her down, even though she could tell this was what he wanted.

Thank God he didn't.

Only... "What now?"

She hadn't gotten her bedroom ready first thing with this in mind, unless it had been a subconscious choice. Either way, there was a queen-size mattress waiting at the end of the hall, but she wasn't quite brave enough to simply take him by the hand and haul him there.

One moment Walker was looking at her as if she were a tasty appetizer, and the next he reached across the distance between them and picked her up. She grabbed his shoulders for balance, but he resettled her quickly, and suddenly she was seated in his lap, tucked up tight against that sturdy chest, his gaze fixed on her lips as if she might vanish at any moment.

It felt right to be in his arms.

He brushed his knuckles over her cheek, his gaze following his fingers. "*What now* is we get reacquainted. I don't think I should strip us down and take you right here on the floor."

It was suddenly very difficult to swallow. "You don't?"

"Not that impulsive sex would be a bad thing, and not that I have anything against floors, but I kind of want to savour this," he admitted. "Take you in one little bite at a time."

He wasn't doing anything except brushing his fingertips over her face, but it was if he'd stroked a match and lit her on fire. Streaks of heat ran down her torso before settling between her legs.

"I'm kind of a sure thing," she whispered.

The resulting shudder made his hand move erratically against her skin as his thumb stroked the side of her neck. "Doesn't mean we have to go all the way right now, Snow."

And even though she really, really wanted to, part of her

didn't. Because stupid as it was, she *hadn't* been with anyone over these years. She'd fooled around a bit, but sex was special, and she'd never found anyone she wanted to share that intimacy with. Not since Walker.

Not until now.

She scrambled to find some kind of mental footing to regain her internal balance. "Not going to go all the way? Are we back to high school and baseball analogies?"

He chuckled. "Maybe. That's a good idea, in a way, although I bet the kids these days have come up with some other lingo."

"Probably computer based, but I don't have the guts to ask my baby sister."

"And I'm definitely not asking Dustin."

His hand had travelled all the way down her arm and landed over her fingers, his thumb stroking her knuckles. She turned her hand over and snuck her fingers into his, and a rush of excitement swept through her.

She was giddy, just like the first time they'd held hands. Him, tugging her with him toward the barns, but instead of letting go once they were in the darkness, he'd held on.

That same sensation of connection and wonder slid up her spine with prickly fingers.

Walker adjusted his chair, turning away from the table so there was more room. "What are we going to tell people? Because you know damn well they're going to ask."

She wanted to say it was nobody else's business, but he was right. "I've already told you that no matter how this ends, I'm not going to be upset."

"I have a feeling your dad has a hole dug in his backyard with my name on it," Walker informed her.

"And I have space in my bed with your name on it," she countered, "and since I'm an adult, I win."

When he spoke, his voice had gone deeper and more rumbly. "You need to stop talking about your bed."

She shivered at the sheer lust in the simple statement. "I think we should let people jump to their own conclusions. You said you wanted to come fix my stairs, and I've got a bunch of other jobs around the place I can't do. I'll pay you to do them, and don't argue with me about that because I'd have to pay anybody else."

"And when I come over we can work on more than the house?" He didn't look entirely happy about the solution. "What're you going to tell your sisters?"

"That you and I are friends, and you're helping me out." She picked up his hand in hers, tracing her fingers over his knuckles. "Look. Just because I love my sisters doesn't mean they or my parents get to know all the details of my life. I don't have a problem with this. I think we tell people we're friends, and leave it at that."

She wanted him to say yes so badly. Or at least she wanted him to say yes to them fooling around.

However she could get him, she would take him. Because she'd told the truth—there'd been too many days when she hadn't known if tomorrow would come. Ivy wanted him, *all* of him, but she'd take him one small step at time if that was the only way to convince him to try.

Only that's when something changed. He was big, and she was small. And sitting in his lap felt as if she were surrounded by a forest; his back a rock wall behind her, the sturdy limbs of his body like a stand of spruce trees, warding off the cold.

So when he shifted position under her it was noticeable, his body straightening just a bit as if the rock wall at her back had risen twenty feet.

"No." The word came out hard. He shook his head, his fingers rising to cup her chin as he tilted her face toward him. "I mean *yes*, we're friends, but that's not what we're going to tell people. We'll figure out what the hell we'll tell them at the end of the summer but for now? I'm not tiptoeing around like some handyman in a bad porn movie, crawling into your bed and being a dirty secret. I'm going to be here anytime I want, and that's not going to be something we can wave away."

He leaned closer, his lips only inches from hers, and she was trapped. He wasn't hurting her, but he was holding her still as if he wanted her to get every nuance of his message.

"Every time I'm in town and have a spare moment I'm going to be here. I want to see you in the daytime as well as the night, and I'm going to take you anyway I want. Not giving this a name means we're sneaking around, and that's not acceptable. You're *mine*. You okay with those rules?"

"I'm yours until you figure out what you're doing?" His eyes burned intensely, stoking the heat inside her. Thank God it had worked. "Yes. Okay."

He leaned in close again, the air from his lungs mixing with hers as she breathed in, searching for control. She found herself shaking as she stared into his familiar and yet brand-new face.

This wasn't how he'd been as a teenager, and she liked the changes. She admired this determined and focused man.

He brought their lips together. It was sweet for a moment, a memory of their past sweeping in, easy yet full of emotion. The next moment it was apparent she needed to put aside the memories and focus on the man here and now, the man kissing her senseless as if he'd been storing up passion for eleven years.

Walker didn't kiss, he consumed.

He breathed her in, using his lips and teeth and tongue until she was gasping for air. Her hands tangled in his hair, her body leaning tight against his as she accepted his demands and made a few of her own.

Walker put one hand on her hip, the other sliding up her

back and into her hair. His fingers tightened as he twirled the strands around his hand, making a fist and tugging slightly to lean her back as he moved away from her mouth. Spending time along her jaw then up to her ear.

A noise escaped her, somewhere between a moan and a squeal as he put his teeth to her earlobe and nipped. Soothing the pain with his tongue then putting his lips to a spot on her neck that set her squirming.

The hand on her hip tightened, locking her in place against his body. She rocked in frustration, wanting to rub against him. Wanting his mouth back on hers.

He worked his teeth along the tendon of her neck. "Oh, yes. Walker..."

It wasn't his name, it was a moan of pleasure as he fastened his mouth and sucked. Her entire body reacted, and the only thing moving against her were his lips. The hand at the back of her head held her, the one on her hip rigid as well, as if she were encased in the stone of his namesake.

And inside the stone, she was melting. Heating up to volcanic proportions, she really hoped he knew how to deal with what he'd unleashed.

She'd been waiting a long time for this.

Walker moaned happily, returning to her mouth as if he simply couldn't stop himself, tasting and dipping, slower now, and yet just as desperate.

Under her hip his erection pressed against her, proof he was as affected by this—whatever *this* was—as she was. She certainly couldn't call it just an innocent kiss.

It wasn't innocent, and it wasn't *just* anything.

Their tongues tangled before he took control, filling her and demanding she let him in.

She'd seen enough porn for that to spark other images of him demanding entry to other parts of her body. "*Please.*"

"Yes." The word came out muffled against her, and she wasn't even sure what he was saying yes to. But the hand on her hip was rising, drifting over her ribs, sliding until he cupped her breast.

She had her fingers tangled in his hair, and for some reason the thought of Brad's shaved head slipped out of nowhere and to her dismay, a giggle escaped.

Walker slowed, his lips against hers curling into a smile. "What?" he demanded.

He pulled back far enough she could look into his eyes. She softened her fingers and let her right hand slide through his dark hair. "I like your hair," she admitted.

One brow arched upward. "That's what you're thinking while I'm kissing you? Damn, I need to try harder."

She tightened the fingers of her left hand that were still tangled around his locks, tugging slightly. Loving the flash of fire in his eyes. "You're getting more than an A for effort, trust me."

Ivy took a deep breath, and that's when she realized he still held her. His hand was cupped around her breast as if he had no intention of ever moving it again.

And yet he wasn't stroking her, and he wasn't teasing, but as he leaned forward and took her lips again it seemed her skin grew hypersensitive. The small motions of their bodies made his hand over her blouse rub her bra slightly.

It was enough friction to tease nipples that had gone tight somewhere around the first *thought* of him touching her. They were sensitive, and they ached, and she really wanted him to do more than hold her, but it seemed he had his own agenda.

She was okay with that, returning her attention to his lips because it was too good to miss a single moment.

Everything in the room sparkled when he pulled their lips apart, but she wasn't sure if it was because the sunlight was hitting a batch of glasses she'd left on the counter or if she was so oxygen-deprived she wasn't seeing straight.

They stared at each other for a while, Ivy taking advantage of the opportunity to touch him. To run her hands over his shoulders and down his back, and when he chuckled and pulled her in tight for a hug, she closed her eyes and soaked in the sensation.

Sex and sexual tension were wonderful things, but his arms around her gave her a firm place to rest, and that was a glorious sensation.

A buzz sounded just before his phone rang, and he shifted her so he could reach into his back pocket to answer the call. "Yeah?"

While the buzz of a voice echoed softly, Walker's gaze drifted over her face. She watched him intently, his eyes no longer soft but growing more focused as he brought himself back from where they'd drifted to together.

"I'll be there." Walker hung up and made a face. "I gotta go."

Which was probably a good thing, even though it didn't seem like it at the moment. "Okay."

She shuffled herself to her feet, his hands sliding off of her reluctantly. "I'll call you."

"When it works. No agenda, no expectations," she reminded him.

His expression twisted as if ready to protest, but instead he rose to his feet then caught her fingers in his as he walked her to the front door. He turned then, looking her over with that strangely serious expression, so different from the carefree boy she'd known for many years.

Walker leaned down and caught her chin in his fingers again, looking her straight in the eye. "No toys."

"What are you talk—?" Oh God. Her cheeks lit on fire and her heart was suddenly racing.

His lips twisted into a smile that was mean and tormented all at the same time. "You know what I'm telling you."

Ivy forced her head higher, the grip of his fingers a sensual control. "Which means you're not going to go take care of yourself, either?"

"You think I'm riding a thin line?"

"You'd better get moving or you're going to be late," Ivy teased. "I have something I need to do."

He growled, and a shiver raced up her spine. "No toys," he repeated. "Not unless I'm here to see it."

Well, that opened up an entirely different line of potential adventure.

"Okay, fine." Her words didn't come out quite as obedient as they might have because she was quivering over her dirty future plans.

Walker stroked his finger over her lips, staring as he swore softly, then leaned in to kiss her one last time. Brief, hard.

Pulling back with a smile as he licked his lips. "Cherry. My favourite."

He turned on his heel and headed out the door, and Ivy wondered exactly what she'd just agreed to.

10

Walker stared over the edge of the pen at the new foal that had joined the Silver Stone ranch that evening, the surprise arrival working out better than they'd hoped.

"Josiah is on his way, but I think we're okay." Luke laid a hand on Walker's shoulder and squeezed. "Thanks for coming back from wherever you were. I appreciate the helping hand."

"Didn't do anything special," Walker said.

Luke cut him off with a shake of his head and a firm tone. "'I swear sometimes you can't see your nose in front of your face. Just having you around helps the horses. Snowflake was a lot more settled after you arrived."

It certainly ended up being a different evening than what it might have, but the praise from his brother sent a different kind of heat through him. Acceptance and a touch of pride. "Glad I could help."

Luke tilted his head toward the exit. "Go ahead and hit the sack. I'll stick around until Josiah shows up."

But Walker was in no hurry to get back to his lonely bunk.

Because even though he had permission to go over to Ivy's, he planned to keep that on a slow track.

It was too tempting to jump in full speed, but he couldn't do that to her, no matter how much she said she wanted everything. Everything could come one step at a time.

God, this was going to kill him.

Instead, he got himself comfy, leaning against one of the upright posts. "What else are you up to these days? I'm only gone for a few weeks at a time, but it feels as if this past year is nothing but a blur."

Luke offered him a long, hard look. "You really interested?"

What kind of question was that? "Of course."

His brother shrugged. "Just asking because it feels as if there's a bunch of stuff going on in your life you're not telling us about. I assumed that meant you wanted space both directions."

Walker cursed softly. "Nothing of the sort."

"So you're not keeping secrets?"

Busted. "There is something I'm working through that I want to figure out on my own," he admitted. "But not because I don't trust you and Caleb. I need to figure out a way I can contribute to the ranch, and it's my issue."

Luke made a face. "Every now and then you and Caleb come up with the most boneheaded comments. You do a lot when you're around, and we certainly don't begrudge the time you're out on the circuit."

"Or the cost for me to travel? Or the equipment I take with me? Or the fact that when I'm out there I'm not here helping? It's not simple," Walker insisted.

"As long as it's something you like doing, it *is* simple," Luke snapped in return. "If you're done because you're done, then stop. But if you think for one minute we want you to give up on your dreams, then you haven't been paying attention."

"There's my problem. I don't know what my dream is anymore," Walker said without thinking. The words slipping from him as if Luke had triggered some *confess your deepest fears* button.

He and Luke stared at each other for a moment before his brother dipped his chin slowly. "Okay. I understand. And if that's what's got you so tied up in knots you're not thinking straight, I'll back off. You take the time you need, but if you want to talk it out, we're here. Caleb or me, or heck, Ashton's got a good head on his shoulders."

"I know." Luke's words echoed for a moment until Walker had to ask. "Not thinking straight? What the hell are you talking about?"

Luke grimaced. "Ivy Fields bought you at the bachelor auction. But you told Josiah you're not seeing each other. Are you out of your goddamn mind? One date and you're done?"

He had been, and he was asking for all sorts of trouble changing paths, but for better or worse Walker had set his boots in a new direction and he was going to enjoy the trip. "Don't you know a tease when you hear one, bro? Josiah fell for it too. Ivy and I are quite happy both being in the same postal code for the first time in a long time."

A slow sort of shock slid over Luke's features before he schooled them back into nonchalant amusement. "Well. I might have to take advantage of this bit of information to make a little money, considering someone was laying odds on you staying single this summer."

Good grief. "Did Kelli start another betting pool?"

"When doesn't the girl start a betting pool?"

They laughed together before chatting quietly about a couple other things. Luke mentioned he could use a hand at the house he was building in a couple of days.

Walker agreed then headed back to his bunk, slipping

through the door and closing it behind himself a whole lot happier than he'd been hours earlier.

He checked his phone before putting it aside for the night and spotted a message from Ivy sent only ten minutes earlier from a messenger account.

Call me.

He opened it, setting his phone down on his night table as it rang. Only when the screen opened, he tripped over his own feet and fell onto his bed because Ivy was naked.

Mostly covered by bath bubbles, but still naked. He snatched up the phone and ogled her. "Jesus Christ, woman."

Her head tilted as she offered the wickedest smile he'd ever seen. "Such language."

Walker recovered enough to pull himself to a seated position as he scanned the picture more thoroughly. She was in her bathroom, in the tub, which explained the bubble-line drifting along the swells of her breasts. She had her legs bent so her knees poked out like two creamy islands. "Is this an obscene phone call? Because I've always wanted one of those."

"I called because you said I wasn't allowed to use this unless you were watching." Ivy leaned forward slightly to reach over the side of the tub, and Walker took advantage of the opportunity to sneak a peek as new skin was exposed.

Ivy leaned back and lifted something purple in the air, and for a second he had a hard time thinking back on exactly who had said what and when.

She clicked a button, and a low vibrating sound began.

He swore again. "You wouldn't dare."

Ivy raised a brow. "It's not my fault if you turn off your phone to come racing over here, because by that time I'm going to be done. So I suppose it's your choice if you want to watch or not, but I was trying to play by your rules."

His sweet, innocent Ivy had developed some kinky edges

over the years. "I guess I should've been more specific with my instructions, but now that you've gone through all the bother of getting warmed up, it would be mean to not appreciate your efforts."

"Exactly." She dipped her chin firmly as if pleased he was falling in with her plans. She let her hand slip under the water, and he realized the flaw in the system.

"I can't see what you're doing," he pointed out.

Her knees eased apart slightly then her lashes fluttered, pleasure streaking across her face.

His entire body turned into one solid rock. He might not be able to see the vibrator touching her, but he sure as hell could see the effect.

"Ivy," he said with a warning tone.

"Hmm?" She opened her eyes, a haze forming over her pupils already. She licked her lips before eyeing him up and down. "You're welcome to join me. I mean right there where you are."

Never had a man stripped so fast in his life. His clothes might have been on fire.

He sat on his bed, back against the wall with his phone propped on the bookcase so he had a good view of the show.

Now Ivy wore an adorable pout. "I can't see you," she complained.

Walker chuckled evilly. "That's too bad."

She winked before wiggling to a more upright position that, glory hallelujah, exposed her breasts. Bubbles clung to their surface here and there, like erotic clouds that refused to let go.

He didn't blame them one bit.

Walker adjusted position until she could see the motion of his arm as he wrapped his hand around his cock. "Put the vibrator between your legs and squeeze it in place so your hands are free."

She flushed, and he didn't think it was from the heat of the water. It wasn't for him as he slowly jacked his hand over his stiff length. Curling his palm over the head and spreading the moisture.

"Like this?" Ivy wiggled again, her hands under the surface of the water as her knees vanished. He could tell the moment she touched the vibrator to sensitive parts. She didn't have a very good poker face, and that was a glorious thing, because Ivy heading toward an orgasm was one of the most beautiful things he'd ever seen in his life.

"Perfect. Now bring your hands up and touch yourself where I can see it."

He considered leaning over to grab some lube but it wasn't going to be necessary. Not with the way his body was getting ready to spill as if he were seventeen again. He wasn't even touching the woman, just watching as she touched herself. Hands rising under her breasts, circling once before she cupped them and squeezed together. Lifting, with her thumbs coming over her nipples.

Part of his brain was watching and taking notes of what she liked and what she was doing so that the first time he got a chance, he could prove how good of a student he was to this particular teacher.

The other part of his brain had shut down completely and was enjoying the show. Pleasure streaked through his body, not only where he applied pressure around his cock but somewhere deep inside where he was tickled that his sweet Ivy had come up with this perfectly dirty scenario.

"Pinch your nipples," he ordered, just to see what she would do.

She obeyed instantly, rolling the peaks between her thumbs and forefingers as her head fell back to rest against the wall, her chest moving erratically with each breath as she panted, the surface of the water shimmering.

He didn't bother to swear he was so mesmerized. "I can tell your legs are shaking. Got that toy right on your clit, don't you? The next time, baby, that's gonna be my fingers. That's going to be me slipping my fingers into you and putting my mouth on your clit, licking until you scream my name."

Ivy moaned, but her lips twitched. "I didn't know you could hold your breath for that long."

He stumbled in his rhythm for a moment, laughing before he picked up tempo again, pleasure rushing forward like a steam train. "Sassy girl."

"Stubborn rock." She quivered, shaking on the spot. "Next time it'll be my hands on you, stroking up and down as you teach me how you like it. Or maybe it'll be my mouth..."

She licked her lips and that was it.

Walker gave up control and let pleasure take him, seed exploding from the end of this cock to land in stripes over his hands and belly. He was done, but it took forever to finish, especially when a breathless cry escaped Ivy's lips, the word turning into his name as a tsunami hit the surface of the bathtub. Bubbles broke into lone icebergs, crashing into her limbs as they escaped.

It took a while for both of them to come back. He bet he looked as dazed as she did when she finally met his eyes.

She smiled sweetly before lifting a hand to kiss her fingers then blow it at him. "Good night."

Ivy hung up and left him with his head ringing and his body reeling.

Whatever was going to happen this summer, they were in for one hell of a ride.

Ivy wasn't sure how she would feel the next time she saw

Walker because she'd used up most of her stock of boldness that night in the bathtub.

She'd had a good time, and so had he, obviously.

But other than texting they hadn't a chance to get together the next day, or the next. And after her little "I'll take as much of you as I can get, but I won't interfere with your life" spiel, Ivy had accepted the gap and dove back into her activities as well. There were a lot of things she needed to accomplish before the fall, all of which created a good distraction.

Tall, sexy cowboys needed to be distracted from.

She worked on her house, and she stopped by her Grandma Sonora's ranch with the delivery of baked goods Tansy had sent from Buns and Roses.

Her grandma looked the same as she had the last time Ivy had visited, and Ivy shook her head as she placed a basketful of treats on the well-worn kitchen table. "I hope someday you'll share and tell the rest of us where the well of eternal life is on this property."

Sonora laughed, the sound dancing brightly off the walls like a reflection of the sun shining off the squeaky-clean windows in her tiny kitchen. "Good living and hard work, sweetie." She lifted the cloth off the top of the goodie basket and peeked in, making a noise of approval. "And just enough treats to make the tough moments easier."

Ivy sat at the table, the sweetness of being there a treat all in itself. This was why she was moving back. *This* was what she needed—her family.

Sonora settled opposite her, pushing a steaming hot pot of tea her direction. "Make yourself useful," she ordered.

It was one of the oldest tricks in her grandma's books. Tongues tended to get looser when their hands were busy. Only Ivy didn't mind. This was exactly why she'd stopped in.

She poured the hot liquid into two cups carefully as she considered. "Are you still happy living out here, Grandma?"

"It's my home," Sonora answered. "I've gotten rid of a lot of the animals, and I don't do as much gardening as I used to, but I can't imagine being somewhere I couldn't get up every morning and go for a ride."

The word *home* was one that resonated the loudest. "That's what I figured."

Her grandma eyed her, suspiciously. "Did your parents put you up to this?"

"What?"

Sonora waved her hands in the air, gesturing around at the small room. "This. They're worried that I can't take care of this anymore, but I'm still capable, so I don't see any reason why I should leave."

"Neither do I." Ivy took a sip of her tea, staring out the window at the familiar rolling hills that backed onto Silver Stone land. It was pretty, and it was wild, but that didn't make it wrong. "I'm sure there will come a time that you need to move, but you're smart enough to make that decision on your own."

Her grandma nodded firmly. "I don't mind a bit of friendly advice, but I don't need to be dictated to. Certainly not by any stubborn, interfering..."

She stumbled for the next word, so Ivy offered a suggestion. "Family?"

Grandma Sonora blinked, coming back from somewhere else with her thoughts. "I was going to say *asshole*, but I didn't want to shock you."

Ivy laughed so hard. "Oh, Grandma. I love you."

She didn't bother to ask *who* her grandmother was referring to because she could guess, and that would be something else she could laugh about with Walker the next time they got a chance to be together.

She visited for a while then got up and headed to her next destination, which was a date with Emma Stone.

The first couple of times they had gotten together, Tamara had sat with them, working on something at the table as Emma went through her exercises. But the last time Emma had been the one to speak up and tell her mom she could go and work.

"Ms. Fields is my teacher, and I like her." Which was as solid a recommendation as anyone could ask for.

Tamara had smiled and offered a wink, and then managed to not hover, which impressed Ivy a great deal.

Then again, it's not as if Ivy and Emma were ever truly alone, not with big sister Sasha on guard duty.

She wasn't obvious about it at first; just had to get something out of the refrigerator while Emma was working through pages at the kitchen island. And when Ivy had suggested they go outside for a walk while they talked, Sasha had magically appeared with an over-sized walking mop at her side.

Emma had rolled her eyes at her sister then dropped to her knees and grabbed hold of the dog's big ears, the move terrifyingly quick until Ivy realized the creature was more sheep than sheepdog. Gentle enough that it didn't matter how much the girls tugged him one way then the other. He just sat there and adored their attention.

Demon didn't like the bonnet Sasha fastened on his head, but other than that, the creature was a welcome part of their new rambles.

The sun was shining too hard today to do any kind of activities inside the house, so it was inevitable they ended up heading toward Big Sky Lake. The few puffy clouds floating overhead reflected in its depths.

"Wanna see our goats?" Emma asked.

"Yes, but say that again, please," Ivy instructed.

Emma frowned for a moment as if she didn't realize what

she'd said. And she probably didn't, because she was so used to keeping her sentences short and sweet, contractions were still absent at times.

"A lot of the ranch hands say *wanna*," Sasha offered. "Kelli says that's because they're being lazy."

"Not lazy," Emma snapped before saying it again with clear enunciation. "*I'm* not lazy. I'm learning."

"Course you are," Sasha said firmly as if that was the end of the conversation.

Ivy hid her amusement, but sometimes she wondered why she was even there. Emma was a charming little girl, and so was Sasha, but it was obvious whatever had caused Emma's speech delays was well and truly dealt with.

It was a bit like being paid to have fun—getting to come out to visit the Silver Stone ranch—but Ivy wasn't going to turn down the opportunity.

They headed over to the goat pen, the occupants of which Ivy had already had the auspicious pleasure of meeting. Only this time, instead of being greeted by a trio of decidedly debonair-looking goats, with their grey coats and upright ears, the pen was partly open. One guilty-looking animal was caught by his collar on the latch of the gate, his back leg stuck in the metal railings.

Sasha hurried forward to set the beast free. Ivy grabbed hold of her arm to stem her enthusiasm. "Go slowly. I'm sure he'll be happy to be free, but he might kick while you're trying to help him."

"Look, there's Meany." Emma was pointing toward the barn.

Sure enough, both of the missing goats were playing some kind of a goat's game that involved hopping into the horse arena then up on top of the nearest gateposts.

They looked like strange yard decorations. Instead of reclining lions, Silver Stone had goats.

Sasha glanced reluctantly at the goat caught in the gate, then at the two that were running free still. "Maybe we should leave Eeny trapped until we get back. Three goats are hard to handle at once."

Emma was already headed toward the arena, and Ivy gestured Sasha after her. Keeping the two girls within arm's reach seemed like a good idea.

She pulled out her phone and hit Walker's number.

He answered just as they reached the fence. "Hey, Snow."

"Are you at the ranch right now? Anywhere near the main barn?" She spoke rapidly, getting a hand on Emma before the little girl could topple over the gate and race after her pets. "Because we're having a goat incident."

Walker chuckled, and she immediately heard a whistle in the background. "Count to five, honey. We're just inside. Tell my nieces to hold their horses."

She hung up and rapidly assured the girls help was on the way. "Uncle Walker will be right here."

Sasha looked a little disgruntled. "They're our goats. We know how to take care of them."

"I'm sure you do, but are you allowed in those arenas without supervision? And I don't count because I'm not a cowboy," she added as Sasha's mouth opened.

He had to have been literally steps away on the other side of the barn wall because Walker's laughter echoed on the open air. "Sasha, someone's got your number, little girl."

Emma snickered, slipping her hand into Ivy's fingers and tugging to get her attention. "Sasha's always trying to get closer to the horses."

"I bet she really loves them," Ivy said in return.

Emma took a glance at her sister then back to Ivy, obviously considering sharing something before changing her mind and staying silent.

Ivy made a mental note to pass on that bit of intel to Tamara.

Meanwhile, Walker had caught hold of the first of the goats and had the creature pinned under his arm. Caleb was there, talking Sasha through trying to coax the second animal close enough they could grab it by the collar.

Emma's gaze was pinned on her sister and her father, so Ivy kept hold of her fingers but let her attention wandered to the tall man damn-near strutting his way to her side.

"Hail, conqueror of goats," she teased.

Walker winked. "Good to see you. You sticking around for a while?"

She checked her watch. "Another hour or so. You?"

The look he gave her was scorching hot. "About the same. And then I have plans."

Oh Lord, she truly hoped those plans were what she thought they might be. "It's always good to have things to look forward to."

She wasn't sure how he could answer in a way that was appropriate for little ears to hear, because she was certain that Uncle Walker wasn't about to break out the dirty talk around his niece.

Unfortunately, they were interrupted in the best possible way.

"Hey, what's a girl got to do to get a hug around here?"

Caleb and Sasha turned from where they'd finally gotten a hand on Meany. Ivy, Walker and Emma rotated on the spot to find a somewhat familiar face marching toward them.

"Auntie Ginny," Emma shouted, breaking free from Ivy's grasp and rushing forward to throw herself into the young woman's arms.

Sasha arrived next. She must've flown through the railings because she was covered with dirt, but still right there in the middle of the pile wanting a hug.

Walker's little sister didn't look exactly how Ivy remembered, but that was because her hair was short and bleached a shocking white with a band of pink at the very front. Ginny looked happy, and as she untangled herself from her nieces, she glanced at Ivy with curiosity,

While Ivy had been watching the reunion, Walker had stepped in closer and slid his arm around her waist. Ginny's brows rose, but she didn't say anything, just moved into Caleb's arms as he offered a hug.

Walker squeezed Ivy then let go to offer a hug as well. "You're early."

"Ha. I thought the complaint was that women are always late?" Ginny said happily. "I decided to come home a month before the wedding instead of sticking around after. That'll give me lots of time to catch up on everything that's happening here at Silver Stone."

She eyed them again, her expression full of questions. Ivy laughed inside.

So much for a quiet afternoon visit with the Stones.

11

Walker shouldn't have been so entertained by the tableau playing out in front of him.

Then again, he shouldn't have been surprised when Ivy took it all in stride and opened her arms, stepping forward with a welcoming hug. "Good to see you, Ginny."

The women stepped apart, Ginny still tossing glances between Walker and Ivy. "Good to see you, as well."

She opened her mouth to ask something else, probably something provocative knowing Ginny, when the girls were back, tugging her excitedly toward the house.

"Mama wants to meet you right now," Emma insisted.

Ginny raised a brow, obviously pleased at Emma's outspokenness. "Well, I suppose you're right. I am a very exciting person to meet."

Emma giggled, and Sasha snorted, and the whole lot of them moved in a wave to the ranch house with a brief stop at the goat pen to free Eeny and lock up the other two escapees.

Walker spoke softly as he walked at Ivy's side. "You ready for the bedlam?"

"Nothing says I have to stay," Ivy pointed out. "She's your family. You should take the time to get caught up."

Screw that. He caught her by the hand and slowed his stride until they were at the back of the pack. "My choice is to say hi, and do the family thing for a bit, but then I want time with you. Something that's an appropriate follow-up to your little toy-shop trick."

Her face told him exactly what she thought of his plans. One hundred percent on board looked good on her.

"Tamara's been talking about having you join us for supper, anyway," he offered. "And I have a feeling neither of the girls will object."

She squeezed his fingers. "Your nieces are adorable. I look forward to teaching Emma this coming year."

He suddenly realized how tangled the summer could become. It was one thing for them to say they were adults, and getting involved shouldn't affect anyone else. But the truth was they were part of two families who weren't about to ignore them, which was both a blessing and a curse.

But at least if he did end up leaving, and this thing between them was just a brief white-hot fling, Ivy would still have a connection to the Stone family. Hell, she'd *always* been a part of their family.

He didn't want Emma or Sasha hurt again.

They walked in the door, the volume in the living room going up as the body count rose. Tamara was talking earnestly with Ginny while Sasha and Emma raced around in circles laughing and dancing.

Caleb pushed a beer into his hand then gestured outside. "You're on barbecue duty. Go get the grill warmed up."

Walker nodded, turning to Ivy, but it was too late. Caleb had already recruited her to do some other task as if he had every right to boss her around.

Come to think of it, this wasn't the first time. She'd always been willing to join in any time they'd had a family event. His earlier thoughts about her fitting in with the family were so true. Back then she'd been so shy everyone had worked to gently ease her along. It seemed Caleb hadn't forgotten, as he sent her off to a moderately quiet corner of the room to work on a salad.

Taking the summer to be with her was one of the best moves Walker could've made, for his own sake. Selfish as that might seem.

He scrubbed at the barbecue grill, content in the mindless action. He waved at Luke as his brother walked by, an armload of steaks probably nabbed from the bunkhouse cook's walk-in refrigerator.

JP wouldn't even miss them.

Dustin wasn't around, since he was still off with Ashton, but Tamara had put speed dial to good use. Cars full of people were pulling into the parking area, including Ivy's sisters.

Kelli came up from the barns, dressed from head to toe in denim with her long, dark braids hanging on either side of her head.

"You dressed up for the party," he teased.

She stuck out her tongue. "I put on new boots." She eyed him a little harder. "Which is more than you can say. Go change, Walker Stone. Those are the same clothes I saw you in an hour ago."

Oops. "Good point. I've got something in Caleb's closet I can use."

She took over for him at the grill, whacking him on the butt with the back of the scrubber before he could get out of range.

He slipped around the back way so he didn't interrupt the party going on in the living room, stealing into Caleb's old room and grabbing the set of clothes hanging in the closet.

He slipped into the shower and scrubbed up quickly, his

thoughts jumping all over like a bull on a good day. His sister being back, Ivy being there, the goats, Kelli teasing him like usual...

There was another one who fit in well with the family. She had been around the ranch for a long time, but she'd shown up after Ivy left. Nobody was even sure who'd hired her, but after Ashton had agreed to keep an eye on her, she just carried on and did her job.

The only thing Walker thought suspicious about the situation was that there was no way on earth that girl was in her late twenties. Oh, he knew sometimes people looked young but had the age on their driver's license to prove otherwise.

Kelli was one of those souls who seemed simultaneously old as the hills and young as a newborn foal. Sometimes innocent and sometimes weary, but he'd never been able to get out of her where she came from or why she'd shown up one day out of the blue.

The girl could keep secrets, that much was true.

He was doing up the buttons on his shirt when the door to the bedroom opened and he glanced up, somewhat surprised to find his sister stealing into the room and closing the door behind her. "Running away from your own party already?"

"Oh, we'll be partying till the wee hours, and this is just the beginning. I'm here for the whole month. Try the veal."

He snickered. "Your standup comedy hasn't gotten any better while you've been out of the country."

Ginny dropped onto the bed, her blonde hair bouncing up before landing in a tousled mess most women would pay a fortune to achieve. "And you've become intriguing while I've been gone. I thought I'd gone through a time warp when I came around the edge of the barn and spotted you and Ivy Fields all cozied up together."

"She's just back," Walker said. "And we don't cozy in public."

Ginny made a rude noise. "Please. You could hardly keep

your hands off the woman back in the day. And don't try to lie, because Dare and I were fourteen when you and Ivy officially started going out, so it was like the romance of the century to us."

"I'm going to gag," Walker warned her.

"What? Because I pointed out how vividly I remember thinking that someday I wanted to have a special someone like my big brother had?"

He paused for a moment, because—wow, that was a pretty powerful statement to take in fast. "It was pretty neat. And Ivy and I have good memories from that time, but then we both moved on and did the next thing."

"Or she went off to do something, and you kinda stayed here and did nothing."

And there it came—that wicked tongue of Ginny's that could cut like a knife.

He made his tone go a whole lot colder than he wished, considering it was her return to the family day and all. "Thanks so much for your vote of confidence in my life choices."

Ginny's eyes widened, and she suddenly looked very apologetic. "Oh, *shit*. I'm sorry. I wasn't talking about rodeo. I meant how you've never had another sweetie after she left. Honestly."

Walker looked at her for a moment, but it seemed Ginny was sincere. Still, it was an uncomfortable truth he'd had tossed his way.

"It's okay. I just wanted to point out that was a long time ago, and while I'm glad you and Dare built such romantic dreams based on my teenage love life, we're here at a different point in time. And you're visiting for the summer, so don't go interfering."

Ginny drew an X over her chest with her finger followed by pretending to turn a key between her lips then throwing it over her shoulder. Which he assumed meant she was going to keep her mouth shut or some such nonsense.

Then she leaned forward with a gleam in her eye. "Okay, fine. But on a different note, I want to gossip about Tamara."

Good grief. "No."

She looked downright pained. "But *Walker*," she whined. "Dare's not here for me to gossip with, and you always were my favourite brother."

He finished tucking in his shirt and looked down at her, putting as much force into the word as possible. "No."

"It's not bad gossip. I like her, but *pleeeease*." She dragged out the last word so it had about five syllables.

He kept the smile off his face with difficulty. "*No*."

"Hmmph." She let the sound out with enough force it ruffled her bangs, but then she bounced to her feet and came over and squeezed him in another tight hug. "I love you, big bro."

"I love you, little brat."

She snickered. "I hear you're in charge of the steaks. Just to let you know, I want mine extra-rare."

"Did you become a werewolf while you were in London?"

They were entering the living room, and she threw back her head and howled. It took Tansy all of three seconds to join in, the two of them sounding as if a demented wolf pack had invaded the house. Yet by this point with the number of people around, it wasn't as if the howling added a lot more chaos to the room, but somehow it still did.

As he made his way outside to resume his appointed duties as barbecue chef, he caught Ivy's eye. She'd found a quiet spot just outside the door and was sitting with Emma. He offered a smile and a promise for later.

Right now it seemed they were immersed up to their neck in family, his and hers. And that was just fine.

~

The sweetness of the evening continued long after the dessert had been consumed. Ginny was a born storyteller, and while she'd been keeping in touch with her family, all the rest of them were an eager audience for the new adventures that Ginny had been involved in over the past nine months.

"But you're going back?" Tansy asked. "You're just here for a month?"

Ginny nodded. "The place I'm staying in Italy extended my program for a month so I could take the time now and come out for Dare's wedding."

"That was generous of them," Caleb said.

Walker's sister made a face before smiling broadly. "Generous, but I'm pretty sure they'll find something terrible for me to do when I get back. Trust me, I'm not sitting back and sipping the choicest of wines. I'm grunt labour, and lots of hours of it."

She was obviously loving every minute.

Ivy was enjoying herself immensely as well, catching up with people who had lived in Heart Falls for a long time, all of whom wanted to have a brief moment with Ginny before she vanished again. She was coping with the wild and rambunctious gathering by staying to the edges and keeping her focus on small conversations. And so far, she'd been successful in avoiding being overwhelmed by the crowd.

But when a certain cowboy slipped his hand around her waist and tugged her back into the shadows from where they were standing by the bonfire listening to stories, Ivy went willingly.

Linking their fingers together as they strolled toward the lake was another tug at her heart's memory strings. She glanced down at their joined hands, a smile rising easily. "Sounds as if Ginny's found something she loves."

He didn't answer, just sighed softly as he brought her farther from the revelry. "I'm glad," he said finally. "She's a hard worker.

When she's done, she'll come back and run the greenhouse again. That extra money will be a lot of help to the family."

Ivy had been thinking more about the courage it had taken for Ginny to up and leave her family. Ivy knew the other woman was a lot more vivacious and outgoing than she was, but still—Ginny wasn't in familiar territory *and* she was facing new challenges all by herself.

She mentioned that to Walker as he pulled her to the grass at the far side of the lake, tucking her between his legs and tugging until her back rested against his chest and she was using him as a recliner.

He made low noise. "Don't know that it's any braver than what you did. You left home, all of your family, and all the rest of us. You didn't have anybody with you then, either."

Truth. And that was only part of what she'd faced alone. She still didn't know how her parents had kept the small-town gossip chain from finding out every bit of her business while she'd been gone.

She leaned her head against his chest, and they watched as the moon rose behind the hills to the east of Silver Stone. "Going to university was busy enough I didn't notice most of the time. But I really did miss seeing the family, and I missed you an awful lot."

Ivy didn't want this moment to be gloomy, but in case he'd been thinking she'd walked away and never once regretted everything they'd put on hold, she had to share.

His cheek brushed hers, stubble scratching her skin lightly. "We're here now, so let's focus on this, not days we can't reclaim."

She tilted her head and offered her lips.

Walker didn't need any coaxing. He leaned in and kissed her, the hand around her back cradling her close as he enticed her with the sweet, addictive pressure of his lips over hers.

The hand at her waist untucked her blouse, his palms

skimming over her bare skin, sliding upward until he was once again cupping a breast.

Just holding her, a tease of an entirely different kind than she'd expected. She leaned back, staring into his eyes. "We're right out in the open so we have to keep this from getting too dirty, but I'm considering not wearing a bra when we get together from now on."

His eyes widened for a second before he chuckled. "Not that I have any problem with those plans, but any particular reason?"

"You seem to have forgotten how to undo them. I'd hate to be the one keeping you from your goal."

"Oh, you mean this?" He rotated his hand slightly, the soft center of his palm teasing the fabric over her nipple. "Ivy Fields, are you saying I'm not moving fast enough for you?"

She was up in a flash, rotating and resettling herself in his lap so her butt rested on his thighs and they were face to face.

"You are going too slowly," she said, enunciating each word carefully.

Laughter burst from him, his eyes bright with amusement. "If you want my hands on your breasts, you're facing the wrong way."

Damn. He was right.

Before she could do anything about it, his strong hands caught hold of her hips and dragged her forward the final couple inches it took for their torsos to connect.

He was hard. The thick length behind his jeans made contact with the sensitive parts between her legs, and suddenly the thin cotton of her slacks seemed far too much of a barrier.

And far too little as their lips met again. Walker took control of her hips, rocking slowly so that the faintest pressure teased over and over. Like a drop of water falling in a steady stream from a leaking tap—enough to be heard and yet not enough to actually fill a cup without waiting a long, long time.

They were right in the open, but Ivy was rapidly losing any sense of propriety. It was late enough Caleb's girls were either asleep or cuddled in arms by the fire, and those were the only people Ivy didn't want to stumble over her fooling around with their uncle.

The rest of them? If anyone else strolled this far from the party, they were probably looking for space alone with someone themselves.

As she untucked and unbuttoned Walker's shirt so she could slide her hands over his torso, the faintest prickle of pride struck that she had moved on far enough from her early years of shyness to be able to have such radical thoughts.

Then she wasn't thinking because her hands were on his body, and *feeling* was so much better than using her brain.

He slid his hands up her back, her shirt rising over his wrists. Cool night air brushed her rib cage and her back. Heat enveloped her from the front as she continued to explore, palms skimming the hair on his chest. That hadn't been there years ago, and she leaned away from his kiss so she could admire him, fingertips stroking through the curls.

His lips twitched. "You're petting me."

She caught hold of his nipple and squeezed, his body jerking under her and making their hips bump.

"I'm exploring," she corrected him.

A low rumble began in his chest, and his hands rose high enough to unsnap her bra. He had hold of her hips again, and the slow, relentless tease resumed. He seemed unaware he was driving her crazy.

Walker nibbled her lips and narrowed his focus to torment her, and he was terribly, terribly effective between his mouth and that rocking motion. Now that he'd unhooked her bra, the cups slowly slid out of position until the strap that normally rested along her rib cage rose to land in a direct line with her nipples.

Every time he moved her, the strap teased until she couldn't take it anymore.

"Not nice," she complained, mumbling the words against his mouth.

"I want to explore too," he whispered.

The next thing she knew, she was rising in the air. Her hand shot out to grab his shoulders, but he was twisting and resettling her in his lap. Once again her back was against his chest, this time with one of his strong thighs rising between her legs.

It seemed a little awkward at first until he sat upright, pressing her forward as he tucked his thigh in tighter, and suddenly pressure bloomed between her legs.

When both his hands snuck under her blouse and shifted upward, she realized the boy she'd had her first sexual experiences with so long ago had grown into a very, very inventive man.

Her bra was no longer tormenting her. Instead it was his hands, cool at first as he cupped her. Firm and steady as if he was weighing his options. Weighing her. Squeezing gently before sending his palms in circles.

Multitasking, his mouth settled on her neck as he kissed his way up to behind her ear.

Swamped with sensation, Ivy still had one complaint. "I can't touch you."

"Relax and enjoy yourself," Walker murmured in her ear before giving it a teasing lick. "I'm having fun."

He copied her move from before, pinching her nipples lightly. Electric bubbles zinged through her bloodstream, setting off sparks. She closed her eyes and rested her head on his shoulder before giving into the temptation to move her hips.

Rocking against his firm thigh increased the ache growing in her sex.

"I wasn't going to do this, but damn if I can resist." Walker's left hand slid back and forth over her breasts, his nails trailing over her nipples and her skin in a way that set her nerve endings dancing.

His other hand? Her slacks gave way too easily. In an instant, he had them unbuttoned and unzipped, and he eased his leg out of the way to make room for his fingers.

Sliding over the front panel of her underwear, he cupped her sex.

She moaned in frustration. "There are no hooks to undo down there. And I don't know that I'm brave enough to threaten to stop wearing panties."

He chuckled softly. "It's not a barrier that's going to stop me for long. I'm enjoying how soft they are. Silk?"

"Yes." She didn't have many vices, but pretty bras and underwear had become something of an addiction before she'd learned to set a budget.

Walker seemed happy with her choices, and she sucked for air as he pressed one finger tighter against her, pushing the thin fabric until he made contact with the sensitive bundle of nerves that was screaming for attention.

"*Walker—*"

It was as close to begging as she could get without actually saying the words.

His finger rotated slowly, the even pressure triggering a needy buzz. His teeth scraped along her neck, and his breathing picked up. "Dammit, Snow. You make me want things I shouldn't want."

Ivy clutched his forearm, feeling the tendons move as he stroked his fingers against her clit over and over again. "There's nothing wrong with what we're doing," she whispered.

Except they might have chosen a wiser location.

"What I want to do is strip you naked, right here and now. I want to drop between your legs and put my mouth on you so I can taste the sweet honey coating my fingers." He growled again, and for one horrible, terrible moment he took his hand away.

Thank God it was to shove aside her panties and slide his fingers against her wet core. He stroked a half-dozen times, slipping in to the first knuckle.

He took his hand away completely, lifted it to his mouth, and sucked his fingers with an appreciative moan.

She tilted her head to watch, uncertain what to focus on. His hand crushing her breasts? The fire in his eyes? His *hmmm* of approval won out as his wet fingers returned between her legs, slipping under the gusset until he could curl his thick digits inside her.

Her legs fell open wider, and when he put his thumb against her clit, she buried her groan against his torso.

Faster. Faster, his hand moved in syncopated timing as the pressure on her clit increased enough to send her close to orgasm. He still held her breasts, his face tucked close to hers as if he were whispering secrets. His arm wrapped around her. From a distance they probably looked as if they were enjoying a quiet moment, innocent and sweet, as the moonrise slid over them.

Innocent. But the dirty truth was that he was fucking her with his fingers in public.

And with that image, the demand between her legs was answered. She sighed out her pleasure, and he swallowed it, mouth meeting hers as he adjusted position enough to roll them slightly, his fingers between her legs still moving, dragging out her pleasure. Making her want to weep because this was *Walker*, and his touch and his kiss were tangled up in all the right kinds of connection and intimacy.

While the aftershocks slowed, his caress continued, delicate now. Softer. Easing her down.

She was embarrassingly wet, and yet too relaxed and content to be worried about it. "Thank you."

Walker pulled his hand from her pants and reached around to put things to rights before twisting them both until they lay on the grass side by side. Pale silver light shone over them and revealed a contented expression on his face. "My pleasure."

He caught her and pulled her against him, and they relaxed in the warm summer air, covered with moonlight, his heart pounding under her ear. Whatever was going on, and whatever choices he needed to make, *this* part was right.

Taking as much of this man as she could and making new memories was right. This time had been his turn to give, next would be hers, but being together—that was what was important. She didn't want to give that up.

Ivy lay cradled in his arms as he played with her hair and hummed softly, the melody escaping him somewhere between a lullaby and the soundtrack to a really heartfelt movie.

12

Walker couldn't remember the last time he'd been so happy.

After their intimate moment down by the lake and the sweet cuddle together afterward, he and Ivy hadn't bothered to rejoin the party. She'd been nearly asleep in his arms, all warm and relaxed when he'd realized she was peopled out.

He'd walked her to her car, stolen another kiss, then given her a pat on the butt before tucking her behind the wheel.

Temptation called him to trail her home and follow up on the rest of the promises their bodies had made.

His cock ached and he wanted more of her, but at the same time the evening seemed perfect, even ending with the edge of frustration on his side. The fact he was choosing the speed, and deciding to take it slow as they rekindled their physical connection, made all the difference.

The next couple of days got busy again, because even though Ginny said she was there for a holiday, his little sister wanted to spend time visiting every bit of the ranch, exclaiming how much it had changed during the year she'd been gone. And she'd decided she needed an escort as she did her reminiscing rounds, hauling one brother at a time out with her for a few hours.

Walker figured it was her version of quality time, which worked for him. They'd always had a good relationship, and even though she and Dare had been tied up in super-glue-strength knots made of female friendship before they'd become family, the three of them were close enough in age that he'd been a part of their mischief for a lot of it.

That was the good part of the days. The bad?

That part came when he walked around the corner in the barn after coming back from the far fields and ran smack dab into Luke and Kelli in the midst of an enormous fight. Only a few words later, it was clear the argument wasn't personal.

Kelli glared at Luke. "You're not my boss. I don't have to tell you anything."

He had her pinned against the wall of a pen, glaring down from his extra foot of height. "I'm one of your bosses, and I want a name, now."

Walker hurried forward. "Luke, quit crowding her."

His brother glanced up, blinking as if surprised anyone else was around. "What?"

"You're scaring her," Walker said softly, stepping to Kelli's side and catching hold of her hand before she could escape. "You okay?"

"She's not okay, and I want to know right now who the hell gave her those bruises."

Oh shit. Walker eased his grasp on her wrist, but he didn't let go. "Kelli? What's going on?"

All the fight seemed to go out of her, and she inched closer to him as if she didn't feel entirely safe with Luke, which Walker didn't blame her for one damn bit.

"It's none of his business," she began.

"Don't go there," Walker ordered. "What bruises?"

She glared at him this time. "Maybe it's none of your business, either."

"Her whole left arm, and the side of her neck," Luke butted in. "And don't try and give me a line about how you fell off a horse, because number one, you don't fall, and number two, the ground doesn't leave finger marks."

"Luke, go away." Walker put as much authority into the command as possible before stepping between his brother and Kelli. He made a barrier so she couldn't escape without crowding her, then bent his knees until their eyes were on the same level. He lowered his voice. "Look, it isn't my business, unless it is. Did you get those bruises from something you didn't mind was happening?"

While she might seem to live twenty-four/seven with the horses, people had different kinks, and he wasn't about to let Luke make her feel bad about it if the bruises were consensual.

Kelli slowed right down as if there were a cone of silence around them, staring into his face as if making a judgment call. She glanced over his shoulder once, but thankfully Luke had taken the hint and disappeared from sight.

She opened her mouth and took a deep breath, and he was sure she was going to tell some bullshit lie when her face twisted up and she stepped against him, curling in like one of the kittens hiding from a predator.

Walker held her until she finished crying, patting her back and making soothing noises as best he could.

He glanced over her shoulder. Luke was there again, grim death in his eyes, and when Walker motioned for him to step away, Luke's expression said more than the shake of his head.

So be it. He had a crying woman to deal with first. Then he'd stop his brother from committing murder.

"Kelli? You've got to talk to me, sweetheart."

She made a rattling sound as she sniffed and brought herself back to vertical, still hiding against him even as she used the back of her sleeve to wipe her eyes. "I didn't want the bruises. It wasn't like that."

Jesus. Walker's gut was somewhere down around his toes. "Who did it?"

"I can't tell you."

She barely whispered the words, but his brother must've had bionic hearing because a curse echoed from a good ten feet behind where Walker and Kelli were huddled together.

Kelli cringed, and Walker glanced over his shoulder. "Shut up. In fact, I told you to go away."

For once Luke actually listened. The sound of his boots stomping faded until the door to the outside closed with a slam.

Walker reached down and tipped Kelli's chin upward. "Why can't you tell me?"

She licked her lips nervously, fidgeting even as she held his arms. "I need to take care of it myself."

Heaven save him from misguided, stubborn women. "I'm pretty sure you can take care of a lot of things, but Kelli, if it was one of the hands around here, that makes it our business and something we need to help you with."

She shook her head.

"Do you trust me?" he demanded.

It was a bald-faced question to ask, and it made her pause. Then her words swept out like a two-by-four and nearly knocked his feet out from under him. "Haven't you ever had a secret you kept to yourself because it was something *you* needed to deal with?"

Damn, he wanted to lie. "Doesn't mean I was right in keeping the secret."

She shrugged.

"Kelli, if someone hurt you, they might do it again. You need to trust us to help you *and* to let you take care of yourself. I know it's a juggling act, but you're smart enough to figure it out."

She let go of him as she stepped back, straightening as if she were an Amazon instead of a teeny bit of a thing. "I promise I have it under control. But no, it's nobody who works here. And I'll be careful. It won't happen again."

Which was a relief and yet a worry at the same time, and it just meant they would all be keeping a closer eye on her for safety's sake. He patted her on the shoulder and gave her a firm nod. "Okay, Kelli. If that's your choice, I'll accept it for now. But any time you can come and talk to me, or you can tell Ashton."

She made a face.

"Or you track down Luke, or you go to Tamara—you've got a whole lot of people who care about you around here."

"I know that." She wiped her nose then grimaced. "You'd better fast-talk Luke, because I don't want to have to put up with him bossing me around unless I ask for help."

"I'll deal with him," Walker assured her. But as she walked away, his gaze lingered on the blue marks along her neck, and he wondered if he was making the right choice.

When he walked outside of the barn and was accosted by his brother, it made it that much harder to stick to his guns.

Luke's eyes were on fire. "Who was it?"

"How did you see the bruises?" Walker wanted to know, hoping the question would distract Luke.

"She was scrubbing down saddles wearing nothing but a tank top because it's stinking hot in the tack room. She jerked that long sleeve shirt on before I could do more than see the damage." Luke caught him by the shirt and didn't let go. "What did she tell you?"

"That she wants you to mind your own business," Walker said softly. "She promised to ask for help if she needs it."

Luke stalked away, swearing loudly before whirling on a boot heel. "That's *bullshit*. Because whoever beat on her is going to stop in the middle so she can come running to get one of us?"

"She's a grown woman, and one of our employees. We don't have the right to run her life," Walker snapped back. "I don't like it any more than you, but it's not our decision."

"Fine. We'll make sure she's never anywhere without supervision," Luke said firmly.

"What part of *grown woman* did you not understand?" Walker said. "You don't think she's going to figure out we've got her under house arrest if there's suddenly someone babysitting her all the time?"

"I don't care if she figures it out as long as she's safe."

Walker stopped then, sudden wonder making him look Luke up and down more thoroughly. "You seem a lot more heated up about this than just discovering a situation with someone who works for us. I mean, it's horrible, and I want to get to the bottom of it too, but is there something going on with you and Kelli?"

The expression of sheer shock racing over Luke's face gave a firm *no* answer, but it didn't explain why he was going off the deep end.

"Okay, forget I asked." Walker rubbed his temples, tempted to haul Kelli in front of Ashton until the woman confessed what was going on. But that wasn't how you treated somebody who was a strange mix of employee and family. "We'll tell Ashton to keep an eye on her, *and* we'll talk to Tamara."

Luke's worry and anger redirected slightly. "Well, damn, you are sneaky. Tamara is the perfect solution."

"But you need to lay off," Walker warned.

His brother nodded reluctantly. "I went about that the wrong way. I was just so pissed."

"But she's not the one you need to be pissed at," Walker pointed out. "And that's the way it sounded."

He put his arm around Luke's shoulders and walked forward,

giving his shoulder a squeeze and trying really hard to force himself to let a few of his own secrets go.

Because Kelli was right *and* completely wrong. He knew what it was like to want to solve a problem by himself, but he was also realizing it didn't always work.

"We're headed to the pub tomorrow. You joining us?" Luke asked.

"Who's we? Because I was hoping to see Ivy."

Luke waved a hand. "Invite her along. It's me, Glenn, and Josiah. Ginny will come, and Kelli said earlier she was going to meet the Fields, so maybe Ivy plans on being there anyway."

Walker nodded. A night out together sounded like a great next step in their summer. If he went home with Ivy afterward, so much the better.

Because while he was enjoying going slow, it was time to pick up the pace a little. It wasn't a secret how much he wanted her, and the best way to tell her was with a full-out physical confession.

Maybe one confession would give him the strength to make a second.

Ivy wrapped her fingers around a glass that held something cool and lime-scented, settling into the comfy chair she'd been pointed at after stepping into the room above her sisters' shop.

A group of women were already assembled, including Tamara and Ginny Stone, Rose and Tansy, and two others.

Ivy remembered one from before she'd left Heart Falls. Brooke's father owned the garage in town. The other woman Ivy hadn't met until that night, but she turned out to be Brad's mysterious Hanna. She was petite and delicate, with long brown hair and haunted eyes.

Ivy took a sip of her drink and scolded herself for letting her imagination take off into flights of fancy. Brad had set his sights on a pretty target, but she did seem quiet compared to Brad's boldness.

Kind of like me and Walker, remember?

"The first monthly meeting is about to begin," Tansy announced, interrupting Ivy's musings. She set off a set of bell-like chimes on her phone to get everyone's attention.

"Thank you, Tinkerbell," Rose snarked mildly.

"And what exactly are we meeting monthly about?" Brooke asked, crossing a foot over her knee as she leaned back in the corner of the sofa and balanced a drink on the armrest. "Because all I got was an email from Tamara telling me to show up and bring a snack, which, hey—I'm good at following orders when it involves food and drink."

"This was partly inspired by you, Ivy," Tamara said. "You mentioned starting a book club, which I still think you should do, but Tansy and I had been talking about other things that would be fun and interesting to learn—"

"From each other," Tansy slipped in. "Because we are awesome, and we've got a lot of talent, so why not share the wealth of information?"

"Share our talents? You guys want to learn how to do your own oil changes?" Brooke made a face. "Okay. If that's your idea of a good time."

Tamara grinned. "Oil changes *and* spending time together. It doesn't always have to be about the project. It's a good excuse to eat and drink with friends."

"Damn you for not thinking of this years ago," Ginny joked. "You're going to have to include me via Skype or something until I'm back for good."

"Long-distance repair lessons in exchange for hints about which wines go best with seduction?" Brooke raised a brow.

Ivy laughed with the group. Surprisingly, Ginny didn't jab back, just winked and rose to get something from the kitchen. Her cheeks were flushed redder than usual.

Ivy tucked that interesting tidbit away to gossip about later with her sisters.

"What's the agenda for today?" Tamara asked. "Oh, and Kelli sends her regrets, but says she'd love to join us next time."

"I was wondering where she was. You think she'll make it to the pub tomorrow night?" Brooke took a sip of her drink. "God, Tansy, whatever we're doing tonight had better not involve heavy machinery. This is like a double."

"Triple, but who's counting?" Rose eyed her sister. "Tansy had a fit of some sort right when the bottle hit vertical. I swear most of the tequila went in the blender."

"Better than on the counter or the floor," Tansy chirped happily. "And since this is our first night we're just going to hang out, drink and eat."

"A worthy agenda," Ivy offered. It would be good to get to know more women in the community.

Rose and Hanna brought out trays with hot food, and everyone loaded up. Ivy avoided the jalapeño poppers but hummed happily as she dug a chip into a cheesy melted dip that smelled like a million calories.

"Oh my word, pass the napkins because I'm drooling."

Hanna's eyes lit up. "You like it? It's pretty much my go-to for potlucks."

"It's gorgeous, and don't you dare give me the recipe," Ivy warned. "Or anyone else. If you're the only one in town making this, I can avoid the temptation to have it every day."

"It's good with vegetable sticks too," Hanna offered, smiling proudly as she settled on the carpet by the coffee table with a filled plate.

Ivy's attempt to stop from making a face failed.

Her sisters laughed. "Ivy, do you still hate vegetables that much?"

"I can eat a salad," Ivy protested. "If I have to. Maybe."

Tansy turned to answer Hanna's puzzled expression. "Our sister does not approve of vegicide. She has no trouble with steak or chicken, but she's like an opposite to vegan. If it doesn't have a face—"

"—it doesn't have a taste." Ivy recited the last bit of her old motto with a sheepish smile. "Really, I am better than I was all those years ago."

Hanna was snickering now with the other girls. "Please don't teach your grade two students to hate veggies. My daughter will be in your class this year, and right now Crissy thinks broccoli is a treat."

Ivy shuddered without thinking, drawing more laughs from the group. She glanced over at Hanna, somewhat surprised the woman was old enough to have an eight-year-old daughter. "They'll never find out from me, I promise. Only if she wants to bring an apple for the teacher, I'd prefer that to carrot sticks."

Conversation flitted like butterflies over a patch of wildflowers; the whole group for a while, smaller twos and threes at moments. Ivy took mental notes, but it was fun to find out more about each woman's personality as well as what they were doing for a living.

Tamara was working at the ranch, and Ginny was helping her get a limited Community Sponsored Agriculture program going while she was in town for a month. Then Ginny would be heading back to Italy and the rest of her apprenticeship time.

Brooke still worked at the garage with her father, and Hanna cleaned local offices in the evenings.

And even though Tansy and Rose were family and Ivy had kept in touch with them over the years, it was good to hear how they spoke about Buns and Roses with such excitement. It pleased her to see the delight on their faces and know the shop was something they wanted to do.

Another happy gear turned in her gut, and the tumblers for "content family" lined up a little tighter.

Rose had just refilled the glasses when Tansy clapped her hands. "On to the final event of the evening, unless you all want to stay for a sleepover."

"I thought there wasn't an agenda?" Ginny was curled up next to Tamara, the two Stone women who'd only briefly met before this week obviously hitting it off.

"No agenda, just fun." Tansy passed a page to each of them.

Rose eyed the offering with trepidation. She knew Tansy the best of all of them. One glance was enough to have her sputtering. "You're so bad."

"What is this?" Ivy glanced at her page and laughed even as she felt her face heat.

"Dirty Minds," Tansy informed them happily. "We take turns. Read out your three clues, Ivy, and we'll all try to guess what you're talking about. First person to get it wins a point."

Oh. No. "I can't read these out loud," Ivy complained.

"A grade two teacher who can't read?" Brooke snickered into her glass. "Hanna, this doesn't bode well for your daughter."

Six expectant faces were turned Ivy's way. Ivy glanced at her paper again. "I will get you for this, Tansy."

"That's not a clue..."

"Or a surprise. Someone is always threatening Tansy." Rose sighed long-sufferingly.

"We need to keep Tansy and my sister Lisa apart," Tamara murmured. She cleared her throat. "I'll start. First clue. I last a long time when conditions are right."

Ginny raised a brow. "Do I want to listen to this bit of gossip? I mean, yeah for you and Caleb, but..."

Rose elbowed her on the other side. "It's the clue. What's that describing?"

"My brother's sex life? Which, ick."

Brooke snorted, her eyes widening as if in shock. "Excuse me."

Tamara kept a far straighter face than Ivy would have been able to. "Second clue. You never know how many inches you're going to get."

"Oh. My." Rose fanned her face with a napkin. Tansy was grinning ear-to-ear.

Brooke dug into her purse and brought out a tape measure. The mechanic pulled on the tape. Slowly. Slowly. A bit more, making faces as she eyed the length.

The first inches got a wrinkled nose, then that expression morphed into a happy smile before turning into wide-eyed shock. And when she pulled her arms apart, stretching the tape as wide as she could reach, a cry of dismay and horror bursting from her lips, Ivy laughed hard enough she was having trouble breathing.

Tansy fell off her chair.

Tamara somehow pulled herself together, and after clearing her throat a couple of times, still snickering hard, she got out the final clue. "You never know when I'm going to come."

Ginny buried her face in her hands, but it was Hanna who brought the house down.

"A snowstorm?"

Ivy wiped the tears from her eyes to look into Hanna's clear, innocent expression. Tansy coughed a few times before they all lost it.

Hanna sat back and quietly sipped her drink while they got themselves together.

"*You* don't have a dirty mind." Tansy raised a glass at Hanna. "But the game is young. We'll teach you, young Padawan."

"But I get a point?"

Ivy's lips curled into a smile as Tansy assured her she had a point, and that it was her turn to read a clue.

The night went on, and it was good to laugh and know there was a place for her within the company of some wonderful women.

A place to build a home and a life. And it might be the tequila talking, but it was too easy to imagine Walker Stone at her side.

13

Walker stepped into Rough Cut, sandwiched between his brother Luke and their friendly neighbourhood veterinarian, Josiah Ryder.

The music hit him low in the gut and set his bones on fire. The familiar words of the song rose to this tongue like sweet honey, and a smile snuck up on him.

They didn't know it, the bodies moving in time with the pulsing beat, but that was *him* in the background. One of the songs that he'd headed out last February to be a part of. He'd hit the studio to help with last-minute backup vocals for a friend of a friend, and it had started the whole singing nightmare.

Production of the song itself had been pretty neat.

A large screen had been added to the interior décor of the pub to the side of the stage area, and sure enough, there was a music video playing in all its glory. The top layer of live-action recording meshed together with the work they'd done in the recording studio, and the magic of music production turned it into one solid performance.

He let himself feel a moment of pride. They sounded pretty

good. Of course that was ninety-nine percent the rising star in the foreground; the man Walker had a chance to do more with than just quietly hide in the background, if he could only handle it.

He must have gotten lost in thought because he was being guided by the arm. Josiah pulled him to the bar where a new face turned toward them with interest. A dark-haired man with Asian features, his hair cut military neat. His sharp gaze took in Walker and Luke, a smile growing as he turned back to Josiah with a nod. "These the Stone boys?"

"You're good," Josiah answered with a nod. "Luke and Walker. Guys, this is Ryan Zhao, the new owner here at Rough Cut. His family's moved to Black Diamond, but he's decided to spend money in our corner of the map."

"As long as you decide to spend some in mine, it'll all work out fine." Ryan spoke easily as he shook their hands. "I've already met Caleb. I can tell that you're family."

Luke raised a brow. "Our big brother was out drinking without us?"

An easy laugh escaped the bartender. "He and his wife were at the community hall on Canada Day. My daughter is the same age as their oldest, and Tamara was suggesting day camps she thought Talia would enjoy."

Of course Tamara was involved, because their new sister-in-law had jumped into the community like it was a lake and she was on fire.

"Hope it helped." Luke was grinning at Walker, the same thoughts regarding Tamara visible on his face. They were both pleased at Caleb's change of fortune, and the woman was definitely at the center of that change.

"Luke can find a ride for your daughter," Josiah reminded him. "Best horseman in these parts, other than me, of course. If he doesn't have one to sell you, he's got the contacts."

"You looking for a mount?" Luke's expression sharpened like it always did at the suggestion of matching a horse with a rider.

"I am, but not until the end of summer. We should talk."

Luke nodded. "I'll give you my number."

Josiah joined in the conversation for a moment, easy and light. Walker met Ryan's dark brown gaze steadily as the other man examined him with a great deal of curiously.

"And you're Walker, the man of mystery," Ryan offered. "I got a call from your manager this morning."

Walker shook his head to clear the cobwebs that had snuck in, because he was lost. "Who?"

"Maxwell Pillion. He's a big fan of yours—definitely thinks you're headed for amazing things."

Oh my God. "He called you."

Ryan's lazy grin tightened with confusion. "Is that a problem?"

"Just not sure what's going on," Walker admitted. "He knows where to find me, and there's nothing going on right now that would require him to track me down."

Because his deadline was still more than a month away.

The sense of confusion was spreading as the dark-haired man's gaze tightened. "He knew I ran the pub here. Said he thought the locals would be keen to support one of their own."

The sense of dread in Walker's gut was growing. "There's nothing to support."

"What's wrong?" Luke laid a hand on Walker's shoulder and leaned in, watching the conversation.

Ryan glanced at Walker, concern growing. "You didn't know about this?"

"I have no idea what Maxwell would have talked to you about."

Curses escaped Ryan. "One second, I need to stop—"

The music changed, the group vocals fading to be replaced

by a guitar strumming a steady beat. A light, happy lilt that danced around the room. They turned together toward the stage area, a sea of backs blocking Ryan's path to the controls for the screen and the new hell descending on Walker...

The music video that had been playing was gone, and this time it was his own damn face that appeared, his voice slipping into his ears to mix with the ringing disbelief.

Damn Maxwell.

Walker stared at the screen in front of them. It wasn't an official music video, but it was far more than just one of those still shots that people tossed up that stayed static as music played in the background. The video itself had been put together with generic scenes from a countryside setting. Big old ranch trucks driving down dusty back roads. Equipment working a field. A group of men dancing back from the gate as a bull burst free and exploded into action. A woman stepping through a swinging screen door onto a porch, looking into the audience with a welcoming smile on her face.

Nothing more than still pictures of Walker rather than live-action shots, but they made it clear he was the singer.

He was simultaneously proud and horrified.

The drinkers and dancers from all corners of the room were raising their voices now, cheering as they recognized him. And damn if it didn't strike him that while Maxwell was the biggest bastard in the universe, he was also one of the smartest.

There was no putting this bull back in the pen without a hell of a struggle.

A fist met his arm. "You crafty devil. Why didn't you say something?" Luke demanded.

"Because—"

Because there was nothing to say the last time Walker had talked to Maxwell. Because he was supposed to still be making up his mind.

But the crowd had spotted him now, and friendly, helpful hands were pulling him to the stage. Pats on the back and admiring smiles landed, and Walker didn't understand how he could feel sick to his stomach and still get a rush from the chaos.

Damn brain. Damn body.

Damn *Maxwell.*

Ryan had made it to the stage, moving quickly to turn down the volume. Displeased shouts rang out. Whistles and jeers.

It wasn't the man's fault, so Walker put on a good face and wrapped an arm around Ryan's shoulders. "Don't worry about it."

A firm head shake. "I took him at his word. I'm sorry you weren't expecting this."

"What did you have planned?"

"Maxwell sent a cut of music. Said you could do the vocals live." Ryan straightened up. "I can deal with this. You go back to your family and enjoy your night."

"I'll do it." Walker offered fast before he lost his courage. "Glad to help out."

Gratitude shone in Ryan's eyes, but wariness too. "Tell your manager I don't appreciate being played. I'm glad you're a better man than him."

"I'll give him hell," Walker promised.

They shook hands quickly as the crowd moved like an impatient bronco, wanting to burst free and explode into action.

Ryan grabbed a microphone from the top of a speaker, chatting easily with the crowd. "You folks got a surprise there. Here's another. Walker Stone is going to sing something for us. It's your lucky night, and this is a first, as far I know. It's something he wrote himself. So put your hands together."

He passed over the mic, patting Walker on the arm. "Drinks on me after. And forever, as far as I'm concerned. Sorry to throw you under the bus like this."

"It's okay," Walker muttered back, forcing a smile to his lips as he faced the gathering of familiar faces.

He could do this. He had done it so many times before. Maybe not with the familiar tune beginning to play behind him, and damn his manager again, because that was him, Walker, on the guitar.

Luke was clapping loudly, encouraging him as Walker lifted the mic.

The crowd parted, and he spotted Ivy at the edge of the room, her confusion clear but with a smile bursting out just for him from where she stood with her friends.

Her silver eyes caught him like an anchor, jerked him to a halt, and held for long enough to give him the strength to start, to sing out the opening words about feeling restless, about being restless.

Being in front of a crowd had never been a problem—until it was. But this time having Ivy there made the words he was sharing sweeter. He could do this, the fear of panicking receding as he stared at her.

Ivy tilted her head as if she were listening intently. Not only to his voice, but to what he was feeling inside. Of course she was. His Snow, the one who'd held his heart in her hands forever...

Someone pushed between them and blocked Ivy from his view.

Instantly, fingers wrapped around his throat. Death's boney grip was back.

Oh God. *No.*

Not now.

Not here.

The room faded.

~

He'd been singing, staring straight at her as if they were alone and this was something he needed to tell her that was urgent and heartfelt.

She'd been jostled to the side, and by the time she'd found room to pull herself free and stop her heart from pounding, something had gone desperately wrong.

The song continued, but the tone seemed off slightly, as if Walker were distracted and no longer concentrating. She tried in vain to catch a glimpse of him, but pressed at the edge of the room, it was impossible.

That sense of urgency grew thicker.

Ivy took a deep breath and headed into the mass of bodies. She ducked under various arms and around enough bodies to put her within a few steps of the stage.

By now the song had faded until only the music remained. Walker wasn't singing. He wasn't moving. He didn't seem to be *breathing*. The music carried on in the background, but he was more like a statue than anything.

People glanced at each other in confusion, but Ivy was already rushing forward.

Maybe she was wrong, but she didn't think so. This was so similar to when she'd watched him climb and then freeze. It made no sense, but right now wasn't about understanding. It was about doing what she had to.

She couldn't stop him from falling, but she could be there to lift him to safety.

Ivy dodged the final few people to reach the edge of the stage. Thankfully there was a step to get up so she didn't have to throw herself on her belly.

She stepped quickly to Walker's side and wrapped her arms around him, tugging hard until she could pull their lips together as if they were trapped in a passionate embrace.

It had been maybe fifteen seconds without singing, but with

something to distract them, the crowd was willing to focus on the kiss she was making look as wild as possible. Which involved a fair bit of dramatic flair as Walker was stiff and unresponsive for far too long.

When he did move it was to catch hold of her hips as if she'd thrown him a lifeline, clutching tight enough she'd have bruises.

She softened the kiss, tugging on his shoulders to pull back far enough to speak to him. She had to speak louder than a whisper to be heard over the crowd's whistling.

"You okay?"

He nodded then shook his head.

"Can you sing?"

Walker looked beaten. "I...can't."

She cupped a hand on his cheek. "Give me the mic."

He handed it to her, fingers stealing around her other hand. Ivy sucked in a deep breath for strength before turning to the crowd.

Curiosity and amusement reflected back. They hadn't expected him to sing in the first place, so this rollercoaster was just one more bit of the entertainment, which meant Ivy could solve this and get Walker out of there.

Only now she had to speak.

She caught Tansy's worried expression before her sister forced a smile and flashed her a thumbs-up. Rose too was offering her support, hip-checking the nearest guy out of the way to get a better view as she put her hands together and clapped.

I can do this.

Ivy lifted the mic. "Hey. Sorry about that."

"If you're done kissing him, can I have a turn?" Kelli James lifted a brow and stuck out a hip.

Laughter rang. Walker took a deep breath and shook his head in amusement.

Ivy stepped in front of him as if claiming territory. "Hands off, chickie."

Walker's hands settled on her hips, pulling her against him.

Kelli made a show of folding her arms and sticking out her tongue.

Ivy smiled, thankful for the extra distraction. "I think we all had a surprise, and this one is my fault. That's..."

Her mind had been racing to figure out a possible solution, and it was weak, but would have to do.

"...that's *my* song. I didn't think Walker was going to sing it in public yet. I wasn't ready to share. Sorry."

Her cheeks must have gone crimson from the rising heat, not just from staring into the faces before her without cringing at her bald-faced lie, but speaking in front of all those faces, period.

She'd learned hard lessons over the years. Lots of coping strategies, but that didn't mean she liked public speaking.

Or in this case, public lying.

Walker leaned in and kissed her cheek, and the music in the background turned to another familiar song. Ryan waved a hand in the air as he stepped forward to take the mic.

"See what I get for not lining up my entertainment ahead of time?" He shook a hand at the complaining people to the left of him. "Another time. But since we can't enjoy Walker, put on your dancing boots. Half-price pitchers for the next half hour, and we'll get some line dancing started early. Where's Carly? Time to do your thing, girl."

A girl in the crowd bounced forward excitedly, her sheer enthusiasm bringing smiles to faces as much as the announced liquor sale.

Ivy took control and pulled Walker with her to the side of the room, ignoring the teasing questions. Walker took the ribbing as well, silently waving off his brother. Luke looked ready to pounce on him both for protection and answers.

Fingers crossed she wasn't about to set off the fire alarm, Ivy pushed through the emergency exit and dragged Walker into the fresh evening air.

He pushed the door shut with her, collapsing with his back against the hard surface. He dragged a hand through his hair then bent over as if he might fall.

Whatever was going on, the rest of this evening needed to happen elsewhere. "Come on," she ordered, offering her hand.

He tilted his head back and stared at her palm before slapping his fingers against hers.

She led him to her car, opening the passenger door before heading to the driver side.

Walker didn't argue, just crawled in, adjusted the seat to make room for his legs, and then settled in. Closing the door, doing up his seatbelt—every step orderly and neat. Controlled.

Ivy held her questions. This wasn't something she wanted to get into while she was behind the wheel.

He stared straight ahead in silence as well. At least until his phone rang not fifteen seconds after she left the parking lot.

Walker glanced at the screen before answering it on speaker phone for some reason.

"What?"

Luke's concern rang like lightning. Sharp and clear. "Where are you?"

Ivy noted with approval that was his first question instead of *What happened?*

Walker spoke softly. "With Ivy."

"Good." Luke was still at the bar, the music loud in the background. "You need me, bro?"

Extra points for that, Ivy noted. Walker's brother was a rock. One who might get leaned on heavily depending on what happened over the next thirty minutes.

Walker glanced at her. "I'm good. I'll talk to you later. Sorry—"

"Nothing to apologize for. But call if you need anything."

Luke hung up. Walker put his phone away and went back to staring out the window.

Thank goodness the town was small enough they were pulling into her driveway within minutes. Ivy stopped and got out without speaking, leaving it up to Walker to follow her or not.

She paused as a faint light shining at the edge of the graveyard caught her eye.

Along the fence, a solar powered light had been placed by someone, tied with a shiny red ribbon. The bright spot glowing with such determination seemed out of place, and yet it warmed something inside her.

There was always a light of hope if you knew where to look.

A hand on her shoulder turned her toward the man she'd cared about for a long time. Cared, worried about...

Loved.

Walker pulled her against him and held on tightly, and in that moment Ivy knew she'd do anything for this man. Anything to help him understand he was valuable and had so much to give.

Help him know he was loved.

Help him see the light.

14

She untangled herself from his embrace and brought him into the house.

Walker followed and sat when ordered to, silence falling as Ivy worked at the counter. Everything he'd walled up was going to come out now. There would be no more pretending nothing was wrong.

Inside he had to admit he was kind of glad he'd been pushed to the limit and needed to confess.

She pushed a cup of tea into his hands. "Drink," she ordered.

"The cure-all tea comes to the rescue?"

She settled opposite him. "It's not a bad solution. Gives you something to hold on to, and something to sip while you're trying to figure out what to say. My mom taught me that."

"Your mom is a smart lady. When she's not being annoying," Walker teased gently.

She wasn't letting him get away with not talking about it. Ivy put her cup down and laid a hand on his arm. "What happened?"

He didn't take the easy way out and look at the steaming

liquid. He kept his gaze fixed on her face, the steely strength in her eyes a contrast with the softness of her fingers caressing his.

"I..." He thought back. Panic setting in, and then—

"I don't know," he confessed. "I lose bits of time. These moments come over me, and suddenly there's nothing there. Then I'm somewhere I don't expect, doing something I don't remember."

Ivy frowned. "What do you remember tonight?"

Walker tried. "Going up on the stage. Thinking I needed to cut Ryan some slack because it wasn't his fault. Thinking I was going to kill my manager the first chance I get. I know I heard the music start."

"And the last thing?"

He took his time, forcing himself back to that moment of blackness. It was like staring into a fog bank, not sure if he was imagining the barn and fence posts he could barely see.

The only thing he knew for certain was the very end. "You were holding me, looking at me as if you were worried, but not about to let anyone else know. Like the time we played hooky and got caught."

Even with concern written on her face, the corners of her lips moved upward in the smile. "We were not playing hooky. We were doing research, and we lost track of the time."

"We had fishing poles in our hands, and the only research we could do down by the lake was how many perch we could catch during math class."

"You don't remember singing?"

Walker felt like an idiot. "I assume I must have gotten something out because the song was nearly halfway done when you woke me up." He turned his hand palm up and caught her fingers in his. "Thank you."

"Of course, but we need to—"

He tugged to get her attention. "Don't blow off my gratitude.

That's twice you've saved my ass. I know how much it cost you. The first time at the pool you could've gotten really sick. This time you were so damn bold when I was—I don't even know what I was doing. Drooling? Making rude noises?"

He shook his head.

Ivy let out a disgruntled sound then stood, crowding forward until he pushed his chair back far enough she could sit on his legs. She caught hold of his chin in her slim fingers. "I'm not blowing it off. I did 'save your ass' as you so eloquently put it. Now I want to know the whole story. That's your payment for making me throw myself at you and kiss you, *again*, in front of a crowd."

"Because kissing me is such a chore?"

She leaned in, her grip on his face strengthening as she added a second hand. Cupping his cheeks and tilting his head so she could kiss him. Tender and soft, a caress of her lips over his. His hands were wrapped around her hips, so they were connected and together, and yet it was almost sweet. Something far more than sexual.

He didn't fight when she pushed back, staring at him, her quicksilver eyes icy cold and burning hot at the same time. "Tell me, Walker. You've had this happen to you before, yes?"

He dipped his head, the scruff of his chin brushing her soft palms.

"Don't make me pull it out of you one word at a time. Consider this like back in high school when I refused to let you copy my English homework."

Good analogy. "You're going to make me do the work myself?" He adjusted his grip on her hips because holding her helped center him. "The first time recently was last fall. I ended up on my ass, but I don't remember starting the ride."

Her entire body tightened. "You've had this happen while you were riding a bull? Oh my God, Walker. That's entirely different than getting stage fright."

"It's only happened a couple of times," he hurried to reassure her. "I can feel it coming on. I've bailed on some rides and in some situations when I can tell it's going to happen."

The furrow between her brows was deep enough to plant potatoes. "Your stomach gets tight, and your heart rate picks up. Your palms get sweaty?"

"My ears start to ring, and I swear it feels as if"—talk about admitting to having a troubled mind—"something is choking me. Right around here, until I can't breathe."

He laid a hand high on his chest, fingers touching his neck.

Ivy's head tilted as she laid her hand over his and stroked softly. "You're not the first person to feel this way. Although I'm sure that's not reassuring considering society doesn't let guys deal with emotions easily."

"Please. I'm man enough my ego can handle knowing my brain is out of kilter, but that doesn't help me fix this." He linked their fingers, hands dropping into her lap. "I know I have a problem. I can't ignore it, and I can't work around it. God, Ivy. I have a chance to go on tour with the same band I filled in for on that recording you heard tonight. Maxwell keeps talking up ideas of things that could happen in the future, but how can I build a career in something that's done in public when I can't tell when I might freeze again?"

She listened intently.

"And I need to do something big, or else I'm not going to be able to help the family."

Ivy gave him a light smack on the chest, lips tucked into a pout as she scolded him. "You're a bigger help than you give yourself credit for."

"If I can't bring in money, I'm not." He caught her hand and returned it to his chest. "Caleb says things don't look good with the ranch. I need to get my head on straight. I need to be able to tell Maxwell *yes*, and he's only given me till the end of summer to decide. If I don't sing, I've got to figure out how to keep my ass down on a bull for long enough to score. Those are my only options."

She was quiet for a while. And just looking at her, he could tell she was working on the right thing to say. The right words of encouragement.

The moment was too familiar.

A memory of their past snuck in. Ivy, fighting back tears because she didn't want to leave, even as everything in her wanted to take the next step.

Him, forcing himself to say the right words. The unselfish ones, the ones that allowed her to follow her dreams, even though it was like tearing out his heart and handing it back to her.

It was clear Ivy had caught the flashback coincidence when she spoke. "Way back when, you asked me what my dream was. You asked me what was going to make me happy heading into the future, and when I said *being with you*, you told me it wasn't enough. That no one person should be somebody else's dream."

"Good memory."

"It's etched into my soul," Ivy whispered. "For a teenager, you were very smart. I needed to go away because there was no other option, but leaving you was the hardest thing I've ever done."

Walker waited.

"What's your dream? What do you want?" Ivy asked. "You sent me off with your blessing, and it took time—a lot of time—but I accomplished what I set out to do. I'm a teacher. That's part of me forever. Now it's time for you to reach for your goals. So, what do *you* want?"

"To be there for my family. To save the ranch."

To be with you.

He kept the last one to himself, because he didn't see any way to make it happen.

But Ivy was shaking her head. "I'm not asking the right question. Do you want to sing? You've always liked music, but a music *career* was never something you talked about while we were growing up. I didn't even know it was on the radar."

"It just happened," he admitted. "I was goofing off at a bar with a bunch of the guys after an event, and Maxwell was in the crowd. It was karaoke gone wild, but you're right. I've never aspired to be a singer."

"What about rodeo?"

He could tell where she was going. "I like the animals, and the guys, and the atmosphere. It's exciting. But I also enjoy being with my brothers here at Silver Stone. I don't need the adrenaline rush."

But Silver Stone could be gone if they didn't find the funds.

Ivy nodded thoughtfully.

"If you don't have a preference one way or another, I'll admit I'd prefer you have a panic attack in front of a crowd instead of while on a bull. Embarrassed is not the same as hurt or dead."

She said it so forcefully her words snapped like a whip.

"Which is why I need to deal with the panic attacks," he insisted. It always came back to the same thing.

But Ivy wasn't done brainstorming. "What about songwriting instead of performing? Ryan said tonight the song was something you wrote."

He'd never thought about that. "It's another option, but that's not what's on the table right now. Right now the offer is for me to travel with the band and sing. When they head to the studio again, Maxwell said he can set it up for me to do a couple more singles like the song I wrote."

Her cheeks were pink. "I'm sorry for lying about it in front of people. I hope that doesn't cause trouble down the road."

Walker thought back to figure out what she was talking

about. "The fact you said I wrote it for you? Snow, I *did* write it for you."

She blinked.

Hell, he'd spilled his guts about everything else, why not go for broke? "I've never forgotten you. You would not believe how often I wished I was with you. I don't think a day has gone by since you left that I didn't think about you at least once."

Everything about her softened, and her eyes went liquid. "I missed you so much."

They hadn't solved anything. In fact, they'd only cracked the door on his troubles, but somehow sharing the burden with Ivy had made it seem manageable. She was such an integral part of his life he couldn't imagine going forward without her.

He shoved that problem to the side and let his heart speak. "I don't know if I want to be a singer, or ride, or just work with my brothers. There's only one thing I know for sure that I want."

Ivy gave him her full attention.

Walker pulled her against him. "I want you."

He didn't need to expand his comment. She already knew from the look in his eyes that they weren't holding back anymore. It was as if the honesty between them had produced this final confession. Their bodies needed to connect like their hearts had so they could commit to the next thing.

Kisses came naturally. The faint scent of tea on the air mingled with the candle she'd left on the counter, the flickering light casting a rosy glow on the walls. A soft radiance that matched the gentleness of his touch as he caressed up her back then down again, his fingers lingering at the top of her hips.

Her pulse danced as his fingers tugged her shirt free and slid under, palms warm against her.

His touch was distracting and enticing, but for a moment her thoughts were still tangled up in what they'd been talking about. His fears—the panic attacks as he called them—weren't something to be lightly pushed aside. She was terrified to discover he'd been missing chunks of time, especially within the arena.

She knew what it was like to feel fear. To feel her throat close up and her tongue tangle until she couldn't speak and to want more than anything for the ground to open beneath her feet so she could vanish away from staring eyes and cruel whispers.

Only she'd never felt *real* fear until this moment. At the idea he was willing to risk his life. There had to be better options.

She couldn't imagine a world without Walker in it.

He'd shared that he'd thought about her daily. It was the same for her, and though they'd been physically apart for years, it seemed everything else about them had remained interwoven, tangled like an intricate artwork where the back was a mess of knots but the front had become a beautiful tapestry. That could be their future.

But not if he was dead.

Walker's grip tightened, and a second later she rose in the air, supported by his arms. He pulled back far enough to look into her eyes. "Where's your room?"

She was so thankful she'd finished that room first. "End of the hall on the left."

Everything was ready. And as Walker carried her down the hall, his strong arms iron bands around her, she pushed aside her plotting and planning and resolved to make *this* a moment he would remember in explicit detail.

His feet didn't make any noise on the solid wood floor, except as he passed sections where the boards squeaked and moaned. As if the house were preparing for a session of ecstasy as well.

Then they were through the door into her cozy room. Walker didn't stop to admire the fresh paint or the pretty arrangements.

He laid her on the bed and covered her with his body and went back to kissing.

She was trapped under him, cocooned in a protective cave formed by his thick biceps resting on the mattress on either side of her. His torso barely caressed hers, one of his thighs slipping between her legs. The heavy weight of his hips and the line of his erection pressed her to the mattress.

It was like being surrounded and entombed in pleasure. The sweet exploration of his mouth as he nibbled his way along her jaw paused as he pressed kisses to her temple then behind her ear, licking her earlobe and making her laugh.

As if the happy sound changed everything, Walker took a deep breath, let it out slowly, and murmured against her skin. "My Snow Princess."

His hand drifted to the front of her blouse, undoing the buttons with far more skill than he'd had back when they were teenagers. Those days had involved a lot of fumbling, including panicked moments of pulling her clothes back into alignment after a session of heavy petting, trying to look as if they were innocently watching a show as her parents reentered the TV room.

No one would interrupt this time.

Still, Ivy felt a swell of jealousy at the women Walker had touched during the time they'd been apart. Oh, it was an irrational thought, but while part of her was glad he'd enjoyed pleasure over the years, she was envious.

Focus on now. Focus on the future.

Walker pushed open the sides of her blouse and pressed his lips just above where her heart was pounding at a frantic pace. "This is how I remember, but better."

Ivy was going to tease him about his words not making any sense when he reached under her and undid her bra, sliding the shoulder strap off one side to expose her breast to his eager gaze.

He rolled slightly, body still in contact, the rock-solid length of him—*all* the rock-solid lengths of him--pressed against her. Walker lifted a finger and slid it down her collarbone, slowly, teasing as his gaze followed the path he was tracing. Up the slope of her breast, around her nipple, around again.

His gaze drifted higher to meet her eyes, a slow smile sliding across his expression. "So damn beautiful."

A gasp escaped her as he laid his palm over her breast and squeezed, rubbing in a circle against the tightening tip. Squeezing again, harder this time, over and over.

Ivy squirmed, reaching for him, tugging at his shirt.

Walker sat back far enough to reach over his head and drag his T-shirt forward, stripping it over his head and throwing it to the floor. The next second he had taken off her shirt and bra completely, humming happily as he gave her other breast the same teasing treatment.

It was good, and made even better because now she could touch him as well. So many strong muscles to stroke her fingers over, sliding down his shoulders, across his back. Caressing his sides and letting herself explore for the first time in forever.

He wasn't a teenager anymore. He was lean and hard, cut beyond belief. The muscles of a man who'd laboured and sweat, one who'd put in the work that was now built into every inch of his body.

His lips were back on hers then traveled to her shoulder. He placed a brief kiss on the top of her breast before he surrounded the peak and sucked sharply, drawing her nipple into his mouth and sending a lightning strike directly between her legs.

Ivy threaded her fingers into his hair, closing her eyes and letting him touch. His lips played over her nipples as he used one hand to cup and stroke, lifting her higher.

One hand disappeared as he continued to tease with his mouth. The teeth nibbling at her skin weren't enough to distract as his hand slid down her belly and under the waistline of her pants.

Strong fingers slipped into her panties and over her mound. Possessive, controlling, one finger pressing hard over her clit before sliding deeper.

"I need to be here. I need to push my cock into your body so we're one."

Honesty rang in his voice with longing and need.

Ivy reached down and undid her pants, wiggling everything off as quickly as she could. Rolling to the side, she pulled open a drawer in her side table to grab a condom, because she was an adult, and this was her house, and she was prepared.

She'd been so hopeful this was going to happen.

She rolled back to discover he'd also stripped, and when he held up a condom as well, their eyes met and they both laughed.

"Remember how hard it was to find condoms for our first time?" she asked.

Walker snickered. "Snow, this isn't the moment to reminisce."

Then he kissed her senseless until she wasn't thinking about the past, no matter how sweet the memories. She was fully engaged in the moment as he went back to teasing, his hands stroking between her legs, fingers slipping into her core then delicately circling her clit.

He pushed her thighs apart, and moved away. But before she could finish protesting, he laid his mouth over her sex and the only sound she could make was an inarticulate groan.

The cowboy side of him had made him good with his hands, or maybe it was the guitar playing, but the singer—oh, what the man could do with his mouth.

Pleasure built rapidly, his teasing tongue combining with his fingertips sliding in and out of her core. Steady yet demanding, changing position slightly as she gave him feedback with a series of desperate noises.

She would've used words if she'd been capable of speaking.

When he pushed two fingers in deep, stroking the front of her sex, an orgasm arrived with a rush, her body squeezing tight around him. Her hips bucked upward, wanting more.

He gave into her demand instantly, replacing his fingers with the broad head of his cock, angling over her until the heat of his torso and the steamy heat of his need were her everything.

Every inch registered sharp and clear as he pressed his thick length into her slowly, joining them the way they were meant to be. The first time in forever, yet so much like coming home.

He rocked slowly, his gaze moving over her face as he held himself with ironclad control. The muscles in his shoulders bunched tightly as he moved into territory that hadn't been explored for a long time. Not by him. Not by any man.

Ivy realized that toys, while fun, truly had nothing on the real thing.

With a final motion he closed the gap, and they were completely connected. He lowered himself the slightest bit, increasing his weight over her, and it was achingly good.

Ivy adjusted her hips, sliding her thighs farther open to give him more room. When she curled her arms around his neck and sighed happily, he chuckled.

"I don't know what I want more. To stay like this because it feels so damn good, or to move because that's going to feel damn good as well."

"Move," she said. "Definitely move."

She tightened around him, and he swore softly before following instructions. Pulling his hips back and pressing in again, a slow, deliberate motion that made her feel every inch.

Ivy stared into the eyes that held so much of her happiness.

Walker's face contorted as if he were in pain. He licked his lips and breathed out slowly as he fought for control.

Ivy squirmed again. "Walker?"

"Yeah?" He continued to move in smooth strokes that felt good, yet weren't nearly enough anymore.

She tangled her fingers in his hair and tugged hard enough to yank his head up so their eyes met. "I need you to move harder."

Another curse escaped him.

"I mean it. I'm not a delicate snow princess—"

He needed no further encouragement. Cutting off her words with his mouth he kissed her greedily, pinning her beneath him. The dusting of hair on his chest rubbed her nipples as his body rocked faster and faster still. Hips pressing forward again then jerking back. Thrusting now, her sex wrapped tightly around his cock as he speared into her over and over.

Walker angled his hips lower so on every thrust he rubbed their groins together, teasing her clit and making pleasure dance over her.

He growled, pausing just long enough to hook an arm under her leg, opening her wider so he could thrust deeper into her willing body.

She was helpless under him and it was perfect. It felt good—no, it felt *amazing*—but this was beyond the physical. He was no high school sweetheart, he was a full-grown man who knew how to take and give pleasure abundantly.

Ivy clutched his shoulders harder, closed her eyes and let the rapid pace send her spiraling back up. He broke, calling her name as he locked their hips together, grinding in a circle against her clit as he jerked inside her.

Another wave struck, her sex contracting around the thick length of his cock, dragging out his pleasure from the sounds of his continued groans. Ivy reveled in the sensation, the goodness of being connected with him.

Walker panted hard, holding himself over her for a moment before settling slowly, carefully, at her side. Still connected, tugging the leg he had control of over his hip. He nuzzled against her neck and peppered kisses over her face. Tender and delicate, and oh-so-intimate with his cock still inside her body.

She watched him, holding back the words that wanted to burst free. Not wanting to scare him, but knowing this was one step to help him see his value. Not just to her, but to himself.

Walker stroked his fingers over her cheek. "That was better than I remember."

Ivy laughed. "We were seventeen. I don't think it could've gotten any better for us back then. You've gained some skills that I appreciate very much."

His expression turned serious. "Ivy? This was the first time for you since back then, right?"

She nodded.

"Me too."

15

The silence in her room deepened. It wasn't what Ivy had expected him to say, but the first rush through her wasn't incredulous disbelief. It was a kind of sweet pleasure.

She laid a hand against his cheek. "Wow."

A slow, sexy smile drifted over his features. Contentment was there, but there was also amusement that seemed just for her. "*Wow?* You're not giving me much to go on. How do you feel?"

"You know very well how I feel. Any woman who's had two orgasms in a short period of time is pretty happy. If I'm surprised by anything, it's how much better that was than when we were young, considering neither of us have been practicing."

Walker laughed softly. "It just never felt right to take that final step."

A flash of memory struck. "That's why you smiled when I told you I hadn't had sex."

He nodded. "Maybe that makes us a couple of old-fashioned fools."

She leaned in tight, pressing her lips to his and kissing him fiercely. "We're the perfect fools together, then."

Walker tapped her on the nose before slipping from the bed to take care of the condom. A moment later he poked his head out of her tiny bathroom with a grin. "You have a shower in here," he informed her brightly.

Ivy sat up, tucking the sheets against her chest. "Good eye."

"Smarty-pants." He tilted his head toward his discovery. "Join me. I've always wanted to have you in the shower."

It was clearly a demand, not a request, but Ivy didn't care. His idea was right in line with what she wanted, so she pushed back the sheets and joined him.

Wet and *sex* turned out to be a lovely mixture when the water was hot and the man was Walker. Steamy pleasure turned into long, languid cuddles in her bed, and he didn't leave until the morning. He'd curled around her and held her all night.

Ivy was thankful she'd wiggled the queen-size bed into the space, even though Walker had to sleep at an angle to keep his feet from hanging off the end.

Ivy was still in a sleepy fog when Walker pressed his lips to hers, kissing her lazily. "I gotta go, Snow. I'll call you later."

"Come over when you're done with work," Ivy offered.

"Wild horses couldn't drag me away," he teased.

"We still need to talk," she reminded him. "We're not done."

His face went serious. "No. You're right. We're not done."

She didn't think he was talking about his panic attacks, and that was fine with her. She gave him a final squeeze then watched him stride from the room.

She fell asleep again quickly enough considering it was four a.m., but her dreams were filled with partial conversations and mini movie clips. Ones that started with a shock and never concluded.

Sweet images from their days in high school. Ivy with her family gathered around. Time from her days spent in the hospital when she'd fallen sick—which was a secret she needed to share with Walker sometime soon. Her dreams turned even more restless and when she saw Walker thrown from a bull—

That was when she gave up altogether, crawled out of bed, and got ready for her day.

She did a few tasks related to the school year, but it still meant that by noon she was headed to her parents.

Sophie greeted her with a smile. "Your father is at the bookstore if you need him."

"I'll stop by later, but I thought I'd visit with you, if you've got time."

Her mom pushed aside the papers on the table before her and gave Ivy her full attention. "Want a cup of tea?"

Ivy laughed. "No, it's not that type of conversation. I just wondered if everything was going well."

"That's supposed to be my question, not yours." Her mom headed to the counter to plug in the kettle anyway. She turned and examined Ivy briefly without staring too intently. The *mom glance* she'd perfected over the years. Ivy knew she'd been checked out closely, but it didn't seem as invasive as when others did it, probably because it *was* a mom thing.

The other mom thing Sophie did? She waited until Ivy answered the question. "I'm fine. No lingering problems from my dip in Heart Falls."

"Nothing physical, but what about—?" Sophie turned her back quickly and pulled tea bags from the cupboard as if it was the most vital task ever. "How is Walker?"

Ivy's cheeks heated, but she was old enough to make up her own mind about how she lived her life. "Are you asking because you don't know? Someone in town has to be keeping you up-to-date with gossip."

Sophie placed the teapot on the table and took her seat again, playing with the spoon. "What do you mean *someone* in town? Your little sister Fern—I swear that girl has a shortwave radio hidden somewhere in that artist's cave of hers. I heard something happened last night at the watering hole you kids go to, and it involved Walker, but I didn't hear how it ended."

"He'll be okay." Ivy hesitated. It wasn't her secret to share, but there were things her mom could help with.

But more than that, Ivy was aware of how much her parents had helped over the years. How strongly they'd fought for her in so many ways.

"I don't think I've told you thank you often enough," Ivy said softly. "You and Dad have been wonderful parents. Not just to me, but to all us girls. The whole time I was gone, I knew I had you to come home to. I knew that whatever happened, you would support me."

Her mother paused in the middle of pouring tea. "Well, I think you've said it often enough. We know you're appreciative, but that's not why we do it. We love you."

"And I have never doubted that, especially not on the days when I would come home sick from crying over being teased at school."

Sophie's expression sharpened. "Oh, a few of those days I got to have a little extra excitement, marching back to school to give some of the other parents a piece of my mind."

"You were fair, though. I hope the parents I have to deal with are as reasonable and admit when their little darlings aren't angels."

Her mother smiled. "The only time you weren't an angel was when you were running around with Walker. But I don't blame your behaviour on him. I think you probably got him in more trouble than he would've on his own. His mother used to ask if we could calm you down a little, which always made the two of us laugh, considering you were so frail."

It was always a little sad to talk about Walker's parents. Their deaths had touched everyone in the community, including her mom and dad, who had been friends with them both.

"I'm glad you adopted us." Ivy leaned forward and gave her mom's hand a squeeze. "I know you said before that you simply picked four girls who needed to be loved, but we were fortunate. You opened your hearts to us, you and Dad."

"It's been worth every moment," her mom said firmly. "On a slightly different topic, not that I don't love for you to come in here and tell me how awesome I am..."

Ivy grinned at her.

"You and Walker."

Her smile slipped slightly. "Yes?"

Sophie picked up her spoon and her cup. An obvious telltale sign she was looking for the right words to say.

"Mom. You're not going to say something embarrassing, are you?"

Her mom's gaze snapped up. "I'm totally going to say something embarrassing. Honey, I know he was at your house last night, and I don't think he was helping with house repair. And I just want to make sure you know that while we like Walker very much... Well, you're a grownup, both of you—"

"Yes, we are."

Sophie gave her an evil look. "Be careful."

Safe-sex talks with her mother. So *not* what she wanted. "I'm pretty sure we had this conversation well over ten years ago."

Her mom looked shocked for a moment before laughing. "Oh, honey. I'm not talking about sex. You're right, if you haven't figured that bit out by now, what with the Internet and everything, you just go ahead and muddle through on your own. I'm talking about your future."

Well that was almost more embarrassing than talking about sex. "What kind of future? Don't you think I should be with Walker?"

It was her mom's turn to reach for her hand and squeeze her fingers tight. "The opposite. I don't want you to miss out on something that could be absolutely wonderful. You had to give up a lot when you went away, and I know with your health problems, it's taken a long time for you to return. He's a good man. An awful lot like his father was. Walter Stone had more heart than anyone we knew, including your father, who has a tendency to get a little too sarcastic at times."

Her mother wanted her to be with Walker. "I always thought you liked him but, you never seem *that* taken."

Sophie looked at her with the solid bluntness that had carried through the years. "For a while we didn't know if you had a future, darling. It wasn't right for either of you to get your hopes up. But it wouldn't have been right to deny you your young love, either."

Cold ripples went through Ivy at the memory of how sick she'd been. "I'm far healthier now."

"You are," her mom agreed, "and you've learned a lot that will help you stay strong in the years to come. But that means you have to juggle. If Walker's the one you want, I don't want to see you miss out on him. Having the right person in your life makes the tough days so much more bearable."

They fell quiet for a moment, the light music her mom always had playing in the background filling the corners of the house with quiet joy. Not loud enough to hear the words, but a distinct enough tune that was uplifting and joyous, so much like her mom.

So much like the household Ivy had grown up in, and once again she was struck by how much she wanted the same thing with Walker.

Ivy picked up her cup, wrapping her fingers around it as she smiled at her mom. "You're a pretty smart lady."

"Damn right I am," Sophie offered in return. "So ignore your father's grumbling, because he's still got his tail out of joint. We should plan a family meal and invite Walker. I promise not to tease, and I'll make Malachi behave as well."

"Are you physically capable of not teasing?" Ivy asked in dead seriousness. "Oh, wait. Let's be sure to ask Grandma to join us. That'll put Dad on his best behaviour."

A snicker escaped her mother before Sophie forced her face back to serious. "Buffalo?"

Ivy smiled and laughed and felt warm inside. "Oh, Mom, I love you so much."

"I love you too. We'll get the guys to barbecue. They can bond over the smoke and charcoal. It's written into male genetics, right?"

Caleb slapped a hand on his shoulder and offered a droll grin. "I can't believe I'm saying this, but can you stop singing?"

Walker blinked in surprise. "Was I singing?"

"It's like working with a cage full of canaries next to me. You keep chirping out this and then the other, and none of it makes any sense. It sounds good, but I don't know that you can sell it."

Luke slipped from a stall on the other side, stepping forward. He looked Walker over closely. "You're okay."

"I am. Thanks for checking."

Caleb looked between the two of them. "Did I miss something?"

Luke hid his grin, and Walker worked on keeping a stone-like face. Their oldest brother had never caught up on the gossip as fast as everybody else, which this time was playing in Walker's favour. "Nope."

"Walker spent the night at Ivy's." This offering came from above their heads, and the three of them twisted to see a flash of a bright red flannel shirt disappearing as Kelli's voice trailed off into the distance. "Not that Caleb would be interested."

Walker glanced at his big brother. Caleb had one brow lifted and there was a smile on his face that involved a fair bit of gloating.

"What're you smirking about?" Walker demanded.

Luke jumped back in. "He's a happily married man. Now his only goal in life is to make sure everybody else gets a ball and chain."

Walker's and Caleb's eyes met, but this time it wasn't amusement that passed between them. Something had changed in Luke's tone, and they turned to face him.

Luke had grabbed a pitchfork, stabbing into the nearest hay pile as if he was defending himself from invading monsters.

"Interesting observation from a man who's engaged to be married," Caleb offered dryly.

That comment should've gotten a snarky response, but Luke quietly lifted a load of feed in the air and walked off, his shoulders stiff under his fleece jacket.

Caleb and Walker stared at each other. "Was it something I said?" Caleb asked. "I was kidding around."

"I don't know what's going on, either. Penny's been gone for a few weeks, so maybe he's missing her." Walker didn't want to poke a sore point by asking, either. But something was definitely wrong.

Shuffling noises drifted from above, and a bit of hay fell from the loft.

Caleb rolled his eyes. "Kelli. Get your ass down here and stop eavesdropping."

She slid down the old water pipe they used to play on when they were kids, riding it like a fireman's pole. A pair of heavy leather gloves protected her hands, and as she landed, a swirl of dust puffed up under her boots. She marched over, slapping her hands together then slipping the gloves into her back pocket.

"Yes, boss?" she asked, all innocent and sweet.

"Don't try that with me, young lady."

Kelli's lips twisted for a second before she outright snorted. "Oh my God, don't. I mean when Ashton gives me hell, I can see it because he's like...*old*. But you're most definitely not the grandpa type. At least not yet."

"Stop trying to change the topic. What do you know?"

Kelli made a face. "Isn't that Luke's business?"

"Kelli," Caleb warned. "You seem willing enough to talk about everything else that goes on around here. Spill."

She cocked a brow. "All I know is he went from bouncing like a frisky colt because he just *happened* to beat me at cards, then his phone went off with a message, and ever since he read the text, he's been a grumpy ass."

"Penny," Caleb guessed. He sighed heavily. "I'll track him down later and find out what's going on." He glanced at his watch. "Actually, I'll track him down now. I promised the girls I'd take them fishing, and we need to get ready."

"You're going in the middle of the afternoon? The fish don't bite until dusk."

"Oh, we're going fishing later, but that means we have to start to get ready this afternoon, at least according to the girls."

He slapped Walker on the shoulder, gave Kelli a warning glance, and then marched off after Luke.

"And he complained I was making noise? His whistling is terrible," Walker muttered. He turned his attention on Kelli who was trying to sneak out of the room without it looking as if she was sneaking away. "I won't call you *young lady*, but don't you leave without talking to me."

Kelli offered him a saucy grin. "Sure, boss."

Walker gave her a dirty look.

She toned it down. "Sorry, it's just so much fun to tease Caleb now that he's all jollified from being married to Tamara and all."

"How're you doing?" He kept his gaze fixed on her face so he wasn't tempted to check her for more bruises.

"I'm good," Kelli said sharply with a firm tip of her chin. "No problems, and I don't see any in the future, either."

"So you're good?"

"Good as gold," she offered, back to full perkiness. "But I'd be even better if you give me permission to ride Storm Dancer. Please?"

The girl had a masochistic streak mile wide. "That horse is dangerous as hell."

"You ride him."

"I'm not five foot and one hundred pounds."

Kelli planted her fists on her hips and glared. "Five foot *two*, and way more than one hundred pounds. But that might make it better because he won't mind little ol' me on his back."

"You really want to ride Storm Dancer?"

"Damn right I do," she snapped back with enthusiasm.

"Tell me who gave you the bruises."

Her face twisted into a scowl. "That's nasty."

"Your choice," Walker said calmly. "I swear I won't tell anyone else, and as soon as you give me a name, I'll supervise your attempt to ride Storm Dancer."

Kelli seemed to think it over, opening her mouth and closing it a half-dozen times before giving her head a firm shake. "I can't. And I think you're really mean to make that a condition, because —well, just because."

It had been worth a try. "You're sure no one's going to come and beat on you again?"

"I'm positive the situation is never going to come up ever again," Kelli said with absolute conviction.

Damn. He wished one of the other hands could give him the scoop, but there wasn't anybody else. Kelli *was* the eyes and ears around Silver Stone. She was the one who found out the gossip, not the one who created it.

"Fine. Tell you what. Next time I have Storm Dancer out I'll let you give him a try. But only when I'm there," he finished, raising his voice to be heard over her high-pitched squeal of delight. Kelli threw herself at him and offered a shockingly strong hug for someone her size.

Then she was off, racing away with the enthusiasm of a teenager.

Walker shook his head. She was a damn fine cowboy, but hell if he knew what made her tick.

His phone buzzed, and he glanced down, excited to see a message from Ivy.

Ivy: *how do you feel about barbecue?*

Walker: *it's good*

Ivy: *chicken or beef?*

He couldn't resist: *buffalo*

Ivy: *LOL. How did you know?*

Walker: *I've seen your house, Snow. Unless you hid it in the graveyard, you don't have a grill.*

Ivy: *huh. Now that you mention it, I'll put that on the list.*

Walker: *you need to fix the porch before you buy a grill*

Ivy: *I have plans to fix the porch, but my handyman has been rather occupied dealing with an emergency in the bedroom*

He laughed: *is this something that happens often? Emergencies in your bedroom?*

Ivy: *I'm not sure. You might need to come over when you're done with work today to see if it's a regular occurrence or just a once in a while thing*

Walker: *honey? Trust me. Regular like clockwork. Daily. Twice a day, or more often if possible*

It was a sweet exchange, almost a flashback to the days before she'd left. And as they made plans to get together when he was done for the day, Walker enjoyed knowing they had parts of this relationship thing down pat.

He still had to figure out what he was going to do with his future. Was it possible to deal with his panic attacks, or was he going to have to find something else to do to help his family?

Unfortunately, no matter how hard he racked his brain, he didn't come up with any other solution. The entire time he was at the bunkhouse to get scrubbed up, he kept mulling over the idea. Something new. That's what he needed.

Yet, he'd already been given a golden opportunity, and was it right to just throw it away? How many people longed for a career in music? And he was being handed one on a silver platter—

Enough.

He threw some things in a duffel bag because he fully intended on staying with Ivy tonight. Not just because they had a lot to talk about, but because he needed to get her perspective. Being able to spend the night in her arms was going to make all of the confusion and the restlessness that much easier to deal with.

16

She didn't bother to pretend she wasn't waiting for him.

Ivy stood on the porch as his truck drove up her long drive. The August heat trailed up from the road and produced shimmering mirages in front of his big tires.

He parked, and his feet hit the ground with a solid clunk. As he reached into the back and pulled out a duffel bag and his guitar, she admired the lean, muscular lines of him. His T-shirt stretched tight around his biceps as he draped the bag over his shoulder, guitar case in hand, walking toward her with a lazy grin on his face. The one that said he couldn't wait to be with her, either.

They stood for a moment and admired each other; her on the porch and him on the bottom step looking up. It was a picture-perfect Alberta day, with blue sky in the background and a mass of spruce trees framing the Rocky Mountains. Even the weathered headstones in the graveyard beside them seemed to fit the moment.

Something old, and yet beautiful. Memories of lives well

lived. That's what she wanted with him; memories that went from now until forever.

"You're looking very *ranch girl*," Walker said, checking her out from top to bottom.

Ivy laughed. "Tansy and Rose bought the outfit. I think my grandma put them up to it. And, yes, I feel as if I stepped back in time just pulling it on.

She tugged the multilayered prairie skirt and offered him a cheeky curtsy.

He put his guitar and bag down on the porch, standing close as he ran a finger along the ruffled neckline of the peasant blouse. His finger was hot where it bumped her skin. "Pretty wrappings on a pretty package."

Walker tucked his fingers under her chin and lifted her face, kissing her softly. Sweet, until it wasn't as he took the kiss deeper, a little more intense, and Ivy felt her bones begin to melt.

He pulled back with a *hmmm* of satisfaction. "I take it we have a barbecue to attend?"

"Later. Mom and Dad aren't closing the store until seven tonight. Some readers are in for a special event at *Fallen Books*. I can feed you now though, since I hear that's something cowboys do. Eat two suppers."

He followed her through the door, glancing around at the totally empty living room. "You went a little wild with decorating, Snow. Very minimalistic."

"I'm getting it ready to do all the repairs to the walls and the floor," she told him, glancing over her shoulder to see him wandering down the hallway. "I don't keep a fridge in my room."

He stopped. "I should ask. Any objections if I toss my bag in there?"

Which meant he wanted to stay the night. A shiver of happiness slid through her. "Sounds good to me. I don't think there's room for you to toss your guitar as well, though."

"I thought I'd bring it to your parents' tonight. Your grandma likes to hear me play."

Ivy paused. "How did you know Grandma Sonora was going to be there?"

He was back at her side, reaching past her for a glass and helping himself. He filled it with water before turning and raising it in a toast. "She sent me a text, of course."

"*Grandma*?"

Walker grinned as he reached for his cell and held it out to show her.

Sonora Fallen: *It's been a long time since you stopped in. Bring that guitar of yours tonight, please.*

Walker: *anything particular you want me to play?*

Sonora Fallen: *Something sweet. And young man, sentences begin with capitals.*

Walker: *Yes, ma'am.*

Ivy laughed. "How long have you been holding secret trysts with my grandmother?"

"Me and Sonora? Heck, we go way back." Walker settled in at the kitchen table, turning the chair so he could stretch his long legs in front of him. "She wasn't doing that well a couple of winters ago with how much snow we got, and I stopped in to check on her. Just kinda hit it off all over again. She asked for help figuring out how to use her phone. Now she texts me off and on whenever the urge strikes."

Of course, she did. Ivy got herself a drink and joined him at the table. "Hungry?"

He shook his head. "I figure we need to talk."

"We do." Ivy took a deep breath. "Do you remember when I first came to Heart Falls?"

His gaze softened, and something in his eyes went dark with memory. "Course I do. The prettiest girl I'd ever seen with the most amazing eyes stepped into the classroom, and I fell in love."

My God, her heart pounded nearly as hard as it had that day. "*Walker*."

"What?" He was smiling now. "That's how I remember it."

"Stop turning your inner eye on me and look around at the rest of the class. Most people were not impressed, especially since I arrived right before Christmas, which meant I didn't have to take any tests."

"They got over it."

"They didn't like that I got to sit at the back of the room at a table all by myself. And when I wasn't interested in sharing my lunch or getting too close to anyone, it was another black mark."

He nodded slowly. "You were pretty frail back then. You had to have room so you could avoid a few germs."

"They didn't know that at first. They just saw a new girl who wouldn't talk to anyone and who got all these special privileges. They called me Icy instead of Ivy."

Walker's gaze drifted over her face. "You had your hair braided, kind of like you had it the day of the auction. Pulled over one shoulder, and the long, white length went down nearly to your waist. And you were all bundled up, lots of layers, and your winter coat was a bright blue. Same colour as the sky on those cold days when we could see our breath when we went outside for lunch."

She was torn between kissing him for the poetry of his words and sticking on topic to get to the real reason she was bringing this up.

"I didn't go out for lunch, though. I stayed inside and sat alone. At least until you decided you wanted to be my friend." It was such a bittersweet memory. "You jumped right in that first afternoon and introduced yourself. I don't know if you realized how scared I was to talk to you."

"I never meant to scare you. Heck, the prettiest girl in the room was willing to talk to *me*? I was damn scared myself."

"But you *did* talk to me, and I made it through without running and hiding, like I had to after meeting the principal." Ivy nodded at the look of shock in his eyes. "And you called me your Snow Princess, which made all of the teasing about Icy fade."

He tilted his head. "You were really shy. You're over that now."

Ivy shook her head. "It's not something that completely goes away. I mean, I got smarter as I got older, and I understand some of the things that scared me aren't valid. Facts help a lot, but I'm never going to be comfortable walking into a room full of strangers. It's a part of who I am. Some people love getting up in front of a crowd—I don't. If I'm in a small, tight-knit group where I can focus on individuals, that makes crowds bearable."

"Yet you got up in front of everybody at Rough Cut to save me."

She nodded. "I can do things when they really matter, but trust me, I wasn't looking at all the people around us. I was focusing on my sisters and your brother. They were my anchors. And you."

Walker shifted forward in his seat. "You're talking about my panic attacks. You're trying to come up with ways for me to deal with them."

Ivy nodded. "We don't know what's setting them off. The best thing would be to eliminate the source, but until we figure that out, the next-best-thing is for you to learn some coping strategies."

"Like picturing people in their underwear?"

She laughed. "If that's going to work for you, yes."

The light in his eyes grew heated. "I might need some visual aids. Maybe you should slip the shoulders on your blouse a little lower."

A trace of pleasure mingled with the shock. "Walker."

"*Snow*," he teased back. "Come on, I'm pretty sure this is a necessary part of my training."

She looked him over for a moment before deciding to go with the flow. In fact, she upped the ante, reaching behind her and undoing her bra, slipping the straps off her arms by twisting free. Thankfully, the elastic and the loose sleeves of the blouse made it possible for her to slip the bra away without putting on too much of a show.

But when she placed the soft cups neatly on the table, folding the straps underneath as if she were tucking the bra into a drawer, it was hard not to smile, especially when she checked the expression on Walker's face.

She sat straight in her chair like an obedient school girl, back arched to press her breasts against the front of her blouse. "Does that help?"

Walker shifted uncomfortably in his chair, rubbing his hands down his thighs as he stretched. The thick length of his erection pressed clearly to the front of his jeans. "Help get my motor going? Hell, I'm always ready to go around you."

"So when you feel a sense of panic begin, you need to have a ritual or routine to follow. Something that's not going to distract you from your task."

"*Now* you tell me. Snow, there ain't no way you can toss your bra on the table beside me and not have it be distracting."

Ivy shimmied the shoulder bands off her shoulders so that the top of her blouse cut straight across an inch above her nipples. "You're focusing on the wrong part of the situation. Stop looking with your eyes."

~

Ivy was right there, only a few feet away from him, slowly removing clothing, and she didn't want him to look? "Hell, no. Maybe picturing people they don't like naked works for some, but seeing your soft skin? Knowing I could reach out and touch you? This is probably not what I should be thinking about when I'm on the back of a bull."

"Are you scared right now?" she asked.

"Only that my balls will explode."

A laugh burst from her, like sunbeams dancing on water. "Okay, let's go with that. No, you don't want to be thinking about sex while sitting on a bull, unless that kind of thing turns your crank. But you don't want to be scared, either. Right now—are you angry? Are you sad?"

She stood and shimmied her skirt over her hips, twisting on the spot as she hummed happily. Dancing in place as the fabric pooled on the floor.

Walker dropped his gaze to her bare feet and the toes that were painted a pale pink. Then he gaped at her long legs that stretched up to vanish under the thigh-length edge of her billowy top.

He stared, mesmerized, as she danced up to him and tipped his hat off. "Right now, happy or sad?"

Somehow he kept his hands off to let the lesson continue. "Happy, and very, very hopeful I'm going to get even happier."

She dipped, bending at the waist. The scoop of her neckline gaped open far enough that the perfect rounds of her breasts swayed forward to display tight pink nipples, begging for him to touch.

Ivy pressed her hands to his thighs and waited until his gaze rose to meet hers. "Hold on to *that* emotion. That's what you think about when the fear starts to creep in. You don't focus on the details of the time and place, but how you're feeling right now."

Like he was the luckiest man on the face of the earth. "This is a good lesson. You're a really good teacher."

Ivy pressed her lips to his briefly, pulling back before he could deepen the kiss. "I *am* a good teacher. I know that when a student is trying their very best, they should get a reward."

Walker's brain muddled through that for a moment, not quite sure what she intended until she pushed his thighs apart and reached for his belt buckle. "Jeez, Ivy."

She got the leather strap undone before fighting with his button. "I need a little help."

As if he was going to argue. It was the one thing they'd never played with back in the day. Oh, she'd touched him, and sometimes just the feel of her soft hand brushing his cock had been enough to make him go off.

But all of their times together had been stolen moments in places where they really didn't feel comfortable enough to linger. They'd never spent a lot of time naked, not until now.

Walker couldn't get enough of it.

He pushed back, stripping out of his T-shirt and jeans as fast as humanly possible. Ivy had settled back on her shins, like a sexy garden fairy who had snuck into the house, amazement in her eyes as she studied him from top to bottom.

"How are *you* feeling right now?" Laughter soaked his voice.

"Scared. Definitely scared," Ivy teased as he stepped toward her, his cock so hard it stood vertical. She took him in her hand and stroked gently, and he was going to lose his ever-loving mind.

"Go to your happy place," he suggested.

Ivy went up on her knees, angling his cock so she could lick it thoroughly. The soft heat and delicate flutter of her tongue wrapped him in a million layers of need.

And when she put her mouth around the head, still twirling

her tongue against the most sensitive spot, the only thing Walker regretted was the fact he was in the middle of the room and had no walls to brace himself against.

She played. Slowly and torturously, throwing pleasure at him with every delicate suck and lap.

Gazing down at her added another level of torment to the lust racing through his veins. They'd called her Icy, but white blue flames were the hottest there were. Watching her touch him so intimately put his feet to the coals and sent fire racing up his spine. She was a delicate princess giving unselfishly to him, dipping down his length over and over. He held himself rigid, not just to keep from pushing deeper than she wanted, but because it felt so damn good he didn't need to move.

Having Ivy give to him was the most miraculous thing in the entire world.

She tilted her head so she could peek up at him, and their gazes met. He memorized the deliciously filthy image of his cock pushing between her sweet red lips, pink tongue lapping delicately before she pulled him deep and sucked.

Walker gave up and let the waves explode from deep within, spurting hard as Ivy swallowed him down until he wasn't sure he could stand a second longer.

He rubbed a hand gently over her head, the silky softness of her hair like spun glass. "I'm going to fall over."

Sunshine echoed in her laughter as she stood. Ivy wrapped an arm around him then pressed her lips to his chest. Walker wavered for a moment, using her strength to keep vertical.

They ended up lying on her bed, him naked, her still covered with the breezy cotton top, her breasts playing peekaboo as the scooped neckline moved with her breathing.

He traced a finger over her shoulder in circles. "As soon as my brain comes back online, I promise to return the favour."

Ivy's gaze danced over him, happiness on her face. "I don't

think you realize how much pleasure that gave me, but I'm not about to say no to anything we do together. But later."

She wiggled in close and laid her head on his chest, and his arms wrapped around her instinctively. The sun shone in the west-facing window, spotlighting the bed.

"I missed you so much," Walker admitted softly, playing with her hair because he could. "I told you I thought of you often, but I had to push aside the part that wanted you back so it wouldn't ache as much."

Ivy went still.

Damn. "I didn't say that to hurt you. I know you had to go, and I know you missed me too. It's kind of like you said, though. Focus on what I'm feeling now and not the memory. When I think about you, I don't think about the time you were gone. I think about how happy I am to be with you again."

"Me too."

She pressed a kiss to his chest, curling against him tighter. "You were so brave when you let me go. I remembered that, especially when things got really rough. I didn't want to fail because you had sacrificed so much by letting me go. It wouldn't have been fair for me to quit."

"Did you want to quit?" Walker asked her.

She took a deep breath then wiggled slightly until her head was on the pillow next to his, staring into his eyes. "I didn't want to quit, but there were times my body didn't cooperate. I got really sick."

What the hell. "How come I didn't know that?"

"Because I didn't think it was fair to let anyone know. No one could visit me anyway, and either I was going to get better or I wasn't."

Walker jerked up on an elbow. "You were sick enough you might've *died*?"

She pressed her fingers soothingly to his lips, making calming sounds the way he would around skittish horses. "It's in the past."

Jesus Christ. "Answer the damn question, Snow."

She gave him a dirty look. "You don't think it took me eleven years to come back because I was gallivanting around the countryside, do you?"

"Teacher's certificate is four years. I figured you'd took a couple of extra years to get what you needed so you could become a principal. Add in on-the-job training." Walker shook his head. "I never did the math.

"Six years of schooling took me eight. I lost a semester every time I got sick. I still did a lot of work and training, but it wasn't specific enough to count toward my degrees." Ivy hesitated, and he braced himself for what had to be the worst of the bad news. "I had a six-month hospital stay at one point. I got really sick and ended up with a bone-marrow transplant that saved my life."

Curses rose that Walker bit back as images flooded his brain. Ivy in pain, alone in a hospital room while he hadn't known. Only she was staring at him with concern, as if wanting to make him feel better. "I... God damn, Ivy."

"It was bad, but honestly"—she swallowed hard, stroking a hand down his cheek—"you saved me, in a way. I refused to give up because someday I was going to come back and get to see you again."

She curled in tight to offer a kiss.

He was still aching at the thought he might've lost her. Might never have gotten to see her again. "I'm glad you made it through, but I think it was a shitty idea not to tell me you were sick in the first place."

"Maybe. My parents and I thought it was for the best."

"You were wrong. I forgive you, but I'm still going to give Malachi a piece of my mind."

She was smiling again. "I look forward to it."

"Troublemaker. You want me and your dad to butt heads?" Then Walker thought of something else. "Did your sisters know how sick you were? Or your grandma?"

Ivy shook her head and then frowned. "The girls knew I was sick, but that it wasn't anybody's business other than family. But I wonder about Grandma Sonora."

He'd fallen into the only family in the world who actually knew how to keep secrets in a small town. Well, he had a few secrets of his own, but nothing like this. He squeezed Ivy tight, holding on to the precious woman in his arms. "I'm so glad you came back."

Truth. One hundred percent truth, but as the summer slipped forward, the question still remained.

After everything that Ivy had fought for, was he going to be able to stay with her?

17

Dinner with the Fields was as bizarre and special as Walker remembered from the past.

Malachi and Sophie greeted him at the door as if he was there for the first time, shaking his hand and asking about his health. Ivy gave him a sympathetic smile as she took off in a different direction, responding to her sister's summons.

"The place smells wonderful," he offered Mrs. Fields.

"Thank you. We just need the steaks done. If you can help Malachi, I would appreciate that very much."

"But did you marinate the steaks? Inquiring minds want to know." All three of them looked up to see Fern peering through the railing. "Hi, Walker."

"Hey, beanstalk. Congratulations on your graduation."

She stood and made her way downstairs, waving her hand at him. "Oh, that's so last month." Fern held out her arms and Walker accepted a hug. She'd only been a little thing, not any older than Caleb's girls, when he and Ivy had stopped seeing each other. He'd seen Fern around town at times, but it hadn't been the same.

She folded her arms and examined him closely. Sophie and Malachi had disappeared into the other parts of the house. "I'm glad you're back with Ivy again."

"You want to come out to the ranch and ride, don't you?"

"Yes. Plus, I'm really glad you're back with Ivy again." Fern grinned. "Hey, did you see my new hand?"

He glanced down at her left forearm which ended two inches shy of where her wrist should be. "It's invisible."

Fern rolled her eyes. "I don't have it on, dummy. You go catch up with Mom and Dad, and I'll grab it from my room."

Ivy's sister delighted in the different technologies that were being made for her missing appendage. "What's special about this one?"

She was already running up the stairs. "You'll have to wait and see."

He stood for a moment in the foyer at the front of the house. Voices and music sounded in the distance, and the scent of food carried on the air, thick and hearty.

He'd always appreciated how welcome he'd felt by the Fields. They'd been protective, yes, but he'd always felt they liked him. Even after Ivy had left, he used to come over...until something had changed and it had started to feel awkward. As if they were uncertain how to treat him. He'd thought the Fields had decided he was no longer good enough to be with Ivy.

Now he realized the change could've come during one of those times Ivy had been sick, and they were debating what to tell him. The bit of past history Ivy had shared changed a lot of things in Walker's mind.

Since Ivy had shared, he'd been thinking hard about the moment he'd meet Malachi again and about the secrets that had been kept from him. And while he was still upset on one level, he had come to realize there had been no easy answers. Malachi and Sophie had been wrong, but they'd meant well, and bringing it up served no purpose. Just knowing, though, made a difference.

It hadn't been anything about him that had changed the relationship.

Walker wandered slowly through the dining room, stealing a few appetizers off the plates waiting there. Then he stepped into the kitchen itself where Tansy was working at the oversized counter, dropping large scoops of cookie batter onto a baking tray.

He stole a piece that had fallen on the counter and popped it in his mouth.

Tansy grinned. She glanced around to make sure no one was watching before offering him another chunk straight out of the bowl. "It's Crispy Crunch macadamia nut."

"Be still my heart." He stole one of the hot cookies off the cooling rack, sweet goodness melting on his tongue. "God, that's good."

"I'd tease you were going to spoil your supper, but I've seen you eat. Here, have another," Tansy offered before turning to put the loaded tray in the oven.

He wandered in a little farther, glancing toward the corner of the family room where an overstuffed rocking chair sat. Ivy had curled up in it like usual, staring comfortably at the fish tank beside her.

In the adjoining open space, Rose and Sophie were discussing flower arrangements. Fern got distracted as she entered the room, stopping to help Tansy open some jars.

The room was full of life, yet there were pockets of quietness, especially around Ivy. A place where she could retreat and still be a part of the whole. Ivy wasn't ignoring her family, she was taking in as much as she could handle, or at least that's how it had been when they were in high school. It seemed that even though she wasn't as delicate now, the family still operated the same way.

Malachi stuck his head in the door and motioned for Walker

to join him. Walker carried out the tray Tansy handed him, joining the man where a barbecue waited, already smoking hot.

Malachi lifted the lid and began arranging thick slabs of meat on the top rack. "Buffalo, but I'm also throwing on sausages and hamburgers. I don't think you'll starve."

Other than delivering the tray, Walker couldn't see anything that needed doing. "What did you want my help with?"

Malachi glanced at him. "God if I know. Sophie seems to think it takes two guys to run a barbecue, and I'm not about to argue with her, so stay and keep me company."

Walker chuckled. "Yes, sir."

He spotted Ivy sneaking out the door. She offered him a wave before making her way to Grandma Sonora's side. The two women sat quietly and chatted under the shade of an oversized umbrella.

Ivy was all drop-dead gorgeous in a buttercup-yellow sundress, and it was only when Malachi chuckled that Walker realized he'd been staring.

"I guess that answers my question," Malachi said.

Walker turned his attention on the man. "Did you ask one?"

"Didn't have to. You figure out what you're doing yet, son?"

Walker dipped his head slowly. "Part of it. Still working on other things. But if you're asking because you're a concerned father, I'll be careful with her. Ivy means an awful lot to me. She always has."

Malachi closed the barbecue lid. Smoke escaped around the edges, sizzling and steam creating an eerie soundtrack to their conversation. "I'm glad you got *part* of it figured it out. You need to talk to someone about other parts?"

Walker appreciated the offer, but this wasn't quite the same as it had been in the old days back when Ivy had left and he kind of just kept coming over to chat with Malachi. Missing his dad, feeling lost.

Missing Ivy like he'd forgotten to take a deep enough breath to get him through the day.

But this was different. "Thanks for the offer, and I do appreciate it, but Ivy is helping me."

Ivy's dad nodded slowly. "Okay. Door is open, though."

They talked about other things then. Malachi's bookstore in town, the horses out at the ranch. By the time the meat was put on a tray and placed on the kitchen table, something inside Walker felt settled and right.

According to the Fields' family ritual, they filled plates and headed off in different directions. The first time he'd eaten with the family, he'd thought something was very wrong considering the Stones sat at one table and waited until their father served them. Here the food was served potluck style then everyone vanished, usually sitting with one or two others to chat as they ate their meal.

It created a different kind of intimacy. No one would ever feel dragged into the spotlight, but it was also impossible to sit in silence and not share.

He loaded his plate then went to sit outside at the small table under the umbrella by Sonora Fallen. The older woman had turned her chair to face the sun, her eyes closed as she sunbathed.

As he sat, she opened her eyes to smile at him. "What a nice surprise. Thanks for picking me for your dinner entertainment."

Walker laughed. "The first time I ate here and everyone vanished into corners I thought—I don't know what I thought. I supposed that I'd offended somebody."

"Sophie and Malachi were brilliant to come up with a solution that meant Ivy had space if she needed it, but there was always good, healthy conversation going on."

It had been a good idea. It was one of those things that taught Walker how a family could be very different from his own and yet still be there for each other.

The Stones could get loud and rambunctious, and when they gathered in one place, it was full of life and energy waiting to spiral out of control. The Fields were more like a wide open space that gave everyone a chance to grow.

Ivy appeared at his side, putting a plate of food in front of her grandma and offering Sonora a kiss on the cheek. "You were too busy chatting to get yourself food."

"Your young man distracted me. Thank you."

Ivy turned her attention on him, her quicksilver eyes filled with humour. "You had no trouble filling your own plate, so I'll leave you two to chat."

She leaned down and gave him a kiss, this one not so platonic. Still sweet, but very definitely possessive. She was claiming him in front of her family.

When she pulled back slowly, her smile was just for him. "I look forward to listening to you play later. It's going to make me very *happy*."

He watched her walk away, hearing the suggestion in her words. Knowing that if for some reason he did have a panic attack—although he couldn't imagine why one would happen in front of these people who were so much like family to him—if he *did* get into trouble, he was going to try her advice first.

And if that failed, she would save him.

He turned back to enjoy his meal and the visit with Grandma Sonora, while part of his brain was plotting what he was going to do to say *thank you* to Ivy tonight when they were alone.

Sexy, sexy Walker Stone sat in her living room, and Ivy was about to experience spontaneous combustion.

Early-afternoon sunshine streamed in, showcasing the two coats of fresh primer they'd painted on to cover the patch jobs in the walls. Ivy had pulled a set of patio chairs in to rest on, but all the fans were turned off to keep dust from flying into the wet paint, so it was stinking hot in the house.

Walker had stripped down to his jeans and boots, and could she really be blamed for getting distracted enough to stare?

She thought not.

Ivy paused in the doorway, a glass of ice tea in each hand held in reserve until she got her fill of looking at him.

Walker wiped his face with his shirt, draping it over the back of the plastic chair before turning back to her. One brow rose sharply. "That's a mighty fine-looking drink, but it's not doing a good job of quenching my thirst from way over there."

"Shhh," Ivy warned softly. "You're interrupting my drooling."

A sharp laugh escaped him as he unfolded himself from the chair, sauntering in her direction to grab one glass from her fingers. He rested his forearm on the wall as he deliberately peered down the front of her tank top. "I'll be quiet as a mouse if you agree to some equal opportunity drooling."

Ivy did her best Spock imitation, striving to lift her brow as high as possible. "You did not mention drooling while you're leaning over me. Because ick."

He laughed, drinking deeply without shifting away. The muscles in his neck moved rhythmically as he swallowed, the moisture on the glass sparkling in the sun that was shining through the window. Ivy sipped her own drink and let him stand there and crowd her, the slick sweat on his muscles making them glisten.

Walker met her gaze evenly. "You look as if you're thinking deep thoughts."

"I really want to lick you," she confessed.

A soft swear rose from his lips. "You're thinking *dirty* thoughts. That's even better."

"Nothing dirty yet. You promised to work on some exercises with me."

Walker dragged the icy cold surface of his glass along the edge of her tank top. "I'd love to do some exercises with you. Do they involve getting naked? Because my favourite exercises are naked exercises."

Ivy reached up and took the glass from him, slipping out of reach as she danced back into the kitchen. "You definitely need to get naked—you need a shower." She pointed at the arm he'd leaned against the fresh paint.

He was cream-white from wrist to elbow.

Walker stepped back quickly, grabbing a wet cloth to wipe it off. "Now, that wasn't very nice. Getting my hopes up and all."

It wasn't time to play, although Ivy was sure temptation would return soon enough. "We need to talk first. Come and sit."

She settled into one of the lawn chairs. Walker adjusted his to face her better, and their knees bumped.

"How did it go the last couple days on the ranch?" She tried to sound as professional as possible, which was hard when he was rocking his heel up and down, causing his shin to rub against hers.

"It was great. We worked with a whole bunch of the stock. Luke, Dustin, and Ashton helped me do some training."

"Dustin is back?" She'd heard about his obsession with Tamara, although everything seemed perfectly normal to her. "I thought he was helping at your uncle's ranch down south?"

"We forgot that Uncle Frank and Dustin don't get along very well." Walker stopped teasing her and looked more serious as he shared. "Uncle Frank thought the younger ones should have moved in with him when Mom and Dad passed away, but Caleb insisted on keeping the family together. I think Caleb was right, but Frank gets his nose out of joint about it sometimes. Frank made the mistake of making some smartass comment about

Caleb, and Dustin gave him what for. I guess things went downhill from there."

"Yeah. I can't see that going over well. Dustin thinks Caleb hung the moon."

"Especially since he married Tamara. The man is brilliant," Walker said with a smile. "But to answer your question, I was fine. I was more than fine—it was exciting. I got in a couple of really good rides."

She let her gaze drift over his body. "Hmmm."

Walker chuckled. "You seem to be losing concentration, Snow. You're not nearly as cool and collected as you were a few minutes ago. Does it make you hot to think of me *riding hard*?"

Oh, my. Ivy fanned a hand in front of her face. "My goodness, repairmen around these parts have such lusty thoughts."

Walker raised a brow. "Repairmen? You really do have a porn-handyman fantasy, don't you?"

She blinked innocently while her insides thrilled at the thought.

He rose to his feet, intent clear in his eyes.

Ivy scrambled upright, chair flying behind her as she ducked to one side and barely made it past him, clearing the back door with Walker hard on her heels.

Ivy made it halfway around the house to where the hose was lying on the ground, water spilling from the tip into a set of pots she was growing lettuce and chives in. She grabbed the hose, stuck her thumb over the end then twirled. The spray of water struck Walker square in the face and brought him to an abrupt stop.

He lifted his hands in self-defense, laughter ringing as he steadily moved toward her in spite of being soaked. "Someone is asking for it," he teased.

She pointed the water lower, hitting him in the groin and soaking his jeans.

Walker stooped and grabbed the nearest section of hose, twisting it until the water cut off. Then before she could escape, he tangled an arm around her waist, holding her tightly against him as he lifted her arm in the air until the tip of the hose was suspended over her head.

"You wouldn't," she begged.

"You did," he pointed out, loosening his grip on the kink he'd formed in the hose and sliding his hand up to help hold the hose as icy-cold water poured down and drenched them both.

Ivy let out a shriek, pressing her face tightly against him as water streamed down the back of her neck. They were both soaked head to toe, the sun beating down like a tropical oasis. By the time Walker tossed the hose away, his chest was glistening, drops of water clinging to the ends of his hair.

She took a peek and discovered why he was staring—her bra was transparent, as was her pale-yellow tank top. All the fabric did was give something for her nipples to cling to.

It was a good thing her house was on the edge of town and that it wasn't the right time of day for anyone to visit the cemetery, because Walker's next move was to drop to his knees and pull her forward to put his mouth over her breast, fabric and all. When he sucked she felt it all the way down to her toes, moisture turning hot as he wiggled his tongue against her.

He teased her a little before tugging her down with him and pressing their bodies together, kissing her hungrily. Ivy gave back as good as she got, no longer shocked her hunger for him kept growing stronger and stronger.

"You know the only thing wrong with my day?" Walker muttered against her neck before stripping the tank top over her head and reaching behind her so that a second later she was naked from the waist up. His gaze fixed on her body as he touched her with a worshipful caress. "The only thing wrong is that it's taken until now to touch you."

Ivy gasped as he brought her close and played with her breasts. Nipping at the tips, kissing the underside as his hands made quick work of undoing her shorts.

She had to help him wiggle the fabric over her hips as the shorts clung to her like wet glue. His hands kept getting in the way, and she giggled as their fingers bumped when she went to open the button on his jeans.

He caught her by the hips and pulled her backward as he lowered himself to lie flat on the ground, shifting her until she knelt directly over his face.

"Oh my *God*."

He devastated her with his single-minded attention to her clit. Licking and sucking, his fingers digging into her butt cheeks until she was squirming, begging for release.

With one move he slid upright, shoving aside his jeans. He pulled a condom out of somewhere, covered himself, and a second later he was back on the ground, kneeling as he brought her over him.

He used one hand to direct the thick head of his cock between her folds, rubbing back and forth a half-dozen times until she was ready to scream.

The next time he was vertical she pushed herself down and trapped him, his length sliding easily into her ready body. Her sex pulsed around him, and his eyes rolled back in his head as he sighed, a sound of complete and utter satisfaction.

Walker held her hips and moved her over him. She clung to his shoulders, nails digging in.

"Use your fingers," he ordered. "Rub that pretty clit of yours. I want to see you come. I want to feel you come all over my cock."

A shiver raced over her skin at his words, and she reached down to follow orders. The first touch was enough to send her racing toward the finish line. And when he increased tempo, driving into her deep and hard, Ivy let her head fall back and gave in to pleasure.

Her body rocked around him. Squeezing tight as he shouted, his cock jerking within her.

The hose was still running in the distance, and there were birds singing as they visited the feeders Ivy had set up around the yard. Somewhere in the distance a tractor motor buzzed, but right there all she heard was the pounding of his heart as she leaned her head against his chest and held on tight.

She didn't ever want to let go.

18

The excitement around the Stone family ranch house had been thick enough to cut. Caleb and Tamara had finally wrangled the girls into the truck and headed north to attend their sister Dare's wedding.

Walker stopped at Ivy's place to tell her goodbye. It was a terrible excuse considering he'd been sleeping at her house almost every other night.

Ivy paused in the middle of painting the shutters on the outside windows. Tansy waved from the top of the ladder while Rose peeked her head around the side of the house.

Ginny, who had decided she absolutely *had* to ride with Walker, rolled down her window and hung halfway out. "So, that's what work looks like. Fascinating, I could watch it for hours."

Rose stuck out her tongue then waved before disappearing from sight. Tansy scratched her forehead with her middle finger causing Ginny to laugh out loud.

Ivy met him on the front walk. "Didn't you have to leave an hour ago?"

"Not the way he drives," Ginny snarked.

Walker turned and gave his sister a dirty look. "If you plan on walking, you'd better start now."

"Oh, you *lurves* me, you know you do." But Ginny wisely shut up and sat back in her seat after giving Ivy a farewell wave.

"We've got lots of time. I don't know why Ginny came back, though. She's been up in Rocky Mountain House for most of the week helping get things ready."

Ivy gave his sister a sharp glance then stepped closer to Walker so Ginny couldn't overhear. "She plans to interrogate you."

Probably. "I don't mind. She's been gone for nearly a year, and she leaves again a few days after the wedding. It's kind of nice to have extra time to chat by ourselves."

Ivy laid a hand on his chest and patted him gently. "Have a good time, wish Dare and Jesse all the best, and I'll see you when you get back."

He pulled her close and kissed her, ignoring the wolf whistles that rose from both sides as their sisters added colour-commentary. And when laughter rang out, he pulled back from the kiss to discover both he and Ivy had lifted a hand in the air, middle fingers raised in salute.

"Ivy Fields, you'd better make sure none of your students catch you doing that," he teased her.

Her cheeks were flushed but she gave back as good as she got. "Walker Stone, you'd better not let my grandma catch you doing that."

He left her after one final squeeze and got in the truck where Ginny proceeded to talk his ear off for the first two hours of the trip. It was fascinating to hear about all of the things she'd seen and the new things she'd learned.

"Once I get back I plan to completely overhaul the CSA garden program. I'm so excited." Ginny leaned back in her seat and guzzled down a bunch of water. She had to be parched after talking nonstop for so long.

There was another reason why they had to keep Silver Stone. Right now Ginny was exploring the world and learning new things, but Silver Stone was home. That's where her gardens were, and the last thing he wanted was for her to come home and have nowhere to put all this enthusiasm.

Ginny reached over and squeezed his hand. "It's good to see you and Ivy together."

Her tone alone said she was gloating. "It's amazing how you make it sound as if you said *I told you so* when those words didn't come out of your mouth."

His sister twisted in her seat so she could face him. "You guys were so cute together before, and now you're even cuter."

"Here's a clue, 'cute' is not usually a description most guys like attached to them."

"Awesome, then. Regal, inspiring. Pick your adjective. But I'm glad you're together. Only, if you can hold off on your wedding until—"

"Whoa. Back up your horses." He glanced at her briefly before focusing on the highway. "We're not getting married."

"Not yet, but since I'm leaving in a few days, there's not really enough time to organize anything. So if you can, wait until next summer. And no going off and getting married with nobody around like Tamara and Caleb did."

Time to change the subject. "It made sense for them to get married on the down-low."

"Of course it did, but when you and Ivy get married—"

"Ginny, you never told me about the men in your life. Is there anyone I need to go over to Europe to beat up?" Not something he'd usually ask her. It was more a ploy to stop her current line of conversation in its tracks.

Only when he expected her to make a snarky joke in reply, she went quiet.

Oh, shit. "What the hell? There is. What's his name? What'd he do?"

"Nothing," Ginny insisted, but her face had flushed bright red. "It's nothing serious, and I'm *not* about to talk to you about my European flings."

Good grief. "*Flings*, as in plural?"

Ginny rolled her eyes and gave him one of her patented duh faces. "Yes, Walker. I've been cavorting all over the European countryside leaving broken hearts in my wake."

Well, that he could approve of. "Broken hearts are fine. But if anybody's disrespectful or needs to be beat on, I don't mind taking a trip."

Ginny's laughter filled the cab as she punched him lightly in the shoulder. "My defender. Don't worry, I'm taking care of myself and being careful. I really am so appreciative of this time to go away. Thanks for helping to make it happen."

He hadn't done anything. "Caleb and Luke are the ones you should thank."

"I have. Caleb at least. Luke has been awfully quiet these days. Is something wrong, other than he's still engaged to the wicked witch of the west?"

"Penny's not that bad."

Ginny sat in silence until he glanced at her so that he could see her face. She'd arched one brow all the way up to her hairline. "*Not that bad*? Ha."

"Luke wants her, and until he doesn't, I'll do what I can to support him."

Ginny sat back and put her feet up on the dash. "Well, I just hope things turn out all right, whatever that looks like. Just like I want the best for you and Ivy. You deserve it."

He wasn't going to argue with her, so they passed the rest of the trip with friendly, generic conversation.

They arrived at the Six Pack ranch and got swept into the horde that was the Coleman clan. It looked as if almost everyone else was already there, and he got more hugs and handshakes in thirty minutes than in a week back home.

Tamara pushed his nephew Joey into his arms. "He wants to see his mom, and Dare was asking for you. She's out back by the garden."

Walker worked his way through the crowds, thinking how good it was Ivy hadn't come. It would've been far too many people.

He looked his nephew in the eye. "You don't have a problem being around big groups, do you, kid?"

Joey smiled then snapped a hand up, catching the brim of Walker's hat and tipping it off in a well-practiced move for a nine-month-old.

Walker laughed as he swooped down, recovering his hat, then lifted Joey high in the air to hear the kid squeal with delight. "Nope. You don't have problems with a lot of people being around at all, which is a good thing."

He found Dare in the garden, where to his amazement, she was picking beans and dropping them into an ice cream pail. "Is this some wedding ritual I'm not aware of?"

She glanced up from her work, delight streaking across her face. "Hey, Walker. Glad you made it." She gave him a hug, kissing Joey on the cheek before going back to her task. "I wanted something mindless to distract me for a while. The beans need to be picked, so I may as well do it."

Walker shifted his nephew Joey from one arm to the other, pulling the tyke's hands off the brim of his cowboy hat before the kid had it on the ground for the third time in three minutes. "Works for me."

"So. If you're seeing Ivy again, how come she didn't come?" his foster sister demanded.

"It was going to be too much," Walker admitted. "Ivy said you'd remember her being uncomfortable around a lot of strangers. I think the Coleman clan qualifies as *a lot*, even though they're not strangers to you anymore."

Dare nodded slowly. "Only she's a teacher now. I thought being shy was something people outgrew."

Just like Ivy had mentioned the other day. It was something everybody assumed. "She can cope, but I didn't want her to suffer through something that should be a celebration."

His sister stopped what she was doing, staring at him before wrapping her arms around him in a giant hug. "Oh, Walker."

He hugged her back, capturing her in a Joey sandwich, not quite sure what was going on. "Oh, *Dare*."

She laughed, patting him on the arm. "You always have been like this."

"Clueless?"

A snort escaped her. "That, plus you're just so sweet."

Walker made a gagging noise because he knew it would make her laugh.

Dare took Joey from him and settled him expertly on one hip as she examined Walker more closely. "I'm serious. You're a pretty special guy. When I think back to those years of chaos after my family died, I get different feelings when I think about all of you. Ginny was already like a sister to me, and that connection got richer. Caleb stepped in and did all the dad things. He made sure everything that had to get done on the list did. And he was stern enough in a good way to make us mind our manners."

"And Luke was mother? He can cook, but he's not really the cuddly type."

She snorted. "But you're right. Luke *was* mother, because he made sure to add fun things to the list Caleb got accomplished. Just like my Mom used to do with my Dad."

A wave of regret that was never going to go away struck again. "I'm so sorry your folks can't be here for this, for *you*, today."

Her eyes got a little teary, but she nodded. "Don't make me cry on my wedding day," she warned. "And *that's* exactly what I mean. You *are* special. You might have been a daydreamer, but you notice things in different ways. You've always understood. Caleb offered to walk me down the aisle. As sweet as that would be, it's not what I want. It doesn't change the fact that they're gone."

Walker nodded slowly. "You've done an awful lot of standing on your own two feet since then. It makes sense for you to do this one under your own power as well. But you know all of us standing out there watching, we're all supporting you one hundred percent."

Dare's lips twisted, and her face screwed up into a rather terrifying scowl. "Damn you. I told you not to make me cry."

Walker opened his arms so she could step into them as he gave her and her son another hug. "I'm proud of you."

She gave a kind of chortling snort with an added sniffle as she gently pounded her fist against his chest. "*Walker*, stop talking."

"Stopping." He squeezed extra tight before reaching into his pocket and grabbing a tissue. They played pass the toddler, Walker holding Joey briefly as he made concerned noises, reaching back to his crying mom.

Dare wiped her face quickly before taking Joey from him and offering the kid soothing kisses. "Don't worry, Buckaroo. Mommy's okay. Her big brother is being all goopy sweet and making Mommy cry, but they're good tears."

Walker watched his foster sister with her son, and truth rang loudly. He was proud of her. Proud of Caleb, and Luke, *and* Ginny for the ways they'd supported each other over the years.

Heck, he was proud of Dustin's enthusiasm that continued to grow by leaps and bounds.

But as she put Joey back in his arms, Walker had to admit that he felt something else he wasn't as comfortable with.

Dare had gone through a lot, and she deserved every minute of the happiness she had right now. But she'd left Silver Stone to find her future, and he was a little sad he didn't get to be a part of her life in the same way anymore.

Maybe he even felt a touch jealous that she'd already worked through a lot of the difficult times and now was getting to enjoy the good parts of finding a partner and raising a family.

Dare took off to do the next thing. One of his siblings took Joey from him, and Walker spent time wandering amongst the Coleman clan.

So much joy surrounded him. Oh, there were a few tears at times, and a few squabbles. It wasn't perfect, but it definitely was family as he watched Tamara hug her sisters tight. And when all of them gathered together to witness the newlyweds' vows, Walker was so close to feeling the solution to *his* problem.

It was like having a word on the tip of his tongue that he couldn't remember. There was a way for him to help his family *and* be with Ivy. But until he could commit to that one hundred percent, it wasn't fair to say the words.

He loved Ivy, he always had. That wasn't the issue. Love wasn't enough, not to help his entire family and be there for them.

Although, as laughter broke out during the wedding ceremony, he had to admit it seemed as if love could accomplish amazing things.

What was the solution? What was the answer?

19

The summer was passing with shocking speed.

Ivy headed back to school the third week of August. She was still on part-time hours for another week, but between getting started there and trying to get as much done on the house as possible, she found she was getting tired.

Which meant something had to go, but it wasn't going to be her time with Walker. That was the main thing giving her joy.

He was busy as well as he continued to train and work long hours at the ranch. Through it all, he kept trying new activities to see if he could trigger a panic attack.

Which is how they ended up back at the base of Heart Falls. Ivy shook her head in disbelief. "I can't believe you're going to do this again."

"Well, it set one off before." He glanced at the top of the falls far above them, water spraying in a glorious arc to create a million rainbows as the sun hit the mist. "If I don't freeze, then I'll make it to the top. I've always wanted to do that."

The only concession he'd made was to tie a rope—a very *long* rope—around his waist. She'd insisted. "Last time you were lucky.

You fell backwards into the water, instead of sliding down the rock wall and breaking your pretty face."

"Because it was so much better to nearly drown."

She gave him a dirty look, and he snapped his mouth shut and stopped joking. That's when he'd agreed to the rope.

"Promise you'll only use it if I get stuck," he said. "Plus you can use it to pull me to shore so you don't have to get wet."

"What else do you think I would use it for?" Ivy demanded.

A grin escaped. "I don't know. I'm sure you'd never get it into your head to pull me off the wall just for the fun of it."

Ivy shook her head in exasperation. "Go do your stupid man tricks. I'll wait here for you to come to your senses."

She had to stand and watch, feeding out rope as he crossed beyond the falls and made his way up the rocky ridge. It was nerve-racking and painful, but he climbed steadily, glancing over and waving at her a couple of times.

When he made it all the way to the top of the ridge and stood with both hands in the air in victory, she felt proud to have been there to witness it.

He undid the rope from around his waist and disappeared from sight, and that's when Ivy realized he hadn't told her how he was getting down—

A loud shout rang in the air as he threw himself off the top of the ridge, flying into the air before dropping like a bomb into the center of Heart Falls pool.

A spectacular splash rose, water spraying far enough to strike her as she stood at the very edge of the water.

Walker popped up from beneath the surface. He flung his head from side to side, and water flew from his hair. Ivy didn't know if she should shout obscenities at him or scream with joy.

He stood once the water was hip deep, dripping wet and grinning from ear to ear. "That was invigorating."

"Walker Stone, did you lose your mind sometime in the last five minutes?"

He came in close. Close enough water dripped from him, splattering her. "Maybe. Want to take me home and give me hell?"

She stepped against him willingly, not caring one bit she was instantly drenched all along her front. "You're lucky the answer is yes."

It was all too easy for the answer to be *yes* when it came to spending time with Walker.

He still seemed distracted. Sitting quietly beside her at the fire pit they'd set up in her backyard. Or early in the morning when she'd open her eyes to find his arms wrapped around her but him staring at the ceiling, deep in thought.

Walker didn't seem to be having panic attacks anymore, which was a good thing. He insisted he could go back on the rodeo circuit without her having to worry about him.

It also meant he could go away and be part of the big adventure being offered by Maxwell. That option she didn't like nearly as well.

Walker gone part-time, she could deal with. Him being gone for a length of time with no definitive stopping point was less possible to bear. It made her think back to the days she'd spent lying in the hospital bed, fighting for strength as her body worked ever so slowly to rebuild her defenses.

Not knowing the future was one of her hot buttons.

Still, she carried on with her different activities, including working with Emma, who was now a fast friend.

Tamara grinned as Ivy walked into the house for the final tutoring session of the summer. "Good to see you. And I'll ask you now so you have time to rearrange things if needed, but we'd like you to stay for supper."

Sasha waved from the table where she was working on some

project that involved multiple glue sticks and pieces of coloured paper. Emma rushed to Ivy's side. "I got to pick what we're having."

"Oh, really. And what is that?"

"Chicken and beans and beans and beans."

Ivy glanced at Tamara who nodded. "It sounds delicious, but you have to tell me what that means. Other than lots of beans."

Sasha spoke without looking up from her task. "Kelli says people should accept an invitation before they find out what you're serving, otherwise it seems—"

"*Sasha*. The timing of your Kelli-isms leaves something to be desired." Tamara gave her oldest daughter a pointed look. "Would you like to reword that?"

Sasha blinked. Then her eyes widened and her mouth dropped open. "Ms. Fields, I didn't mean that *you* were waiting to find out what we're having for supper before you said yes or no. I just kind of..." She glanced at Tamara, who was waiting patiently, a kind smile on her face. Sasha nodded then focused back on Ivy. "I'm sorry. I spoke before thinking. Would you like to join us for supper? I promise that it will be delicious."

They were so delightful. "I would love to stay, and now, Emma, you have to tell me what we're having."

She knelt down so she was eye to eye with the little girl, who raised her fingers to announce very seriously. "Roast chicken and green beans and baked beans and jelly-bean cake for dessert."

Emma shoved her hand into Ivy's and led her to the table where they were going to work. Ivy looked back to see Tamara smiling in approval as she bent down and gave Sasha a kiss on the cheek, pausing as the little girl wrapped her arms around her and kissed her back.

It was a little bit of perfection, and something ached inside Ivy, literally ached, as if there were a hole desperate to be filled.

She ended up helping the girls set the table for eight, chatting with Tamara, who seemed easily distracted while staring out the window with a soft smile on her face. Her lips widened to a full grin, and Ivy slipped up to peer over her shoulder to discover Caleb and Walker side by side, chatting easily as they approached the house.

"Just looking at him does something to me," Tamara confessed softly, glancing over her shoulder at Ivy. "Mine, not yours."

It was another confirmation that everyone thought Walker was hers. And he was, yet as the end of summer arrived, there was still that tiny piece of unknown.

She wanted him. She wanted the best *for* him. And once again Ivy realized exactly how much Walker had sacrificed to let her go off to find her dream.

She wiped at her eyes carefully, hiding her emotions as she stepped back to allow Tamara to greet Caleb first, two little girls dancing around him and squeezing him tight before backing up with wrinkled noses.

"Daddy. You need a shower," Emma informed him before turning her big blue eyes on her uncle. She took a delicate sniff. "I'll go get you a towel, Uncle Walker."

Walker chuckled as he leaned down to bump noses with her. "You're very sweet to tell me so politely that I'm stinky."

Emma lowered her voice, but her whisper was still clear across the entire room. "Mama says it's important to be polite *and* it's important to be truthful."

Caleb had removed his boots and was now chuckling in the background. "Yes, your mama is right. Now, we'll go have our showers and then we can come back to enjoy supper. We have a special surprise for you, later."

The girls squealed as they ran to finish their chores.

Walker gave Ivy a steamy look full of promises then disappeared into the basement.

Tamara turned back to her. "Walker reminded me you sometimes have problems with big groups. If you need to leave the room, go ahead, we won't be offended. Tonight there'll be me, Caleb and the girls, you and Walker, and I asked Dustin and Luke to join us."

"That's sweet of you to be concerned. I take it we're having a typical Stone dinner?"

Tamara grinned. "Yes, which means I can't guarantee the volume will stay below ear splitting."

"I think I'll be okay, but if you don't mind, I'd like to sit between Emma and Walker." She'd gotten past the point of feeling it was rude to ask for what made her the most comfortable.

Which was how she ended up joining the family at the table. Sasha chatted excitedly at her and at her uncle Dustin, who was across the table. Emma joined in occasionally, her comments bringing a smile to everyone's face.

Walker stuck his hand under the table and rested it on her thigh, squeezing as he leaned in. "I didn't get a kiss when I came in."

He hadn't spoken softly enough, because Emma turned to answer him. "You were stinky, remember, Uncle Walker?"

Ivy lowered her eyes to her plate and fought to keep from laughing.

"I was stinky, but I'm not anymore."' He placed an arm along the back of Ivy's chair and curled up against her as he leaned in to talk to his niece.

Emma glanced at him then at Ivy, and then she shrugged her shoulders. "You should give her a kiss. Papa kisses Mama all the time."

Laughter trickled around the room as everyone else paid attention to the conversation. Ivy felt herself tensing up, but instead of pushing his point and kissing her, Walker gave her shoulders a squeeze then slipped back into his chair.

He glanced across the table to where Caleb and Tamara were exchanging loving glances. "I've noticed that. It seems there's an awful lot of kissing going on. More kissing than serving up supper."

Ivy relaxed as attention swung away from her and Walker.

Dustin snickered. "You forget something, bro?" He pointed at Caleb's empty hands. "Are you scooping up with your fingers today?"

Caleb shook his head. "We wanted to share a bit of news with you, and I figured telling you before we give you food means we'll have your full attention."

Something on their faces made Ivy suspect what they were about to announce. Tamara had a secret smile as she glanced at Caleb then nodded.

Caleb looked directly at Sasha and Emma. "Your mom and I are going to have a new baby brother or sister for you next year."

Emma blinked hard.

Sasha tilted her head as if trying to put this announcement into perspective. "I get to be a big sister again?"

Emma elbowed her in the side. "I get to be a big sister for the *first time*."

Sasha turned to her. "I can show you what you need to know, because it's a lot of hard work."

Masculine laughter was kept to a minimum, but everyone abandoned their chairs to give Tamara a hug and pound Caleb on the back.

The expectant father was grinning unashamedly. Ivy offered Tamara a tight hug, somewhat surprised she'd been included in the announcement but honoured as well. "I'm very happy for you," she said softly.

Tamara nodded. "I'm happy and scared at the same time.

There is nothing worse than someone with a medical degree getting pregnant."

Ivy reassured her everything would be fine, then they grabbed the food and put it on the table and the real meal started. Caleb filled plates and passed them around like in the old days when Ivy would visit the Stone family.

And just like in the old days as she sat next to Walker, his hand stole under the table to find her fingers, holding tightly. It was perfect, and it was sweet, and it made something inside her sad in the midst of her happiness.

She couldn't give this up. She wanted Walker. She wanted to be a part of this family, but the last thing she wanted was to be an anchor, holding him back.

At the end of the meal that was full of all kinds of memories, Luke and Dustin took control of their nieces and dealt with cleanup. Caleb and Tamara slipped out of the house to go for a walk around Big Sky Lake.

Walker stood next to her on the porch as they watched his brother and sister-in-law sneak away hand-in-hand, no doubt whispering together about their future.

He turned her toward him. "I'll take my hello kiss now, but it's got to be goodbye as well. I have chores."

"I'll see you tomorrow?" she asked.

"After you're done with work? Definitely. We can finish fixing your stairs."

He kissed her, sweet and lovingly, and somehow she kept her emotions from bursting free.

He headed toward the barns, and she took a slow drive down the long road to the highway, leaving Silver Stone in her rearview mirror.

She didn't go home.

She drove to Buns and Roses and used her key to sneak up the back stairs to her sisters' apartment.

Rose was there, glancing up from the knitting project she was working on, quiet music playing in the background. "Ivy? What's wrong?"

Ivy shook her head, unable to speak. She joined Rose on the couch and leaned against her, accepting a strong hug as her sister folded her in her arms.

They sat there quietly for a while before Rose pressed a kiss to the top of Ivy's head. "Do I need to go hit somebody for you? And by somebody, I mean Walker?"

An inelegant snort escaped Ivy, somewhere between laughter and tears. "It's not him. It's me. I love him so much, Rose. But that means I have to let him go."

Arms tightened around her in a comforting grip. "Oh, honey. The way that man looks at you, I doubt very much he's going anywhere."

"He might have to, and I have to be okay with it. I never realized how hard it is to be the person left behind. It's going to require more strength than it ever took to leave."

Another squeeze, another kiss. "Well, no matter what happens, I know you're strong enough to handle it. And you've got all of us to help hold you up when you feel wobbly."

Ivy nodded. That much she knew to the depths of her soul. "I love you, little sis."

"I love you too. Now, let me hold you. It's going to be okay. It really is."

20

Walker had to give Maxwell a decision sometime in the next twenty-four hours, and it still felt as if he needed more time.

He'd spent the last couple of hours sweating it out in the arena, but even being worked over until his spine felt as if it'd been driven up into his skull, his brain ached more than his body.

Ashton slapped him on the shoulder as a *well-done* before heading off to deal with the hands. Luke worked beside Walker to brush down the horses they'd used as backup, the curry brush creating a soft melody, repetitious and soothing.

Caleb had joined them, grinning good-naturedly at the teasing he'd been getting from everyone concerning the baby on the way. Dustin had been there as well, working hard until he started peeking obsessively at his watch. He checked in with Caleb to make sure it was okay to leave early then rushed off to join his friends.

Caleb caught Walker watching the interaction, and grinned. "Dustin is killing me. He's nearly lost his mind over the idea that Tamara's having a baby. It's ridiculously sweet."

Which made sense considering Caleb's first wife hadn't been too pleased with the idea of being pregnant, or being married, come to think of it. "He's behaving himself?"

Caleb made a rude noise. "He's always behaved himself. It was me who had a stick up my ass. We're good."

The three of them finished their work, chatting quietly. They were ready to head in different directions when Luke cleared his throat.

"Got something to tell you."

Walker and Caleb exchanged glances before moving into position on either side of him.

Luke's usual happy-go-lucky nature had been a lot more reserved the entire summer. They both figured it had something to do with Penny, but every time they'd asked, Luke had put them off.

Until now. He took a deep breath and looked up at Caleb. "You told me once I should think long and hard about what I was doing."

"With Penny?"

Luke nodded. "I really thought it could work out, but after seeing how things are between you and Tamara, and then you..." He turned his attention on Walker. "With you and Ivy getting back together—I see what it looks like when people belong together."

That's what it felt like. That he and Ivy *belonged* together.

Luke straightened his shoulders, staring into the arena. "That's not what I see when I look in the mirror. I don't see myself madly in love with Penny, and I don't think that's acceptable anymore. I thought it would be enough, but it isn't."

Caleb looked thoughtful. "What are you going to do?"

"I called it off. That's where I went yesterday. I didn't want to do it in an email or text, so I went over to her place."

"How'd she take it?" Walker asked quietly.

A bitter laugh escaped Luke. "She was fine. Barely even blinked, to tell the truth, and then she asked if she could still have Red-Hot Whiskey's foal when it arrives in the spring. Insisted she'll pay full price, no problem."

A soft curse escaped before Walker could stop it. The focus now wasn't on Penny being a rotten human being, it was about Luke. "You okay?"

Luke shrugged. "In some ways it doesn't feel as if anything has changed. We didn't have the same kind of relationship you and Ivy already share. As if you can't get enough of each other and can hardly bear to be apart." Luke jerked a thumb toward Caleb, a momentary flash of his usual smirk reappearing. "Which seems to be a lot like this one and Tamara."

Caleb stepped forward and grasped Luke's shoulder, squeezing tightly. "I think you deserve someone who wants to be with you all the time. Someone who is stupid in love with you."

"Yeah, well, that's not what I had, so it's good that it's over." Luke frowned again. "But even though Penny isn't pissed at me, I can't guarantee what Mr. Talisman is going to be like to deal with in the future. It's entirely possible I just jettisoned our hopes of getting ahead as horse breeders."

Another rude noise escaped Caleb. "He's only one man, and if he's got any kind of eyes in his head, he already knows you and Penny didn't belong together. There're a whole lot of other buyers out there we can work with if he does turn out to be an ass."

"I didn't want to do anything to hurt Silver Stone," Luke admitted softly. "I didn't want do something that makes us lose our home."

"Bullshit on that," Caleb snapped with uncharacteristic heat. "Is this why you've been hanging on to that broken relationship for so long?"

Luke glanced at Walker before nodding guiltily at Caleb.

Caleb stomped away a few steps, cursing loudly before turning around and fixing his gaze on his brothers. "Let me make this clear, to both of you, in case you get some harebrained idea like this as well, Walker. Trying to save the ranch at the expense of everything else isn't worth it."

A shocked sound escaped Luke, but Caleb carried on, ignoring the sound of a door opening somewhere behind them.

"Having somebody center you is—there are no words. I love the ranch. I love that it's a legacy we can pass down to our kids. And it's a piece of Mom and Dad I would miss a whole hell of a lot, I'll admit that. But we're building a new legacy, Tamara and me. If that means we'll have a ranch for my little girls and the coming baby, so be it. If it means we'll be making a new start in a new place, I'm okay with that too. Our happiness is worth more than history and memories. *Your* happiness is worth more."

Walker was still trying to take in this unexpected speech, full of wisdom and nearly scandalous ideas, when Tamara appeared from around the corner.

She'd obviously heard the last part of Caleb's proclamation. She went straight up to him, grabbed him by the lapels and pulled him to face her. "I love you so damn much."

Then she kissed him, arms wrapped around his neck, oblivious to the fact Walker and Luke were there as spectators.

Or maybe it was part of her message.

Luke tilted his head toward the corner, and Walker joined him as they gave their big brother and his wife some privacy.

As they walked past the arena toward Big Sky Lake, a little piece of the puzzle slipped into place. "We got lucky when it came to being handed Caleb as a big brother."

Luke slapped Walker on the shoulder, nodding as they walked. "Too damn right."

Walker took a deep breath. "He was right, you know. I was planning to do something stupid. Just as stupid as you."

His brother stumbled for a moment before he caught himself, stopping to look at Walker with confusion. "There's nothing wrong with you and Ivy, is there?"

"Only if I stay on this path. You asked me before if there was something you could help with, and I told you I needed to deal with it myself. I was wrong."

Then he spilled the beans and told Luke everything. All about his panic attacks and the things he felt he needed to do in order to help save the ranch. About disappointing their father, and the fight that was the last thing he remembered.

Luke listened in complete silence. His jaw dropped the longer Walker spoke, and when he finished, Luke nodded once. Then he sent a fist flying against Walker's shoulder, hard enough to rock him back on his feet.

"Dammit. What was that for?"

A scowl covered his brother's face. "Because you were a stupid shit. But since you've told me everything, and because I *was* being stupid as well, I didn't think I should hit you in the face."

Walker snickered. "Thanks for that."

"But you haven't had any panic attacks recently?" Luke waited until Walker shook his head firmly before going back to the same question that Ivy had asked him after the troubles at Rough Cut. "Stop thinking about saving the ranch. What do you *want* to do?"

It was an easy answer. "I want to be with Ivy. I want to stay here and work with you guys, and if by some chance we do lose the ranch, whatever we do next, I want it to be as a family."

"Then let's make that happen. One step at a time."

As plain and simple as that.

It seemed impossible, but after so long, and so many lost nights of sleep, this much was true. Walker didn't have to know all the answers—he just had to know this part.

Walker took a deep breath. "Let's start with me being with Ivy. I have an idea, but I need your help to set it up."

He held out his hand. Luke grasped it, shaking firmly before pulling Walker in for a brotherly hug that involved a lot more back pounding than squeezing.

When they separated, Luke was smiling for real for the first time in what seemed like forever. "And for the record? Dad loved you, and he was damn proud of you. You only got one fatherly warning from him? Hell, I used to get scolded weekly for not taking life seriously enough. So you can put that worry out of your mind. You've done your share over the years, whether you think so or not. We're *all* proud of you."

Walker's chest went tight again. "Thanks."

"We'll make this work. I know we can."

"And...the King of Optimism has returned," Walker teased.

But this time, he really hoped it was true.

THE CRYPTIC MESSAGE Ivy got from Walker intrigued her, and so it happened that at nearly nine p.m. in the evening, instead of getting ready for bed, Ivy was working to put together her best happy face.

Tansy lay on her bed, feet kicking lazily as she watched Ivy apply makeup. "Did the school year get off to a good start?"

"That's not what you want to ask," Ivy pointed out.

Her sister laughed as she pulled herself up to a sitting position. "Just trying to keep you distracted."

"Not working," Ivy said dryly. "I can tell when I'm being set up for something. Just tell me you'll be there in case I get overwhelmed."

Tansy drew a cross over her heart. "I solemnly swear you have backup."

"It would be a whole lot better if I knew what was going on," Ivy suggested.

Her sister shook her head. "Probably, but that would require *me* to know what's going on, and for once, I don't. I'm just following instructions."

"Where are you guys?" Rose called from somewhere near the front door. "Fern is waiting. I'd make her drive around the block a couple of times, but if we're late, I expect something cataclysmic will happen."

Ivy grabbed a coat off her bed and gave Tansy a warning look. "*They're* involved with this too? That doesn't make me feel more comfortable."

Tansy held her hand as they walked down the stairs, and crawled into Fern's ancient Volkswagen bug.

It was late enough in the day that the sunlight was fading. Twilight lingered, with only faint traces of red and gold remaining. Small lights twinkled in the graveyard—there were a half-dozen of them now. Ivy still hadn't discovered who was putting them up, but she had to admit the results were pretty.

When they pulled up in front of Rough Cut, Tansy didn't do anything more than tug her out of the car and up the stairs into the cool interior.

The sign outside the door had said *Closed For The Evening*, but the doors were unlocked. Ryan was nowhere in sight. Music played a lot quieter than normal, and voices carried from the main dance room. Familiar voices, like Tamara and Caleb and their little girls.

"What are the kids doing in a bar?" Ivy asked as they rounded the corner to discover a whole bunch of chairs had been set up on the dance floor. The entire Stone family was in attendance, and she noticed with some shock that Rose and Fern had made their way forward to find places next to her parents and Grandma Sonora.

Butterflies took off in Ivy's stomach, her chest tightening as Tansy led her to a chair. A few people glanced her way but quickly returned their attention to the stage, leaving her safely isolated in the very back row.

Ivy held onto Tansy's fingers as she sat down to discover her chair was right smack dab in the middle of the open aisle, giving her a clear view of the stage where a lone figure sat on a tall stool, guitar in hand.

He was wearing his cowboy hat, a dark, long-sleeved shirt rolled up to expose his forearms, crisp new jeans, and boots she could see the shine on from this distance under the couple of spotlights that had been aimed directly at him.

Walker Stone looked every inch the cowboy. Delicious and rock-solid to the core.

The music from the overhead speakers faded as Walker placed his fingers on his guitar, but it wasn't the steady pace of the cording that had her mesmerized. It was his eyes, staring straight at her as if there was no one else in the room except the two of them.

Tansy gave her fingers a squeeze before pulling away. She whispered softly in Ivy's ear. "I'm right beside you, but I think you've got this."

Then she was alone. Alone except for Walker, who was playing a soft riff over and over again, watching her as if she were a miracle.

"The last time I was up on this stage I had a bit of a rough tumble." Walker spoke quietly yet clearly, his words carrying over the guitar. "But I remember Dad talking about how important it was after a fall to get back up on the horse, and I suppose in a way, that's part of what I'm doing right now." Walker's gaze moved for a brief moment to his brother Caleb, then to the other side as he dipped his head in Malachi's direction. "It's pretty much what some of the smartest men I know have always told me. It's not easy to do the right thing, but it's worth it. So buck up, and get it done."

The music changed under his fingertips. Gentle sweeps now, like the wind blowing over the prairies. Soft and low. Restless.

His gaze returned to her. Not exactly a smile, but something sweet and full of promise shone in his expression. "But instead of telling you a bunch of words, I should do what singers are supposed to do, and let the music tell the story."

The tightness in Ivy's chest wasn't there from fear anymore. It was hope and anticipation as Walker looked into her heart and sang for her.

Just for her.

There might've been a dozen other people in the room, but they were alone.

Do tumbleweeds feel restless,
following the wind
longing for a place to stop
torn up once again

I'm tired of being a tumbleweed,
it's time to put the road away
want to come and live beside you
want to stay another day

The only path I want to walk
is the one to our front door
A well-worn track by your side
I can't roam anymore

Trails out to the swing set,
where we push our little ones
Muddy ruts down to the river

when the day is done

The only path I want to walk
is the one to our front door
A well-worn track by your side
I can't roam—

Walker stopped. Right in the middle of a sentence, but it wasn't the same as it had been before. Not like last time when he'd been on the stage singing and frozen, because now, while the words had stopped he was still looking at her, a slow smile taking over his face even as he swallowed hard.

He wasn't panicking, he was unable to speak, which she pretty much understood because she was in the same condition. She felt as if she were tied up with a hundred million ropes, but it was okay, because even as she struggled for air, they were connected.

It was the two of them, and they were together.

His fingers stilled, the sound of the guitar fading as he cleared his throat. "There's more, but I don't think I can finish. Not without you, Snow. You're the only way I *have* a song to sing. You're the one thing truly worth fighting for."

Ivy lifted a hand to her chest, her heart pounding against her palm.

"We'll figure out together what the future looks like, but I need you by my side. I love you, Ivy. I want you in my life from now 'til eternity, and I want it all. You, a family, whatever that looks like."

He got to his feet and laid the guitar aside, jumping off the stage and walking toward her. He came all the way up and caught one hand in his as he knelt at her feet.

Ivy caressed his cheek. "I love you too."

He lifted her other hand to press a kiss to her knuckles. "I don't know what I have to offer except my heart, and it's always belonged to you."

Okay, she was now officially crying. "That's more than enough."

"You going to marry me?"

Ivy nodded.

Soft clapping started in the background. Amazingly controlled, considering it was her family and his, but even more shocking was the fact she'd totally forgotten they were there.

As the noise level rose, she didn't feel any sense of panic because she was staring into his eyes, completely anchored by his love.

Rooted and centered. The tumbleweeds had come home.

21

As Walker had asked of them ahead of time, everyone stayed out of sight and didn't overwhelm them with congratulations.

He knew he needed to make his statement in front of their families, but the rest of this time was for them. And as he stole Ivy away from Rough Cut and headed onto the street, he realized he still had one problem.

Ivy read his mind as usual. "My house?"

He was already on the road. Ivy snuggled up against his side, the two of them quiet as he drove, when she tipped him for a loop.

"Wait. Not there. Where's your horse trailer?"

He wasn't about to argue with the lady, not now. "It's back at Silver Stone."

There was a smile on her lips. "I'm pretty sure we're guaranteed privacy even if they do spot your truck. Plus, no one is going to give us hell this time if we lock the door."

Walker put his foot down on the gas way harder than he should have, but he didn't care. He parked his truck as far out of sight as possible, though, because he didn't quite believe his brothers would be as charitable as she seemed to think.

Thank God he'd left the trailer in some semblance of order.

Ivy didn't even notice. She stepped into the small living quarters at the front of the trailer where Walker lived while on the road, turned without a word, and threw herself into his arms. Their lips met, and it wasn't hard to follow up on her encouragement.

Tangled lips rapidly became tangled limbs, and they were lying on his far-too-small-for-two-people mattress, not caring one single bit because they were content taking up only one person's space.

Ivy broke away long enough for them to catch their breath, laughter dancing in her eyes. "You know why I wanted to come here?"

"That's a trick question. I'm not supposed to say so we could have sex, right?"

She stripped off her shirt and her bra, straddling his hips as she did so, erasing his worries that this was going to be a figure-out-the-future, conversation-only time.

She dragged a finger down his buttons. "It's a three-part answer. That's the first part."

"It's really difficult to think when you're right there in front of me, partly naked."

"Then you better answer the question before I get all the way naked, or you're going to get an F on this exam."

"Tough teacher," he complained cupping her breasts gently, sucking in a breath of air for control as her nipples tightened. "Part A. We're going to have sex because we're in love. Part B—this had better be the answer to part B—you want to fool around in a horse trailer because that's where we had sex for the first time."

"Made love." She leaned over and pushed his shirt aside.

Tricky woman had undone all his buttons without him even noticing. "Full points for part B."

She pressed a kiss to his chest and then another a little higher, working her way up his neck to his jaw, biting down lightly before swinging up to look directly into his eyes.

Her bare breasts caressed his torso, and he was going to lose his ever-loving mind. "I need a clue for C, Snow. Let me look at your cheat sheet. I promise I won't tell the teacher."

She licked her lips, licked his lips, and then darted out of reach. "We're here because while I can't physically go on the road with you, if rodeo is something you need to do, I promise to support you. If travelling to be a singer—the same. Whatever it is, we'll find a way to make this work."

He lay there absolutely floored by the love in her eyes and the gift of her sacrifice, part of which he had no intention of accepting, and he planned to make that very clear right now. "I'm not leaving you. I still might do something with singing, but becoming a star isn't my dream. Being on the road, and being away from you? Or down the road, being away from our family? I know some people do it, and I'm not saying they're wrong, but it's not right for me. It's not right for *us*."

She was staring at him as if he'd hung the moon, and everything in him that had ever been cold was now warm and happy. Content.

Enough talk. He rolled them, pinning her to the mattress so he could offer her a wicked smile. "That's a sweet, beautiful gift to offer me. And I love you even more than I thought possible."

"I want to—"

Her words vanished into a gasp of surprise as he stripped away her pants and left her naked on the mattress. Surprise turned into soft noises of pleasure as he dropped between her legs and used both hands to lift her knees into the air.

With gentle caresses along the outside of her thighs and then back again, he teased her, staring into her eyes as he touched her with increasingly intimate caresses. Closer and closer to her sex, then away, never quite touching.

Her belly was quivering by the time he actually let his fingertips make contact.

"Walker," she begged.

"Nothing doing, Snow. The last time we fooled around in a horse trailer, it was all fast and fumbling. You're going to enjoy it, more than once," he promised before pressing a kiss to the inside of her knee.

It was fun to watch her wiggle on the mattress as he worked from side to side. One knee then the other, higher on the inside of her thigh. Closer, ever closer to where she'd grown wet for him. And when he used his thumbs to push aside the pale curls covering her, she damn near sang.

His tongue, his fingers, his whole body, every bit of him was involved in making love with her. When he teased her to a gasping release, it was just the first time.

Stripping off his clothes—

Coming to a rip-roaring stop. "Umm, Ivy?"

She looked at him with pleasure-glazed eyes.

"Condom?"

A soft laugh escaped her, and she pointed to her purse that hung from one of the wall hooks. "And before you ask, yes I always carry condoms with me. At least recently."

He dropped her purse beside her, and she reached in, bringing out what he needed. He tried multitasking, pressing her to the mattress as he kept their lips together, but after he fumbled with the wrapper for the third time, cursing in frustration as he had to scramble to find it, Ivy pushed his hands away and took control.

She ripped the package open and slowly covered his hard length, teasing him to the point of no return. So when she lay back, opening her legs and welcoming him over her, he had no more control left to lengthen their lovemaking.

He pushed into her wet heat in one slow, relentless stroke until he was buried to the hilt, completely connected, his gaze fixed on her face.

She dug her fingernails into his shoulders, lashes fluttering with pleasure. "*Yes.*"

It was one word. One simple word, but it meant absolutely everything. It was them together. It was this act of intimacy they were involved in, but it was so much more. It was acceptance and joy in their past and their future all tangled together.

They moved together until they were one breath away from completion. He slid a hand between them and pressed hard over her clit, and that was it. She ripped a climax from him with her response.

A soft sigh escaped her, a *hmmm* of satisfaction, followed by a set of quick gasps as he pumped the last few times, pressing as much pleasure on her as possible.

When they were done, he held her and was held by her, in that tiny space that was a bit of him and that she'd turned into a bit of her.

Now they just had to decide their future.

THE ONE SMALL overhead light was not enough to brighten the inside of the trailer past candlelight levels, which was fine by Ivy. Maybe it wasn't the most romantic of spots to celebrate getting engaged, but it was special for all the right reasons.

Walker's heart was still pounding, and so was hers, but it was so right to lie there in the dark listening to each other breathe and feel the heat between their bodies. It had been such a long time coming.

The thought might've been hokey, but somehow it had felt different. Making love had been better than any time before.

But they did have to talk, and they did have decisions that needed to be made. "Thank you for singing for me. Was that one of your songs?"

He nodded. "I had the idea before, but today after talking to my brothers, it kind of all fell into place. All the words were right there waiting for me once I was ready."

Ivy pushed up, one hand on his chest as shock struck. "You wrote that this afternoon?"

"Some of it. I already had the tune worked out, and the feelings have been there forever."

She shook her head in amazement. "You have a gift, Walker. And I know you said you don't want to go and travel, but I really hope you keep doing something with music. Songwriting or whatever it is that you can do and still be happy with your goals."

"I know. I have to talk to Maxwell. I'm going to tell him no to the tour, but if they ever need me for studio work, I should be able to do that. At least until things change with our lives."

He was talking about children, and she was fine with that. She had to make something clear to him as well. "I do want a family, but I might not be able to have babies myself."

The look he gave her was pure admonition. "You of all people know that kids don't have to come out of your body to make them yours. Your parents have been good examples of that for years. And I don't see Tamara loving Emma and Sasha any less because she didn't carry them for nine months."

Ivy shook her head, loving him more every minute. "I knew it wasn't going to be a problem, but it had to be said."

"Then here's another thing that has to be said. I have no problem planning to adopt from the get-go, because I don't want to do anything to put you at risk."

"You really are an amazing man."

"What? Because I understand how precious you are? Because I know how precious every single baby is out there?" He pulled her tighter against him, the heat of his body like a furnace. "When we think the time is right, and we know we can keep a roof over their heads, we'll do what we can to build our family."

Lights flashed against the trailer windows—some of the hands coming home. Maybe Luke. "You locked the door, right?"

Walker laughed. "Yes."

She sighed happily and snuggled up against his side. "You didn't panic today."

"I was looking into my happy place, and it didn't matter how many people were around because you were there."

My goodness, she was going to die of sweetness. "I really hope that they're done and you never have another attack, even if we never figure out what caused them in the first place."

"It was just recently they got bad," he reminded her.

Something about his statement tugged hard, and Ivy sat up to concentrate. "Wait. *Recently*? Right. That's what you said before when we talked. 'Most recently it started in the fall.' But Walker, when did you have panic attacks before that?"

He folded his hands behind his head, gaze lifting to the ceiling as he considered. "I don't know if they were panic attacks, but I remember losing track of time. You know, like Ashton giving me hell for staring into space when I was supposed to be getting chores done, but I swear to God I wasn't slacking off. He said I was daydreaming."

"When was this? Because I don't remember you telling me, and I'm sure you would've said something."

His face tightened. "After Mom and Dad died, I guess, and the first summer after. It didn't happen very often, and after a while it went away. I figured it had something to do with them dying so suddenly."

Which made all sorts of sense, but now she had to wonder.

"When did Ginny leave?"

"Last September. Right around now."

"And when did Dare leave the ranch?" Ivy ignored the fact she was stark-naked as she grilled him.

He curled upright as well, his frown of concentration increasing. "July sometime."

"And the first time you had a blackout was after that?"

He stared at her with growing disbelief. "You think this has something to do with the girls leaving?"

"The girls, me," she stroked a hand along his cheek. "Your mom and dad. We all left you and didn't come back."

He leaned against the side of the trailer looking into the distance as if he were considering. "Makes me sound as if I can't function without having you around."

"What's wrong with that? I mean what's wrong with feeling something's wrong because the people you love aren't there anymore?" She shook her head, catching hold of his hand. "Maybe I'm off-base, but the timing makes sense."

"Dare didn't leave completely. I get to see her anytime I want. And I talk to Ginny sometimes."

"Which also makes sense because you didn't shut down one hundred percent. I mean, you've done amazing things."

They stared at each other.

Then he shrugged. "You're right. It's possible I was thrown for a loop hard enough it came back and bit me. But I don't really need to know why for sure because I know you're not gone anymore. I still have you."

"Forever. You've got me forever," she promised.

He pulled her into his lap and kissed her, long, slow and sweet, until the heat between them rose again. Which was all of maybe ten seconds.

Then he murmured against her lips. "That means I know exactly where my happy place is. Let's go there again, together."

22

November, Las Vegas

Walker headed from where he'd been warming up toward where he needed to be in less than an hour's time. Around him, the scent and sounds of the rodeo filled his ears and upped his excitement. He waved at some of the other competitors before sliding into one of the holding rooms to collect himself.

The past couple months had been simultaneously amazing and rough. He'd chipped in what money he could toward the mortgage on Ivy's house, and now it was *their* house. The tiny thing would last them at least until they decided they wanted to start a family.

Caleb had begun to walk around with a decidedly tortured look, one minute thrilled by the slowly growing bump in Tamara's belly, then worried as hell the next as bills continued to pile up. Which was when Walker called a serious discussion with Ivy, and they decided he had to try.

So here he was, ready to head out on the back of a bull, and it wasn't concern about blacking out that had him twisted up, it was sheer, straight-up worry.

He had a hell of a lot to live for, and bull riding was damn dangerous.

Still, over the past month he'd attended five rodeos and not only survived but covered all but three of the bulls he'd attempted. He'd earned enough to tuck away some money, but he'd also scored enough points that with what he'd piled up before the summer, he'd confirmed a spot in this final championship.

The door opened, and Luke marched in. His brother had joined him on all his recent trips as support, backup, and all-around pain in the ass. It'd been perfect having him along, and somehow it made being away from Ivy that much easier.

Especially when it turned out Luke and Ivy had chatted before they'd left and made plans. Plans that made Walker grin every time he thought of them.

Luke strolled forward, checking the time on his phone. "Good thing I saw you duck in here, Dynamite. Can't let you go off on your little bumpily-bumpy ride without a final cheer."

Screw it. Walker knew he looked eager, but he didn't care. "You have no idea how much this means to me."

Luke nodded briskly. "Sure I do. Now shut up, someone wants to talk to you."

He held forward his phone, already open to messenger, and there on the screen was Ivy's pretty face, smiling sweetly at Walker. "Hi, love. That's a strange rodeo ground. It looks more like a school room. Maybe I should take up bull riding."

Walker took the phone from his brother then ignored the fact Luke was there. "Good to see you, sweetheart."

She looked him up and down. "You handsome thing."

"Sweet-talk. I like it."

"You'll get more than sweet-talk when you're home next

week, but for now, this will have to do. I know it seems as if I'm not there, but I am. I'm right there beside you the whole time," Ivy told him. Complete confidence shone on her face. Although she had to be concerned, she didn't look like it.

She looked like a woman in love, and that was just fine by him.

"I feel good," he told her. "I pulled a great bull too. He turns back a lot, and I like that, so we should get some good numbers."

She nodded as if she knew what he was talking about. "Well, go have fun. Call me when you're done."

As if he were off to round up calves or something. "Yes, dear," he said with a laugh. "I love you."

"I love you too. Go to your happy place."

She hung up, and he stood there staring at the empty screen for a second before handing the phone back to Luke. "I laughed when Dare told me you had maternal instincts, but I'm sure glad you're taking care of me, bro."

Luke smacked him on the shoulder, shoving Walker toward the hallway and back to the noise and the chaos of the bull riders prep area. "I'm damn maternal. I'm not even going to tease you about *happy places*, whatever the hell that means. You're going to do great. We're here for you."

He knew it. He knew it to the very depths of his being, which was why, when it was his turn and he climbed on the back of the beast that was ready to do his damnedest to get rid of him, Walker felt a strange sense of peace.

The noise from the arena faded into a peaceful melody. The song playing matched the beating of Walker's heart—faster than usual, but that only made sense.

He was on the back of a bull. No man did that without his heart racing.

But in the almost-stillness that came over him, it wasn't a lack of connection to what was going on. It was a complete and utter meshing of all the notes of the melody; the bull, himself, the announcer, the crowd.

And when the gate opened and the bull exploded out, there was nowhere to go except with the music. Staccato, full of life, with an ever-changing rhythm as the animal rose and fell. Through it all, one sensation surrounded him.

Walker was happy.

He was utterly aware of every single second ticking by, as though they passed in slow motion. Glimpses of people in the crowd, flashes of white cowboy hats and dark vests, lights flickering, metal railings and belt buckles. The bull under him raged—

No, it danced. The animal was dancing to a melody Walker could hear, and he was dancing along with the bull.

When the eight second buzzer sounded, Walker dismounted in one smooth motion, walking away with his hands raised to the roar of the crowd. The bull rushed the opposite direction, tangling with the bullfighters.

It was going to be a very good day. A very *happy place*, because Ivy was there with him. She was always going to be with him.

~

EMMA HELD the belt buckle that Walker had given her with a bit of suspicion. "But that doesn't say *champion*, Uncle Walker."

Walker glanced over at Ivy, who had curled up on the couch in Tamara and Caleb's house. He'd just got back from the rodeo, and after they'd celebrated his success at home, she'd insisted they accept the invitation from his brother.

"Well, it's not a champion belt because I didn't win," Walker told her.

"You didn't win the entire thing," Caleb corrected. "You did damn good."

"Caleb."

"Daddy."

"Papa."

Three female voices sounded simultaneously in warning at his swear. He glanced at them with suitable guilt. "Sorry. He did damn *well*?"

The girls still looked scandalized, but Tamara laughed, in spite of looking a trifle green around the gills. "Yes, Walker. You did damn well."

"*Mommy.*"

"*Mama.*"

Ivy couldn't take it anymore. She laughed out loud, so glad she was a part of this household of joy. "Emma, let's not repeat that word in class, okay? But yes, Uncle Walker came first in some of his events, but they only give a champion belt to the one person who wins the whole contest."

Luke had slipped into the room during the conversation and dropped onto the couch next to Emma. "I gave that buckle to Uncle Walker. Isn't it pretty?"

Emma held it up in the air. "It's not as big as his old one, but I like the bull. And I like it that it says *Happy Place* on it in big letters. Is that the name of the bull, Uncle Walker?"

He grinned. "Sort of."

"You earned it," Tamara said, passing the buckle back to Walker. "But I hear you're not planning on riding next season."

He shook his head. "I had fun, but it's time I did other things. And the money I won gives us time to come up with new plans for the ranch."

The doorbell rang, and Emma popped up like a jack-in-the-box. "It's Crissy," she shouted as she raced for the front door

Tamara glanced over at Ivy. "Crissy is sleeping over for the night. Her usual babysitter cancelled on Hanna, and she's got to work."

Walker slipped his fingers into Ivy's as they rose from the couch and headed outside to the fire pit with the rest of the family.

Late November meant there was plenty of snow on the ground now, and their breath showed on the air. But overhead the stars were sparkling and while cold, it was beautiful out.

Ivy tucked into the bench space next to Walker and let him wrap his arm around her, talking quietly as the rest of them brought out chairs and marshmallow roasting sticks.

His lips brushed her cheek. "You look good in your sky-blue coat, Snow Princess."

She smiled at him. "I needed a new one, and I remembered it was your favourite colour."

"Well, now, I wouldn't say that."

Confusion struck. "I was sure you said that blue coat I had back when we first met made you think of winter skies."

"It does, and it looks good on you, but it isn't my favourite colour." He pulled off his glove and put his warm palm to her cheek. "My favourite colour is silvery. Like your eyes—always changing, and yet the most beautiful part of them is always there."

Every time he broke out the sweet talk, her heart pounded. "What's always there?"

"Love. An everlasting love, just for me."

"Sounds like a song lyric," she teased.

He shrugged. "Maybe. We've got an awful lot of pages to fill going into the future. I'm sure a lot of them are going to be covered with beautiful melodies and memories."

"I love you," she told him again, touching her forehead to his and whispering the words as the fire flared, hot-red comfort washing over them. The heat between them was more than enough to keep her safe.

A little-girl whisper carried from across the fire as Emma and Crissy roasted marshmallows, their feet kicking freely where they dangled down from the too-high-for-them benches. "Does Ms. Fields kiss your Uncle Walker an awful lot?" Crissy asked.

"Lots and lots," Emma informed her. "Almost as much as Mama and Papa kiss."

Ivy kept staring into Walker's eyes. He was listening to the conversation as well, a soft smile twisting his lips as they waited quietly, not wanting to embarrass the girls.

Crissy didn't say anything for a minute, and when she did, she sounded sad. "My Mommy doesn't have anyone to kiss."

Emma had a solution. "You should ask Santa for somebody for her for Christmas. That's what I did. I mean, I asked for Mama, and I didn't get her until *after* Christmas, but it worked."

Ivy couldn't take it any longer. "I should warn Hanna," she whispered.

Walker gave her a quick kiss before accepting the bag of marshmallows that had finally made its way around the circle. "I don't know. It sounds like a pretty good thing to wish for. Someone to kiss. I'm glad I've got you."

Ivy had to agree. They had so many things to look forward to, and although some of it was up in the air, there was a lot of good they already knew. The first and foremost—they were together. That wasn't going to change.

And as she leaned against Walker's side and stared into the flickering flames, she sent up a word of thanks for all the good things that had come her way.

Going away and learning so much.

Returning home to find her heart waiting for her.

A thought occurred to her, and she couldn't stop from

giggling, which meant Walker kept giving her looks until he finally caved.

"What's so funny?"

"I'm calculating exactly how much I paid for you. One thousand dollars divided by eternity—I got a pretty amazing deal on a bull rider."

Walker laughed so loud all eyes turned toward them, and she didn't mind one bit because she was right there with the other half of her heart.

He leaned in and looked her in the eye. "I'm a *damn* good deal. Yours, forever. And I'll even sing for you."

EPILOGUE

Luke stomped through the mudroom door of his not-yet-finished house as another long day came to a conclusion. He was starving, and he ached from head to toe after getting bucked a half-dozen times from the new ride he was training, which meant he was also filthy.

Food, then a shower. Then he'd figure out something to pass the rest of the evening. Something he could do alone considering two of his brothers were happily wrapped up with family and wife and/or fiancée, and Dustin was off with his friends.

Luke plugged in his battery-dead phone then opened the laptop on the kitchen counter. He kicked away the bits and pieces underfoot from the packaging that had held the overhead cupboards he'd finally put in place that morning before heading to work. He grabbed a plate of leftovers from the fridge, pulled a stool over with a foot, and dropped onto it, checking his emails as he ate one piece of pizza cold while the rest heated in the microwave.

Junk, junk, emails from his sisters, more junk...

Triple Crown Gala.

He paused, snorting around a mouthful of pizza. "Yeah, me at a gala. Good one."

But the email was from Bertram Cooper, someone Luke trusted a great deal. Silver Stone had done a ton of their top value sales through the man, so he clicked the message open. Bert was probably setting him up for an all-you-can-eat chicken wing night and pulling his leg with the subject title.

Five minutes later, the microwave beeped another reminder which Luke continued to ignore, astonished at what he'd just read.

It *was* a gala, a buyers-and-sellers gala. An invitation-only gathering of the elite horse breeders of North America. It wasn't a buying event, but a meet-and-greet with spouses and families, and Bert had wrangled him and Penny an invitation to the event.

Holy freaking shit.

The rough weather they were having with Silver Stone was put off for a short while because of Walker's gift, but they weren't nearly out of the woods. They had to take that next step with the horses if they were going to make it, and this was like a golden ticket had fallen into his lap.

Luke shuddered at the cost of the event. Thank God it was being held just hours away in Kananaskis country, which meant they'd be able to drive and not have to fly to Texas or Alabama. But the oversized price tag would vanish if they got one new sale, and these kind of events built relationships that were kingmakers.

Years ago, Penny's dad was one of the ones who'd been in the right place at the right time, and they'd never looked back.

There was a message from Bert.

Got word of this shindig. Organizers asked me for a couple of recommendations of up-and-coming breeders, and I thought of you. I don't have to tell you this is a Big Deal event. If I had an operation like yours, I'd be drooling at the opportunity. So yes, feel free to send me a bottle of the good stuff down the road.

Heads up on a couple of things: The group is a bit old school, which doesn't mean they expect you to bring a wife, but a fiancée is better than a girlfriend. And while they're up-to-date enough they won't make you sleep in separate rooms, they do want to deal with family *operations. So for fuck's sake, be sure you bring your fiancée. Don't let her give you grief on this one.*

Best of luck, and I'll see you in the new year. I've got a couple of requests I'll send your way come the spring. Touch base if you need anything sooner.

Luke didn't think about it too hard. The invitation truly wasn't something he needed to consider—the gala could save the ranch. He absolutely had to be there. It wasn't his fault Bert wasn't up to date on the fact he and Penny had called off their engagement.

He filled in the application.

Name of the ranch, their top horses and studs to date.

Personal history.

Name of spouse/significant other—Luke paused.

Contact Penny and ask her to do him a favour? Possible, but risky. She was unpredictable, and he didn't trust her. Plus, he didn't think he could stand to be all cozied up to her again after calling things off, and a *family* event would mean they'd have to at least pretend to like each other.

Nope, there was a far simpler solution right at his fingertips. He filled in the blank with a firm stroke on the keys.

Kelli James.

He hit send.

~

New York Times Bestselling Author Vivian Arend invites you to Heart Falls. These contemporary ranchers live in a tiny town in central Alberta, tucked into the rolling foothills. Enjoy the ride as they each find their happily-ever-afters.

~

The Stones of Heart Falls
A Rancher's Heart
A Rancher's Song
A Rancher's Bride

~

ABOUT THE AUTHOR

With over 2 million books sold, Vivian Arend is a New York Times and USA Today bestselling author of over 50 contemporary and paranormal romance books, including the Six Pack Ranch and Granite Lake Wolves.

Her books are all standalone reads with no cliffhangers. They're humorous yet emotional, with sexy-times and happily-ever-afters. Vivian pretty much thinks she's got the best job in the world, and she's looking forward to giving readers more HEAs. She lives in B.C. Canada with her husband of many years and a fluffy attack Shih-tzu named Luna who ignores everyone except when treats are deployed.